The Billionaire's Board

Also By Lark Anderson

The Beguiling a Billionaire Series

The Billionaire's Board
The Billionaire's Fixer Upper
The Billionaire's Funding
The Bad Girl
The Dis-Graced
The Trainwreck

Reckless in Love
eBook Only

Love you…not!!!
Trust you…not!!!
Tempt you…not!!!

Savage in Love

Savage in the Sheets

The Glow Girlz Series

Stacey's Seduction
Tempting Teysa
Desiree's Delight

If you'd like to become an ARC reviewer for Lark, please email her at: mims@mimsthewords.com.

BEGUILING A BILLIONAIRE
BOOK 1

THE *Billionaire's* BOARD

LARK ANDERSON

Lark Letter Press

THE BILLIONAIRE'S BOARD

Copyright © 2019 by Lark Anderson
All rights reserved.

Lark Letter Press
131 Daniel Webster Hwy # 166
Nashua, NH 03060
www.larkandersonbooks.net
mims@mimsthewords.com
Edited by: Melodie Price

All rights reserved. No part of this publication may be reproduced, distributed, or transmitted in any form or by any means, including photocopying, recording, or other electronic or mechanical methods, without the prior written permission of the publisher, except in case of brief quotations embodied in critical reviews and certain other noncommercial uses permitted by copyright law. For permission requests, write to the publisher, addressed "Attention: Permission Coordinator," at the address above.

ISBN: 979-8-6433124-4-4
eISBN: 978-1-7333579-4-4

Any references to historical events, real people, or real places are used fictionally. Names, characters, and places are products of the author's imagination. The following story contains mature content and is intended for mature readers.

Intro

Remi gets promoted...

Oh my GOD! What the heck just happened?

One minute, I'm presenting to the board, the next—BAM—I'm a director. Appointed by none other than Gabriel Icor himself, or shall I say—Gabriel the 10!

That's right, I was promoted by Icor Tech's billionaire CEO in front of the board and directors alike, and boy oh boy—were they mad. I'm talking raised voices, glaring daggers, spittle slinging grey-hairs that are having none of my shit.

Except—there was that one guy, Tom—the solid 9.

He wasn't so upset by my promotion. In fact, he seemed rather ecstatic. If it weren't for him, I would have been laughed right out of that boardroom.

Gosh, promoted by a 10 and saved by a 9—all in one day. Both ridiculously handsome, oh so sexy, with way too many zeros in their bank accounts for me to count.

How am I supposed to get anything done working alongside THEM?!?

Mental note to self: Lookup company policy regarding directors dating board members.

Who am I kidding? It's not like either of them are going to be courting little old Remi Stone anytime soon.

Chapter One

*Twenty-Four hours earlier, **Remi** is the WORST kind of millennial...*

BUZZ.
Who the hell is calling me this early?
BUZZ.

I swear, there's a special place in hell for people who interrupt a woman trying to get a full night's sleep before an important meeting.

BUZZ.

God, why won't they just quit? The building better be burning down, or better yet, we better be going into nuclear meltdown. You just don't wake a woman up this early on the morning she has a—Oh my God! The meeting!

How could I have overslept? I mean, I've been waiting for this day to come for two weeks.

I hop out of bed, blanket wrapped around my body and immediately fall to the floor. One might think with how often we meet, the floor and I might be good friends, but the reality is, she's a cold-hearted bitch.

I reach on top of my nightstand, to the angry buzz of the alarm, and hit END. The time reads 7:05—a whole hour later than I'm supposed to wake.

Most days, this wouldn't be a big issue, but today is the day I give my presentation in front of the directors and board members of Icor Tech at the quarterly Innovation Meeting. When I'm done with them, they'll know that taking a chance on still wet-behind-the-ears Remi Stone wasn't a mistake.

I wish I could say I had time to shower and set my hair before one of the most important days of my life, but that would be a lie. The truth is, it was an accomplishment that toothpaste made it in my mouth. I'm a woman with time anxiety, and when even the whiff of a time constraint comes on, I panic. I mean full-blown running around, half dressed, brush in hair, one leg shaved panic.

As the youngest program manager Icor Tech has ever had, my life is basically one part working my ass off and one part trying to prove to everyone that I'm not just some lucky idiot. At twenty-three, they figure there's no way I could have actually earned my position as program manager and chalk it up to luck and who I know—I wish it had been that easy.

You see, I'm kind of a genius. I know how that must sound, cocky and arrogant, but I promise you, that's not how I see myself. I see myself as a total, complete, epic mess hobbling on two legs, trying to avoid disaster. I just so happen to test well.

I throw a coffee mug under the Keurig nozzle, hitting the only button in the world that can see me through the day. Then I rush to my closet to find something to wear.

Why didn't I just lay my clothes out last night? I ask myself, but of course, that would make my life a little too easy.

Rumpled lavender flowers—nope. Bright blue asymmetrical neckline—nope. Black floor-length dress that looks like a curtain—double nope.

Why don't I put more effort into my wardrobe?

Unfortunately, I've never put much energy into thinking about what to wear. Before I got my corporate job, I was shopping at Goodwill for most of my clothes, Target for socks and underwear. A trip to the mall to buy real adult attire for work had given me a major panic attack. Nothing was 'broken in,' and just one suit cost as much as my entire wardrobe. But it was what was expected of a professional from Icor Tech, so money was spent, and discomfort was had.

I finally settled on a knee-length white skirt with black and pink flowers throughout paired with a black dress shirt.

My phone buzzes again—the holy shit you're late alarm I have set to go off when I'm supposed to be walking out the door. Instead, I'm slapping on deodorant and looking around for my glasses.

This is exactly what they expect from a millennial. Shitty work ethics, entitlement, living in my parent's basement. None of those traits fit me, but the room full of grey hairs I'm about to brief don't know that. They don't know that I tested out of high school at fifteen, received my Bachelor's in Engineering at Cornell by nineteen, and my Masters by the time I was twenty-two. They just see a young, fair-haired woman and assumed I got my job because of who I know or some affirmative action bullshit.

Kibbles! I can't forget to feed Kibbles, the aging cat my dearly departed grandmother left to me. The cat hates me, looking for any reason to shred my bedding and furniture. She's possessed, more than likely by my dear dead grandma, who was never very happy no matter how much I called, visited, or wrote. Not that she ever really wanted to see me, but she sure did like the checks I was writing for her. I swear, she left me Kibbles just to spite me.

It isn't enough to leave one bowl of food out. Kibbles demands three, placed strategically around the apartment, filled to capacity. If the kibble level so much as lowers by half an inch, Kibbles goes into an angry panic. She dug up every single plant one day and shredded my shower curtain on another. The last thing I need is another Kibbles meltdown.

Oh, wonderful, the cat's glaring at me. Don't panic. It's not a big deal. It's just a cat.

Just a cat. Ha! That's like saying, 'Oh, it's just Satan, Lord of the Underworld.'

Pull yourself together, Remi. You're facing the board and a room full of directors today. Don't blow this!

I try to exhale my stress away, all my worries, but when you're a perfectionist that wakes up an hour late, all you know is panic. You are a literal ball of stress spreading chaos wherever you go, so I walk to the mirror and try my best to make myself presentable.

I have no time to flat iron my hair, so I throw it up into a clip, trying to pull off a shabby-chic look. Next, I apply cover up to the lone pimple that decided to claim my nose. But that's as far as I get. I have to be at that meeting at eight, and I still have a twenty-minute walk ahead of me—time to get going.

Kibbles is standing in the doorway, paw raised, a guttural grown emanating from her massive 30lb. body. For a fat, overfed cat, she's fast—and vicious. She could win wars. I don't know why they're training soldiers and not cats, for real. She could fuck some shit up and then puke a hairball on your bed.

"Be nice, Kibbles. Your new mommy needs to go to work so she can feed you."

Kibbles is uninterested in my needs and wants. She only cares for herself.

"You like your little toys, don't you? Your catnip? You want some catnip? You want your kitty high?"

Pass her slowly, force eye contact, keep talking.

"Maybe momma's gonna find you a hot young man-cat. A stud. Whaddaya think about that, Kibbles?"

Her growl deepens. Kibbles is not easily persuaded by lustful pursuits.

I leap, trying to clear the danger zone, but Kibbles lashes out with her claws, and one gets stuck in my black stockings.

"Crap!" I say as I pull them off and rummage through

my drawer for another pair, but they were my only clean pair.

Maybe they'll assume I'm wearing nude pantyhose.

I pull on my shoes, grab my laptop bag, my keys, and my access badge and head on out.

I live in an old building that is in desperate need of updates, so I don't wait for Boxy Bessie, or as most would call it, the elevator that takes about five minutes to climb between floors. Instead, I rush down five flights of stairs, nearly tripping over Mr. Sokolov, the building handyman, as he's on all fours eyeing a crevice for roaches. Another fantastic aspect of living in an old building.

I dash out of the building onto a bustling sidewalk, nearly barreling over Porn Star Meg, my next-door neighbor. I've never so much as exchanged a word with the chipper woman, our only interaction being the many times I've nearly crashed into her.

Now, I should clarify something. My nickname for her is Porn Star Meg, but I haven't actually confirmed that she's a porn star. I passed by her room once, and there was a camera set up and ring lights, all facing a giant leather couch with boas on it. I'm highly analytical, and I think it's safe to say that my assumption is correct.

Some nights, when I'm lonely, I think about going over there and asking her to hang out. The problem is, she's pretty and muscular and all things beautiful…and, well, I'm a brain and all the things that come along with being annoyingly smart. We just wouldn't mix.

Shit! My coffee is still sitting in the damn Keurig. Not much I can do about it now.

"Watch where ya going!" a man shouts. I look back

to see him hunched, fist raised, glaring at me.

The streets of New York City are no joke, and when you're like me and your situational awareness is lacking, you tend to make some enemies.

Why did I have to pick an apartment that has me walking against the flow of traffic?

I slip my earbuds in and lose myself in Imagine Dragons, the only thing that calms me. Listening to Radioactive, Thunder, and Demons helps my anxiety fall away, and my heart rate begins to enter the realm of 'normal.' Not that anything about me will ever be normal.

Do I have time to stop at a coffee shop? I stare at ImPressed longingly, the slight stabbing of a caffeine headache threatening to take over.

There is no time! You have a meeting at 8! It's 7:50, and you still have 15 more minutes of walking!

I suck in a breath, wish myself luck, and dash through the busy sidewalk. My stride feels off, like something is in my shoe, but I have no time to investigate as I'm dodging pedestrians.

Then, something magical happens. The world seems to open up for me, almost as if I'm in the Matrix. People step aside, the white hands bid me to walk across streets, and nothing gets in my way—for a time.

Then a big German Shepherd sets his sights on me.

The dog is bounding for me, clearly intent on knocking me over. All I can do is stop and bring up my arms to shield myself from the slobbering blow.

BAM! The dog connected with my petite 5'3 form, nearly barreling me over. I am lucky he's not aggressive, just curious. The little old lady walking him though does not share his pleasant disposition.

"Leave Jasper alone!" she croaks, tapping a cane near my feet.

Between the dog and the old lady, I am a bit overwhelmed, almost dropping my laptop bag.

I push at the dog, but it's no use. He just keeps sniffing. Finally, a little boy squeals when he sees the dog.

"Jasper! Jasper!" he enthuses, and the dog loses interest, but not before slobbering all over my left breast. That's right. I am going to be walking into the boardroom today, 5-10 minutes late, in a black shirt with slobber splattered across my tits. Great!

I continue on, cautiously now, wary of every person, every animal, every potential interaction. My earbuds fell from my ear blocks ago. My focus is entirely set on getting to Icor Towers and making the presentation.

They don't take me seriously. I've been sidelined on projects and underestimated at every turn. This is my chance to let them see me, see my strengths, and what I can do.

I may have graduated from grad school just over a year ago, but I had interned with Icor Tech a year before that, so I've actually been with them for just over two years. I started in at a position higher than most, but I never get the projects I want. Sure, I get promotions, and I'm great at my job, but it's always 'someone else's turn,' or the assumption is made that I am in over my head. Here I am, genius-level intelligence, constantly in rooms where people merely considered me subpar.

Oh my God! I finally made it!

I look up at the building I spend 50-plus hours a week

at, a wave of relief washing over me.

I can do this. People are late for meetings all the time, why shouldn't I be extended the same courtesy?

This meeting is different, though. This meeting, I will be presenting. This meeting, they will see something they don't expect. Something I hope they will like and wish to see more of.

I push my way through the huge doors of Icor Tower, lost in thought. My shoes echo on the tile, which isn't at all normal. Usually, the clicks are drowned out by other sounds, but today, the entrance seems cavernous. I look around, it's dead. Security eyes me suspiciously from behind the welcome counter, but other than that, no one.

That's weird.

I have no time to think on it. I walk to the elevator, scan my access badge, and wait for my carriage to arrive.

Everything seems to take too long. Each passing minute feels like ten, and I swear, by the time the elevator door opens, I've aged at least ten years.

I hustle into the elevator, surprised I don't have to share it with anyone. I push the button to go to the eighth floor and run through my speech for the millionth time.

Ladies and Gentlemen, I know we've been using Telwire for as long as Icor Tech's been established, but after some digging, research, and yada yada yada I found if we switch to Expression we will streamline five central core processes, produce reports in greater detail, and save the company over five million dollars over the course of ten years.

I've been practicing the speech for over a week, and now I get to blindside them. Technically, my actual job involves mechanical engineering, but I noticed a few of our systems were inefficient and lagging. On my own time, I researched it and developed a few automated reports on my own, catching the attention of some of my superiors. It was the first good thing they ever attributed to me, but it wasn't even within my job description.

Initially, they weren't even that impressed, but when my reports started saving several man-hours and increased data accuracy, well, that caught their attention, and that's why I was asked to speak at the meeting.

But instead of simply telling them my recent innovations, I'm going to tell them they're working with outdated systems. There's no doubt I'll be stepping on some toes, but this is just the sort of thing it takes to get noticed.

I exit the elevator after an eternity and practically run down the hall to the double doors of the boardroom. It is dark, too dark.

It's probably just some energy efficiency measure. Stay calm. Act natural. You got this.

But of course, I never listen to myself, and as soon as I walk through the door, I'm stammering my apology.

Except, I'm in an empty room. The lights are off. No one's here.

Where is everyone?

A chair pivots, it's spinning around, and I see... *Chance Crawford?*

"Oh, hi. I didn't expect anyone to be in here today," Chance Crawford says.

"There's...there's the quarterly Innovation Meeting...at eight. I'm late," I stammer.

Chance's mouth twitches to the side as though he's amused. He rises from his chair and says, "An innovation meeting? On a Sunday?"

Sunday? Holy mother of Jesus, it's Sunday. And that's NOT Chance Crawford.

"Oh no," I gasp, my eyes grow wide as my glasses slide halfway down my nose.

Gabriel Icor is walking towards me, hand outstretched. As though I'm supposed to touch him!

He is the twenty-eight-year-old grandson of Icor Tech's founder and has been running the company for just over four years, since his father passed away.

I take a step back, startled, and look for an escape.

"You don't have to rush out," he says. "I'm glad for the company, actually."

Gabriel isn't dressed in a suit, which is what he's wearing in every image I've ever seen of him. Instead, he has on blue jeans and a white cotton tee-shirt. A tee-shirt that clings to his tightly-toned physique.

This is the first time I've ever seen him in person, and as far as I know, he's not scheduled to be at the meeting. Now, standing here in the boardroom, on a Sunday, I am staring at one of the richest men in the world, a billionaire, having to apologize for being a fucking idiot.

He's in front of me now, donning a friendly smile. "I'm Gabriel. You may have heard of me."

"Of course! I mean, yes, sir. I mean…" I look down at his hand, knowing I must complete the formality, no matter how embarrassed I am, but instead of completing the handshake, I accidentally grab his right hand with my left hand, creating the most pretentious looking shake imaginable.

"May I have your name?" he asks.

"Oh, uh, yes. My name is Remi. Remi Stone."

Gabriel chuckles. "No need to be nervous. You know what they say about the early bird."

He frowns. "God, that's so cliche, sorry. My granddad was full of sayings like that."

"Yes. I mean, I'm sure he was. I mean—"

"STOP!" He gestures frantically with his hands. He's apparently very articulate with them when he talks. "Stop being nervous. I'm just like everyone else."

No, he most certainly is not. He is tall, tanned, well-muscled, with dark hair and a sexy five o'clock shadow and two baby-blue eyes. He is NOT AT ALL like anyone else. He's a 10 for crying out loud. Oh, and he has billions of dollars.

"I'll try, sir. It was nice to meet you." I turn, sweat pouring down my face, and begin walking on shaky legs.

"Wait!" Gabriel calls from behind. "If you don't mind, I'd like to ask you a few questions."

Ask ME a few questions? Gabriel Icor wants to ask little ole Remi a few questions? What dimension did I wake up in? This is stranger than the whole Avengers timeline bullshit.

I turn to him, swallowing nervously. "What would you like to know?" I ask.

"How do you feel about the company? About the processes?"

"The processes?"

"Yes, I feel things have gotten a bit stale around here. We need to keep up with the times. If we fail to adapt, to evolve, we will eventually become obsolete."

Is he really saying this? I think to myself. I want to tell him the truth, tell him what I found, but I'm scared.

My hands are shaking. And why is he looking at my feet like that?

I look down, and a wave of horror washes over me. I'm wearing one black shoe and one pink shoe. I had traveled the whole twenty minutes from my apartment to work completely unaware I was wearing mismatched shoes.

"Oh, I…oh, wow."

Gabriel purses his lips to stifle his laughter, but the look on his face gives his amusement away.

"When I woke up today, I thought I was going to be late for the Innovation Meeting. Then I got attacked by the Godzilla of all cats. I forgot my coffee. I haven't eaten. A dog jumped on me, slobbering on my," I look down, suddenly growing even more mortified, "but I'm here, a whole 23.7 hours early. If you're wondering what the early bird gets—just take a look."

He stares at me a moment, donning a sly grin before finally saying, "How about the early bird gets treated to breakfast?"

Chapter Two

*That shirt did nothing wrong to **Remi**...*

I follow Gabriel Icor to the elevator, hopeful that he will indeed take me to get food and not to a looney bin. But really, who can blame him if he does? After all, I show up on a Sunday, hair unkempt, mismatched shoes, slobber on my breast, and unable to form a proper sentence.

We step inside the elevator, and he pushes the button for the fifty-seventh floor, and I sigh in relief. I'm pretty sure there is no looney bin anywhere on the upper levels of Icor Tower.

Gabriel looks over at me, and I estimate he's somewhere in the ballpark of 6'3. A giant compared to my below average 5'3.

"Have you been with the company long?" he asks.

Be calm. Answer his questions.

"Two years, sir." I manage to get out after entirely too much thought.

"Please, call me Gabe."

He wants me to call him Gabe? Like, not even his full first name. A nickname.

"Yes, sir. Oh gosh, I mean, I...uh."

He chuckles, looking at the floor.

How on Earth have I managed to make such a fool of myself?

"What is your position at Icor Tech?"

"I'm...I am a program manager. I oversee certain programs in Mechanical Engineering."

His eyes light up, an impressed look spreads across his handsome face. "Wow! I mean, you look young. I hadn't expected you to be a program manager."

"I'm twenty-three."

Gabe's brow wrinkles in confusion. "Twenty-three?" he asks, eyeing me suspiciously.

Oh great, he thinks I'm a nut that can't even figure out my own age. Wait! Did I get my age wrong? No...I'm pretty sure I'm twenty-three.

The elevator door opened, and he gestured for me to exit first.

Stepping out onto the landing, my breath catches in my throat. It looks as though the whole foyer is encased in golden decadence.

"I know, it's tacky," he says sheepishly. "My grandmother's doing."

"It's nice," I say, ogling the fine art hanging on the walls. I swear on Kibbles, it looks just as lavish as the Vatican.

"Follow me." He saunters down a hall to the left, and I realize he's taken me to his actual apartment.

I follow closely, but not too close. I don't think I've ever been so scared in my life, not even during finals week in college.

He walks with a swagger, the sexiest gait I've ever seen. His shirt is half-tucked into his jeans, revealing the hint of a worn, brown leather belt. He looks more like a ranch hand than a billion-dollar heir.

He brings me to a huge kitchen that belongs in a fine dining restaurant. The appliances are huge, some I don't even recognize. An oversized island, larger than some family-sized dinner tables, sits in the middle, and I swear there's a walk-in freezer off in the corner.

"What would you like to eat? Are you a bagel and cream cheese kind of girl, or a yogurt and fruit?"

"Yogurt and fruit," I reply, clutching my laptop bag as though it's my security blanket.

"Take a seat. I promise not to keep you waiting long."

Is my company's billionaire CEO really making me breakfast?

"How do you take your coffee?"

"Black. No! Cream and sugar."

He puts a cup under a fancy contraption, and within a minute, he has it ready, sitting in front of me with a coffee caddy.

I take a sip as he goes to the refrigerator, which looks

like a small cave, and soon the countertop is stacked with various yogurts that all looked completely foreign and very expensive.

I chose one with strawberries, something safe and familiar, and he holds up a piece of bread with a cocked eyebrow.

"Please," I say as I twist the top off the jar of yogurt.

Who buys yogurt in glass jars? I think to myself, studying the packaging. *Fancy, high-classy people do, that's who.*

Gabe puts the bread on a conveyor toaster and grabs his own blueberry flavored yogurt.

"This meeting must be a big deal to you," Gabe says as he scoops a spoonful into his mouth.

God, his mouth is perfect.

It takes me a moment to realize I'm staring, and of course, I overreact, and a large gob of yogurt falls onto my slobber stained black shirt.

I look up to see Gabriel staring at me, his brow raised, a slight smile playing on his lips.

Oh, no! Oh, no, no, no!

I turn a dozen shades of pink and reach for a linen—my hand clashing with Gabriel's.

"Well, I guess I should let you take care of that yourself," he says, releasing the linen.

"There's a bathroom right over there." He points to a large wooden door that looks like it belongs on a castle.

"Well, there's already dog slobber on my shirt, and nothing I do in that bathroom is going to get it clean, so I'm just going to finish my yogurt and hightail it outta here."

"I was hoping you wouldn't be in too great a hurry."

I swallow, saying a silent prayer to whatever is keeping me upright and functioning. Gabriel Icor wants to spend time with me. Remi Stone. Genius nobody.

I push my hair behind my ears, reposition my glasses, and dabbing at the slobber and yogurt stains on my shirt.

"Don't be embarrassed," he says. "I live where I work, and I have considerable help. I imagine you must have to wake up super early to get ready to catch the subway."

"No subway for me. I walk to work. It's about twenty minutes away. This was actually a pretty important day for me. I mean, tomorrow is."

"Oh?"

I don't know what I should say, or how I should say it. I don't want to offend him, calling his systems and processes inefficient, but it's the truth.

"Are you going to make me beg?"

The thought of Gabriel Icor begging makes the temperature rise at least ten degrees, and I start fanning myself with my hand. "Oh, God, please," I say without thinking, and suddenly, Gabriel is staring at me.

I wish I could say this is the first time I've ever blurted something out without thinking—but it seems I've made a habit of it over the years. This is by far the worst instance of my blurting.

Gabriel puts down his yogurt and leans on the island, the muscles of his arms bulging. He's smokin' hot, making me breakfast, and listening to me babble. I must be trapped in an episode of the Twilight Zone.

Suddenly, my hands are in his, and he's staring deeply into my eyes.

"Remi, please, I beg of you, tell me why tomorrow is

THE BILLIONAIRE'S BOARD

so important to you."

I sit there, gawking at him, completely mesmerized by his touch.

Then, he giggles. "You're nervous. I get it. Let's start over, and you can pretend like I'm a janitor."

His hands withdraw, and I focus on what he just said, so I can properly answer his question. But his suggestion has its flaws, and now I'm imagining him without his shirt on, sweating, as he mops the floor.

"So, what has you so eager to be on time for the meeting?" he asks again.

I exhale, trying to get my thoughts in order. "Well, Mr. Custodian, it's just that I'm so young, and most of them already have a negative outlook on millennials. I just don't want to give them more ammo."

Gabe frowns.

"I didn't mean to make it sound like they are bullies or anything, quite the contrary. It's just that—I feel like I don't exist to my superiors."

He smiles. "Believe me—I know exactly how you feel. I'm young, and it doesn't matter what I've accomplished when I walk into a room with people who have been in the business two decades longer than myself. It's like I'm relegated to the kids' table."

I picture Gabriel sitting at a 'kid's table,' without his shirt—*Oh, Lord, what's wrong with me?*

"So, how'd you become a twenty-three-year-old program manager?"

"Well, I don't mean to brag, but my brain's kind of big. Like, super big. Gigantic."

Gabe let out a sigh of relief. "Oh gosh, I'm so glad I don't have to pretend like I don't notice. I must say, I'm a bit nervous about it. Is there going to be a 'Reasonable Accommodation' request that I enlarge the doorways or something?"

"I assure you, all my requests will be within reason."

He pulls his phone out, glancing up at me every few moments as he types into his keyboard.

"Wow…I guess I owe you an apology."

"An apology?"

"I thought you were lying about your age. Women sometimes do that, ya know, but I see here, all your information checks out."

He holds his phone up for me to look at, and I see the picture on my badge, to the right of it my general information filed with HR.

"Level with me. How the hell did you get that position at my company at such a young age?"

"Your headhunters. They circle the ivy league schools, and cases such as mine are rare. They set me up to intern, and I did exceedingly well. After I obtained my bachelor's, I received tons of offers from other companies, but Icor Tech is where I really wanted to make my mark. When I finally graduated with my masters, I was fielding offers left and right, but I decided to stay with Icor Tech on the condition they gave me a program manager position, but I'm still treated like a child due to my age."

Gabriel walks around the island, taking a chair next to mine. He sits so close to me, I can feel his breath washing over my neck. My heart's thumping so loudly in my chest, I'm positive it could register on the Richter Scale. I struggle to regulate my breathing, so he doesn't get to witness me hyperventilating over his close proximity.

"So, why were you at the Innovation Meeting?"

I clear my throat, then I clear it again, and again. Finally, I say, "Well, sir, I was there to brief a database I've been developing to shortcut some of our redundant processes."

"So, what you're telling me is that you're a mechanical engineer briefing on business analytics? Did we put you in the right position?"

God, don't be an idiot! He doesn't care about your boring job. He has people hired to care.

"It's a little more than that," I say with downcast eyes.

"Gosh, I must make you really nervous."

I reach out to touch his forearm, a natural reaction that leaves me mortified. "Oh, ummm…It's not that. I just feel like your time is important. And I'm wasting it." I awkwardly fold my hands on the island in front of me, disallowing them from wandering further.

"Nonsense. I could have just sent you on your way back home. I invited you up for a reason."

It's as though his words push a crushing weight off my chest, and I'm suddenly calm. I smile. Something about Gabriel makes me feel at ease. Like he is actually interested in what I had to say.

"Well, I had decided to go a little bit beyond the scope of the presentation."

"Oh, really?" He turns, facing me squarely in the chair. "How so?"

"Well, I couldn't help but notice that some of the systems we use are inefficient and not as capable as other platforms."

"Which ones?" He spoons a yogurt-covered blueberry into his mouth, raising his brows.

I pivot my chair towards him and pick up my handbag that's sitting at my feet.

"Would you mind if I pulled out my laptop?" I ask.

"Not at all, I love visuals."

What's unfortunate about how he says this, though, is his line of sight. Pivoting to face him puts his gaze directly on my breasts while he's mumbling about how he loves visuals. I realize this immediate, hoping it will pass over unnoticed. But Gabriel soon realizes his folly.

"Oh gosh! I sound like a creep." He turns to face the island, and now we're both sitting awkwardly as I navigate my satchel.

"It's okay, we all like visuals," I say, trying to play it off.

Gabriel's staring at me now, critically, then he bursts out in a fit of laughter.

Way to up the creepiness factor, Remi!

With shaky hands, I pull my MacBook Pro from my bag, turning it on to even more laughter from Gabriel.

"Really?" Gabriel says, looking at the image of The Golden Girls that appeared on my screen.

I smile, though it is more from nostalgia than humor. When I was growing up, I watched The Golden Girls with my mother each night. That was before she passed, when I was seven.

"I learned everything I know about love from Blanche Devereaux."

"That minx."

I turn to him, surprised. "You know her?"

"I used to watch it with my grandma. It has probably

given me unrealistic expectations of older women in bed."

My eyes grow round. I certainly didn't expect to hear that coming from his mouth.

Gabriel Icor, my billionaire boss, just told me he has expectations of older women in bed.

A worried look flashes across Gabriel's face. "Oh no, you've gone pale. I'm sorry. It was just a joke. Forgive me."

"Well, to be fair, I guess I started us down this path."

"Yes. Yes, you did. We'll stick with that when HR calls us in for questioning."

I can't help but smile as I pull up the slideshow presentation I had ready.

He slides his hand to the touchpad, and for a moment, our fingers connect before I retract my hand, vowing never to wash it again.

"Oh," he says, his face a display of confusion, "you're recommending Expressions?"

"Yes," I say, nervously. "I've figured out that it can help us streamline some practices and eventually save us—"

"Millions of dollars," Gabriel cuts in.

Well, that kind of takes the wind from my sails.

"Yes, sir. How do you know that?"

"Because I've also been looking at Expressions, but my old, crusty board can't seem to see at my level."

Maybe I should be happy we've come to the same conclusion, but right now, all my work looks unnecessary.

"Oh, so all this—"

"Is brilliant. You're brilliant. Tell me, how did you

figure all this out? I have access to data and reports and all the other crap that comes with access, but you shouldn't be able to see across systems like this."

"It really wasn't that hard. I knew how to find the numbers, and the ones I didn't have access too, I went to the department heads. Some data is also available from old presentations, so a few of the figures are a quarter off."

"God, that brain of yours, it's huge."

I feel myself blush, as if I could grow any redder. For the first time at Icor Tech, I feel truly appreciated.

Gabriel leans back in his chair, an easy grin on his handsome, perfect 10 face. "So, you're hired."

"Pardon? I've been working here for two years."

"Yeah, but…you've been working as a program manager. I think you need a different position."

The blood drained from my face. I no longer have to worry about looking like a lobster because now I look like a ghost.

"Sir, are you offering me a job?"

"It's a small one, and I'm not offering—I'm demanding you take it."

"I…this…"

"There's a whole floor of office suites for directors and board members—one of those has your name on it because I want you working close to me as an assistant."

Gabriel Icor, heir to the Icor Tech and his family fortune, the perfect 10, wants little old Remi Stone working closely with him, and I am honestly worried I might be having a heart attack. I mean, I am the youngest program manager his company has ever had by two years, and now I'll be working closely with the head of the company as some type of systems analyst or something!

"Sir, are you sure you don't want to think this over?"

"First—I told you to call me Gabe. Second, not one other person has given serious thought to switching platforms. All they do is talk about the cost, having to teach a new system, ignoring the data I shove in front of them. They're so scared of change. Did you know one board member is literally waiting for the day we no longer have computers? He keeps a contingency plan. Seriously, if there is ever a time computers don't work, Icor Tech is going down. After all, we're called Icor TECH for crying out loud."

"Wait, you mean to tell me that a high up member of Icor seriously believes we'll one day wake up to none of the computers working?"

"No joke. I often imagine he watches porn only on VHS. His selection must be lacking."

I blush again, disbelieving that Gabriel Icor has uttered the word porn in my presence.

"Oh, gosh, I'm sorry. I really shouldn't have said that."

"No—no. It's okay. It was funny."

"But it was inappropriate."

I bite my lip, heart leaping into my throat. Oh, to be lucky enough to have Gabriel Icor actually be inappropriate with me. I mean, even if he weren't worth billions, he'd be a catch with his well-formed body, his dark shaggy hair, and his stunning blue eyes.

I give him a wink. "Well, if you'd like, I can sit down with him and bring him up to DVD era technology."

Gabriel let out a hearty chuckle, hands covering his

face. "Oh boy, what have we gotten ourselves into."

I smile, reveling in the thought that Gabriel Icor and I now share a personal, inside joke—not that he will remember it after today, but it is surely something I will be repeating to my grave. All my grandkids will be gathered around while I'm on my deathbed telling them for the hundredth time how I offered to teach a board member of Icor Tech how to watch porn on DVD, to Gabriel Icor himself.

His voice lowers, he looks nervous.

"I need to ask you a favor," he says, leaning close to me.

Oh, God, we're practically touching. Gabriel Icor is so close I can feel him next to me.

"W...what d...do you want?" I stutter like a complete fool.

"Here's the situation…"

Chapter Three

Gabriel's no good, very rotten board....

It's not every day that an enigma walks through the doors of your boardroom, but when one does, you take notice.

When Remi Stone barged in, my first thought was that she was lost, or even drunk. She was disheveled, with a stained black shirt and mismatched shoes. It would have been easy to dismiss her, and on another day, I probably would have, but she came into that boardroom at a time of perfect chaos, when I desperately needed a distraction.

As it turned out—she might be the solution to my problems.

Icor Tech didn't become the juggernaut that it is overnight, and it took quite a team to get Icor this far—an aging team that isn't changing with the times.

Whenever I see an opportunity, I have to fight my way through red tape, or rather, silver tape—the aged board members that just won't let go of the past.

Now, in truth, they are one of my company's most valuable assets. Icor Tech wouldn't be what it is today without the remaining original board members, and they still provide valuable insight.

The problem is, when it comes to upgrading old tech, they keep insisting that the new programs lack support, they're so new they must have bugs, or, my personal favorite, our workforce of almost exclusively engineers can't possibly learn a new system!

And, if I'm being honest, it's not just the older board members that are a problem. Tom Wellington, our CFO, is the biggest thorn in my side.

The board was originally comprised of the original five board members, called the Big 5, and my grandfather, Maxwell Icor, who was the sixth board member. Whenever a board member retires or passes, a new one is appointed. For some reason, my father had Tom appointed to the board when a position wasn't available, bringing the board to seven members.

Tom's just a little older than myself, but he's determined to be an obstacle to every success I try to make. He schmoozes with the other board members, sucking up like a big leech, turning their votes against me, and there's nothing I can do about it.

The problem goes deeper than just old tech, though. It's change in general. They seem to have a problem letting go of ANYTHING.

I've been working for Icor Tech since I was sixteen, even through college, and it hasn't changed.

I was twenty-one when I took my first real stand. I demand we switch from single-ply to two-ply toilet paper. And so the tissue wars began.

Everyone picked sides. I was told I was being gratuitous, that I would one day run the family business to the ground with my desire for luxury. Um, excuse me. Two-ply toilet paper isn't a luxury. It's like a bare minimum expectation for a billion-dollar corporation to have.

With my stance, I solidified the loyalty of the underlings. Then a group that went around calling themselves the Toilet Trio came in and TPed one of the board member's offices. It was a mess—that I had to fix, mind you.

In case you're wondering: no, high-level grey hairs cannot take a joke. The Toilet Trio was put on probation, but in the end, the cause prevailed. One of my only real successes at Icor Tech is literally getting two-ply toilet paper to the masses.

That's why I need Remi on my side. She doesn't just stop with an idea. Based on her spreadsheets, she takes care in conducting research, not jumping to any unproven conclusion. Her thorough research will hopefully convince the board better than I can.

This would all be easier if she wasn't so damn distracting, though. Does she even realize the effect she had on me? How utterly charmed I was?

She only has to make it through tomorrow, and make no mistake—tomorrow is going to be a doozy for her.

I feel bad, really, I do. Remi and her twenty-three year old, bright-eyed self does not deserve the shit storm that's about to be thrown at her. And she's so unsuspecting.

It's the only way.

Remi deserves an office with underlings and access to all the systems and data her little analytical heart desires, but first, I have to see if she sinks or swims. So yes, I'm about to toss her out to sea, but the greater the risk, the greater the reward. Or at least that's what grandpa Max used to say.

I just hope she doesn't hate me afterward.

Obviously, I don't want her to hate me because of her stellar work ethic and results—but I can't deny that she's also kind of hot. Beneath her disheveled exterior is a body most men would be eager to get their hands on. Who could blame me for thinking about what's underneath that sexy, tight skirt of hers? I mean, she wasn't wearing hose, did she forego panties as well?

Oh, my God, am I really thinking this? Am I sitting here, at my desk, wondering if the twenty-three-year-old clumsy genius is wearing panties or not?

She's the kind of hot you see on The Big Bang Theory. Big glasses, dated clothes, quirky, and what's the word? Oh yeah, adorable. What a catch!

My phone buzzes, and I push to connect the line, wishing I had a few more moments to think about the brainy beauty.

Gabe: *What is it, mom?*

Mom: *The flowers are arranged. Lilies and alstroemerias—roses are so dated.*

Gabe: *Mom, I don't care about flowers.*

Mom: *Well, you should! This is a very important family you're marrying into.*

Gabe: *Yeah, but I have bigger things to worry about than flowers, which will no doubt be dead within a week.*

Mom: *We can make a show of the flowers, have them sent to gravestones after the event.*

Gabe: *Don't you think that's a bit tacky?*

Mom: *You're right. I'll run it past PR first. Sayo's mom said something about having an herb in the arrangement. Isn't that wild?*

Gabe: *Well, is it cultural?*

Mom: *I don't know. I figured it was a millennial thing.*

> **Gabe:** *Well, if Sayo's mother is the one—*
>
> **Mom:** *I just want this special day to be perfect for you. I can't believe in two short months…*

My mother's sobs carry over the phone, tugging at my heart.

> **Gabe:** *I know mom. I'm all grown up.*
>
> **Mom:** *She's so beautiful. I can't wait for my grandbabies.*

I clutch my chest. I mean, this is a lot of pressure to put on an only child—the sole carrier of my parent's combined DNA.

> **Gabe:** *Well, I gotta go, mom. Love ya.*

I press disconnect and shove all thoughts of weddings and flowers aside, trying to focus on my current problem—how I'm going to save Icor Tech from going under, which will be inevitable if I can't get these dinosaurs out of the prehistoric age.

I walk over to an antique cabinet and pull out a cheap bottle of scotch. Funny how everyone assumes I drink only the high-end brands. Sure, I have those at parties and business dinners, but Cutty Sark does the job just as well.

I take a long sip, allowing my mind to settle on Remi again, her large doe eyes, her messy blonde hair. Utterly charming and completely unlike any woman I've dated.

In a few short days, if all goes as planned, she'll get her promotion, and it won't just be a new office she'll get. She'll move into Icor Tower as well. Close to myself.

What if she has a boyfriend?

The thought makes me anxious, jealous. She didn't wear a wedding ring, but with her clear disorientation, she might have forgotten to slip it on in the morning. It really shouldn't bother me, not with my own nuptials just around the corner, but it does.

You just met this woman! What is wrong with you?

It's true, I've just met Remi Stone for the first time, and it's not like me to think on a woman too hard. It's just, I don't remember ever having so much fun talking with a woman before. And she's just so smart. I admire her.

My heart feels heavy, an unfamiliar ache. I suddenly realize I'm doomed, having to work with her—closely even, hearing about her dates, her eventual marriage, and one day, her children. She'll no doubt ask me about mine, and what will I say? Will I lie and say everything is fine? Or will she know?

I take another sip, determined to keep my heart at bay and focus on the problem I can actually do something about. Saving my company.

Chapter Four

Cregor is a Grumpy pants...

God, why must we sit through another 'innovation' meeting? People trying to fix things that aren't broken, so that they can get a bullet on their resume or a promotion.

I'm seated with five other board members at the table: Tom, Jim, Essie, Lindel, and Barry. Several directors are seated along the wall, waiting for the meeting to begin. The seventh member of the board, Gabriel, won't bother showing up—he never does.

These meetings will be the death of stability. Very

few of these changes are actually good, and even fewer pan out. I've been on Icor Tech's board for forty years—from the very beginning. There's a reason I'm still around when others are long gone.

Two unfilled seats. What the heck is taking them so long? It's 7:58. Back in my day, it was fifteen minutes early or don't bother showing up at all. These damn millennial XYZers think they can show up a half-hour late and get a trophy just for being there at all. Well, that ain't how it works around Icor. Icor Tech didn't rise to the top from lax worth ethics. Oh no! Sixty-hour workweeks and steadfast resolve are what separated us from the herd.

It's 7:59, and one seat is still open. If I had it my way, doors would be locked at 8, but no. We wouldn't want to hold anyone accountable for their actions now, would we?

The door opens, and a mouse of a woman steps into the room at 8:00 on the nose. Her head is down, glasses sliding off the bridge of her nose, wavy blonde hair framing a delicate face—far too young to be invited to these types of meetings.

Tom Wellington rises to shake her hand, ever eager to make the pretty woman feel at home.

"Remi, it's good to have you up here," he says.

Now, Jim is rising to shake her hand as well. The directors that line the back wall are waving, smiling at her—trying to make her feel welcome.

My eyes stay glued to my paperwork as names are called out, Barry and Lindel follow my lead. We are what's left of The Big Five, the first five employees of Maxwell Icor.

Barry had been Maxwell's best friend in high school, the first of us. Then came Christopher Bass, may God rest his soul. Dean Whitmore, now retired. Myself, then finally, Lindel Sampson.

When Maxwell hired Lindel all those years back, it was a shock to 'The First Four,' as we so-called ourselves back then. Not so much that she was a woman, as someone had to keep the coffee coming, but because she was black.

When we voiced our opinions, Maxwell simply dismissed them. And boy, did we not like our thoughts being taken so lightly and more than one of us thought of walking.

It was a different time then, and I'm not too proud to admit that I was wrong—about so many things. Lindel ended up being the glue that solidified the team—solidified the Big Five. She focused our efforts, the epitome of 'work smarter, not harder.' If Maxwell was the brains of the operation, Lindel was the heart, and boy could she cut a rug.

"And this here is Cregor," Tom said, bringing the mouse to my side.

I keep my eyes on my papers, disallowing the woman the satisfaction of my welcome. These 'innovation meetings' as they call them, have largely been a waste of time, rarely resulting in any lasting changes. It was Gabriel Icor, bane of his grandfather's name, that started them, thinking he knew better than us 'old folks'.

"Don't mind him," Tom said. "You can take a seat. We'll have the slides up in just a moment."

The mouse doesn't sit. Instead, she says, "Actually, Tom, I have some things on my laptop I'd like to share."

"Oh? You didn't have them available Friday?"

"Well, I did, but I couldn't submit them. They require a bit of explaining, and they wouldn't have made it past review."

Damnit, as if I didn't need any more of my time being wasted. It's bad enough this is likely to run over an hour.

"I have these sheets here for everyone to review along with the presentation."

Papers are flying around the room, and I have to grit my teeth to hold my tongue.

Tom opens the meeting, explaining that Remi is here to brief a database she had developed and how training will be rolled out.

What a relief. For a moment, I thought she was going to try to do some big overhaul of a pertinent system. Efficiency is good, though, and if she's found a way to automate a few processes, good for her. Give her the damn raise she's gunning for and let us get on with business.

Tom gives Remi the floor.

It's a lackluster opening from the mouse. A brief discussion of her work. Training times. Man-hours. She's rambling on, and I'm nearly bored to tears.

Then the hammer falls.

"If we were to switch from Telwire to Expressions, we would go from eight core systems down to three, and —"

"Bollocks!" I yell, jumping from my chair. "Is this a damn salesman or an employee?"

Her eyes grow wide, flashing with fear.

The board members are looking at me, as are the directors. I imagine they are rather grateful I have said what they felt they could not. It's what comes with being one of the Big 5. You say what you want, when you want to say it.

"I'd like to hear a little more of what she has to say," Tom says with his usual good-natured grin.

Damn, Tom Wellington. He'd be good for nothing if it weren't for the barriers he creates for Gabriel.

I throw the papers in the center of the table. "Of course, you would. You just love wasting company resources."

Others are chiming it, but it isn't until Lindel speaks up that I hear anyone making any sense.

"Now, how do we know we aren't going to end up with some obsolete tech again," Lindel says, raising a valid concern.

Over the years, the trap Icor Tech fell into time and time again was wasting money on technology and software that was eventually rendered obsolete. Initially, we wanted to be first movers, getting the products before the competition, and at a discount. The number of times we were burned and the dollars wasted—uncountable.

The mouse clears her throat, forcing her voice louder. "Expressions is owned by Fingor Inc., and as we all know, they aren't going anywhere. Expressions also solves seven of the Ten most common complaints raised by people working with Telwire. If anything, Fingo—"

"You're probably having us look at a small snapshot of what, the last two years?" I interject.

"If you look at the papers I handed out, you will see it's been going on for five. Five long years of lackluster performance, and five years before that of merely adequate. And from what I see, they don't have anything scheduled to launch. They're basically staying afloat."

I look around, gauging support from my fellow board members—from Lindel. She looks deep in thought, pursed lips, brows drawn in. She never speaks unless she's had time to thoroughly mull that data.

Barry is red-faced, fist pressed to stomach. Damnit, Barry has gas again, which means he's not paying attention. At least not to us. He's probably paying considerable attention to his clenched spinster. If there was ever a reason to clear out the boardroom, it was Barry's gas.

"Gabriel might want to see this," Tom finally says.

"Why? So he can upgrade the bathroom to cleansing butt wipes?" I say.

The girl starts to sputter, and I know it's time to close in and pounce, but then Tom speaks up.

"I think we need to get Gabriel on the line."

The boardroom falls silent.

No one can come out and say, "No, don't call that idiot," but it's what we're all thinking.

Maxwell Icor was a genius, but his son fell a little further from the tree than expected, and because of that, Gabriel cannot be trusted.

The monitor flickers, Gabriel's face filling the screen. *Damnit!*

"What's up?" he asks casually.

He's the damn CEO of Icor Tech answering a business matter with 'what's up?' I sure do hope Maxwell Icor is not haunting these halls.

"Gabe," Lindel enthuses. "How are you doing?"

Lindel acted as a mother to Gabriel, but unfortunately, for as much time as Gabriel spent with the cunning woman, he didn't take on many of her qualities. Still, he was like a son to her. Her own granddaughter had dated him, and boy did Lindel have strong words with her when she broke it off.

"I'm well. Sorry, I couldn't make it to the meeting. I'm a little busy as of late."

"Gabe, we have a program manager here, Remi Stone, and she has a proposal, and I gotta tell ya, I don't think I've ever been so impressed before."

Tom's looking at the mouse, or rather leering. He does enjoy himself a pretty woman, making his way through the New York City socialites at lightning speed, but he should know better than to look that way at an underling.

"Well, what does she have for me, Tom?" Gabriel asks.

I sigh, rather vocally. I'm not known to suffer silently.

The mouse proceeds with the proposal, stopping to answer questions from time to time. I initially assumed most of the data was estimated, but it turns out, she actually called around to get most of the figures.

Gabriel takes interest, asking way too many questions regarding something that should have been tabled immediately. The damn fool just likes to hear himself talk is all.

Finally, Gabriel says, "I think it needs to be brought before a vote. It's solid research and definitely headed in the right direction. Why don't we give it two weeks to chew on?"

Go before a vote? A vote? Damnit, they're taking the mouse more seriously than I had anticipated.

A vote such as this involves more than just the seven board members. It would involve the directors' input as well. Countless man-hours will be lost on this endeavor. I can't stay silent.

"Not so fast!" I speak up. "Do you realize just what this will entail?"

Tom smiles that ridiculous grin of his and says, "It looks like Remi's done most of the research for us."

"I'll say," Gabriel says through the monitor. "I'm rather impressed by the slides and the accuracy of the data."

"I knew you'd want to see good work, Gabe," Tom says, leering at the mouse.

"Thank you for finding Ms. Stone. But looking at what she's put together and her actual job description, well, needless to say, they don't align."

Tom frowns, glaring at the monitor. "Well, I don't think we should hold a go-getter attitude against her. Let's not discourage innovation."

"Oh, certainly not. But as CEO, it's clearly within my right to make adjustments to the org chart. And I must say, the position that suits Remi Stone best is director."

Chapter Five

Remi needs better stress management…

Oh, dear God, thank you for helping me make it out of there alive. What are you going to request of me? My firstborn child, not that I'll ever get to consummate anything with how much time I spend at work, but there's always the dream.

I stand alone in the bathroom, hands clutching the sink. I fight the waves of nausea threatening to overwhelm me, but I'm losing, and bile fills my throat. I choke it down, not wanting to soil the executive bathrooms.

I was only supposed to be an assistant. Nothing was said about me becoming a director.

I just faced the entire board and a bunch of directors and told them they were working with dated systems.

Then the head of the company, Gabriel Icor, got on the line and promoted me to a sea of mixed reactions. I just became public enemy number one to a bunch of powerful people, and the only ally I have, couldn't bother to be there in person.

Well, there was Tom. He seemed to be delighted in what I had to say and my promotion.

The door opens, my breath catches in my throat. The last thing I need is to be caught off guard. I press the soap dispenser, filling my hand with too much suds, but I can't help myself. I'm in a daze, shaking, and more than a little terrified.

Oh, God! It's Lindel Sampson!

Lindel Sampson is a known woman, and not just around Icor Tech. She has a New York Times Bestselling novel out based on her life, one that I have read half a dozen times.

At fifteen, Lindel dropped out of high school, taking odd jobs to help care for her eight brothers and sisters. When Maxwell first hired her, it was merely to bring them coffee and take memos. Since she was black, not as many people were willing to hire her, so she worked for scraps.

But when Maxwell started to show earnings, he paid her double the average salary for her position, and eventually, she became part of the board. When Maxwell talked, the world listened, and he said in front of everyone that his company would not be where it was without Lindel. And now, here I am crying just thinking about it.

"You okay?" Lindel says, eyes narrowed.

My jaw drops.

Lindel Sampson is talking to me, Remi Stone, who has worked at Icor Tech for just over two years. Lindel Sampson, who wasn't afforded the benefit of a college education—a high school education—yet helped grow an empire, is talking to me.

I can't say anything. I can only stare. Now, she's looking worried, gazing at me critically, and I realize what a creep I'm being.

"I'm sorry," I finally say.

"Sorry for what? Your rudeness?"

"Yes, I mean, I just can't believe I'm in here with—"

"Lindel Sampson. You think I don't get that everywhere I go? You should see me walking into innercity high schools. They scream louder for me than they do for Justin Bieber, but that's not what I'm here to talk about."

"Pardon?" I look at her, confused.

"You go waltzing into that boardroom, telling your superiors about their inefficiencies, end up sweeping the room—getting a director position."

"I'm sorry? Oh, gosh—"

"Why you sorry for? That shit is rude as hell, but do you think I got to my position by being polite?"

I stare at her blankly, unsure of what she's getting at.

"Look, what I'm trying to say is don't go all acting like everyone's friend. You aren't. If Gabe hadn't been wired in, you would have been chewed up and spit out. We'd all be laughing, talking about how you came on into our room, our board, and told us how to run things."

I stare at her, even more confused than I was a moment before if that's even possible. Everything she says seems to contradict itself, and I'm left unsure of what to say in return.

"I don't like you, but I don't dislike you. Ya got that going for ya. People like you come and go. Bright young things. But if this idea of yours turns out to be bad, to be a fluke, based on a little blip in the radar—well, you'll be leaving Icor Tech and flipping burgers at McDonald's."

I'm unsure of whether Lindel's giving me a warning or issuing a threat.

"Dry your damn hands," Lindel says and turns to exit the bathroom.

I mull over her words, and suddenly, I can no longer keep the bile at bay. I rush to a stall, narrowly missing the floor as my stomach overturns.

When Gabriel asked me to keep his knowledge of my presentation a secret, I thought it was to allow me to retain credit and make it less likely people would think he manipulated the data.

I had not expected him to elevate me to the position of director. I merely thought I was getting a slight promotion to work on similar projects. And I certainly didn't expect the chaos that ensued.

I had to stand there in a sea of angry voices, Tom being the only shelter in the storm. I honestly don't know what I would have done if he hadn't calmed the crowd.

My phone vibrates, and I pull myself up from my kneeling position, turn, taking a seat on the toilet. It's a text from Gabriel Icor himself.

Gabe: *You did great!*

I wanted to throw my phone in the trash—no—in the toilet. I'm so angry, but I have no idea where to direct it towards. I mean, Gabriel gave me a director position—at twenty-three! I had thought it was a big deal when I became a program manager at twenty-three, but that's nothing compared to becoming a director. I should be thanking Gabriel, but with the way the position was presented, I can't help but want to go back to being a program manager.

Remi: *Thanks.*

What else am I supposed to say? I can't just ignore him. After all, judging by what the other directors make, he did just give me a six-figure raise.

Gabe: *Would you join me for coffee Friday morning?*

Coffee? Gabriel Icor would like me to join him for coffee?

It's almost too much, and I fear I'll be found dead, slumped over on a toilet seat. Forever the joke of Icor Tech. I'll be like that ghost haunting the bathroom in Harry Potter.

I recall the way his blue jeans sat on his hips, his sexy saunter, his taut muscles.

He's your boss! Stop this! Stop it now! You don't want to be sitting in meetings, undressing him as he's giving a presentation.

But…that's exactly what I want to do. I mean, what heterosexual woman wouldn't want to have sex with Gabriel Icor? He's charming, hot, muscular, and sexy as hell. And—a billionaire! The question is, why would he want to have sex with me?

He has taken an interest in you.

I dare to dream for just a moment. Gabriel looking at me with lust-filled eyes, taking off his shirt, his pants, his —

Then reality hits.

It's because you're a genius, nitwit.

Oh yeah, of course. How could I forget? For a moment, I had dared hope that he just might fancy me, but that would be absurd. I mean, Gabriel Icor has dated supermodels. There is no chance he'd ever want anything more than a professional relationship with me.

He's my boss. I must say yes, I tell myself, but I really don't need convincing. Gabe is a perfect 10 in looks and smarts. Of course, I want to have coffee with him.

Remi: *Sure.*

Gabe: *Great! I'll show you your new apartment next week. I'm having it readied for you.*

New apartment? That's right, Icor Tower houses several suites at the upper levels reserved for board members and select directors. I guess I'm going to get to move.

Right now, I'm living off of just over 500 square feet, my monster cat Kibbles claiming around 150 of it for herself. With any luck, I might gain a few hundred.

> **Remi:** *There's something I haven't told you.*
>
> **Gabe:** *Oh? Do you have a fiancé or something? If he passes the background check, you're welcome to have him come live with you.*
>
> **Remi:** *No, it's not that. It's worse.*
>
> **Gabe:** *Oh, dear, what is it? Are you some kind of sex offender? Damn it. I shouldn't have ignored that vibe.*
>
> **Remi:** *No! It's just that—I have a monster cat, bigger than Godzilla even.*
>
> **Gabe:** *How big can this cat possibly be?*
>
> **Remi:** *30 lbs. It's haunted by the ghost of my dead grandma. She's ornery.*
>
> **Gabe:** *Well, you're in luck, because if anyone can afford an exorcist, it's me.*

Butterflies are fluttering in my stomach, making me giddy. I can't believe how funny he is and that he's wasting his jokes on me.

Now, I just need to go back to my tiny office four floors down, pack up, and wait to be escorted to my new office.

I shove my phone in my bra, cursing the fake pockets on my black pantsuit and exit the stall.

Standing before me, clipboard in hand is what can only be described as a supermodel. At least five-foot-nine, flawless skin, and perfectly proportioned.

"I hope you didn't get any in your hair," she says.

"Pardon?" I reply.

"Puke. I thought that was obvious."

I turn red, willing my legs to navigate around the woman to the sinks but fail entirely, and I stand there staring, mouth gaping like a fish.

"So you're Remi Stone?"

I blink. She knows me. She's been waiting for me. While I've been throwing up in the executive bathroom stall, this Amazon had been silently standing outside.

"Was it Cregor? I bet it was Cregor. Shining beacon of antiquity that he is. You should have seen him after we toilet papered his office—he went ballistic! He wanted me fired."

My brows raise, my stomach is released from the iron grip clenching it. "You toilet papered his office?" I ask.

"Yeah, but it was during a different time. Coffee wasn't free, timecards were highly scrutinized, and toilet paper was so thin it was like wiping your ass with your bare hand."

I stare at her, unsure if she's being friendly or

sarcastic. Part of me wants to laugh, but if this woman ends up being a snake, I am quite positive she has awfully long fangs.

"My name is Analise, by the way." She holds out her hand, revealing a perfectly filed set of nails, then suddenly retracts it, a sneer crossing her face.

"Yeah, maybe I should wait for you to wash your hands."

My legs grow bold, and I find myself navigating to the sink to take her suggestion. When I'm done, I turn back around to restart our introduction.

I take her hand, shaking it with the firmness I hear is desired in the business world, but the sight of her grimacing lets me know I'm being way too over-ambitious.

"I'm here to take you to your new office, and boy, are you lucky." The side of her lip cocks up into a smirk.

"How so?"

"You're up in the 'Shark Tank.'"

"The Shark Tank?"

"Yeah, the executive level."

"Can you tell me something?" I ask.

"Sure thing."

"Am I on some kind of reality television show?"

The pretty redhead scrunches her brow.

"I mean, are there hidden cameras everywhere? Is Ashton Kutcher going to jump out and yell surprise? Because surely this has to be some kind of prank, and people are laughing at me from their televisions."

Analise's eyes grow round. She blinks.

"Or worse, is this the Truman Show? Has my whole life been some big joke?"

She clears her throat, looking at her clipboard. Then she turns ever so slightly to the side, brings a hand up to her ear and says, "Lunchbox, Lunchbox—do you read?"

What the hell is she doing?

"Lunchbox, this is Pumpkin Spice, do you copy?"

I stand there looking at her, trying to figure out what the fuck is going on.

"Lunchbox, we've been made. Repeat we've been made. Abandon ship"

I laugh, realizing she is jesting, and for the first time, I see a genuine smile cross Analise's face. I like her, even if she doesn't like me. She's not fake, and I'm pretty sure whatever her intentions are, she'll make them quite clear. The devil you know is definitely better than the devil you don't, and by the look on her face, I am assured she's quite the demon.

"Let's get you up to your new office," she says.

I finally muster a smile. "Lead the way," I say and follow her from the bathroom.

Chapter Six

***Gabriel** wants what he can't have…*

I pace my office, just as my granddad had when he was my age, trying to fix company problems.

The innovation meeting went perfectly, solidifying key players onto my side of the court without them even realizing it.

Although it may seem silly that I have to work political angles to get common-sense initiatives passed, that's just the boat I'm in. It's impossible for me to get anything done around Icor Tech. If I have an idea I try to push, I'm seen as vain, trying to change a company that climbed to the top over the years with no good reason.

And it's getting exhausting.

It's the reason I was in the boardroom on Sunday. I was planning on going to the meeting and bringing up a couple ideas. When Remi came into the picture in her mismatched shoes and drool-stained shirt, she was the answer to my prayers.

Recognizing the ideas of an underling will get me much further than promoting my own, as crazy as it sounds. Half the board thinks I'm some kind of megalomaniac, the other half remembers me from when I was still in diapers. Remi stumbling in a day early allowed me to enact a few items on my lesser agenda, and if things continue to go well, I'll be able to pass along some of my other ideas to her as well.

And it doesn't hurt for the message to get delivered in such a pretty package.

I was up half the night thinking of her, and not in the way I should be. Her shapely legs played a starring role in my distraction. They really should have had hose on them, company policy, but I'm so glad they didn't. Her eyes were another distraction. Her lashes are so long, I swear they reached the lenses of her glasses.

I pull up the video feed of her leaving my suite on Sunday. Somehow she managed to stumble walking from the elevator.

That's how I knew I was in for trouble. When I replayed that scene no less than fifty times.

I exhale, defeated. Why couldn't Remi have come in the form of an aging 40-year-old man? Why does she have to be so sexy, so smart, so—unattainable?

It must sound silly for any woman to be unattainable

to me. After all, I am a billionaire. A handsome one, so I'm told. But my life comes with complications.

I take a picture of Sayo off my desk, a beautiful woman with the likeness of Gemma Chan. Her ruby red lips against her pale white flesh are striking. So dramatic. So exquisite. A true prize for any man.

Except, I'm the one that has to marry her, and well, she's a lesbian.

I put the picture back, face down, trying to push all thoughts of nuptials from my mind to focus on business. Switching to Expressions is one of the smaller issues on my plate, and there are so many other initiates to pass. But I have a feeling that things are going to get a little easier, with how taken Tom is by Remi.

Like I said, pretty packaging.

So now I'm a pig, having sexy women present for me so I can get things passed. How the hell did I ever get into this mess? Oh, yeah, dear old dad.

Christian Icor, man's man, and possibly one of the most incompetent people to hold a position of power. He lost us prestige, power, and pride—and most importantly—the trust of the Big 5. Winning it back is not easy.

Maxwell Icor surrounded himself with friends and people he could trust. He was the brains of the operation, but he'd often tell me that Icor Tech wouldn't be what it is today without those five steadfast friends of his. Each member of the five lives in the Tower, as they always have, though before it had been at a different location.

At the start of Icor Tech, Maxwell rented out a stodgy building by the docks, converting the top levels into apartment buildings. He couldn't pay the 5 well, so he allowed them to live rent-free. When Icor Tech moved across town, they came with and now reside near the top of the Tower.

The newer board members and many directors have suites as well, though none as nice and lavish as those that belong to 'The Remaining 3'— Lindel, Cregor, and Barry. Now, Remi will reside in one of the suites as well.

I go back to mentally undressing Remi. Stripping her of her black shirt and helping her wiggle out of that sexy floral skirt—and then my phone rings.

Damnit! I think to myself, not wanting to abandon the image of Remi Stone's legs splayed as she sits on my desk.

It's mom—my dear, sweet, clueless mother.

My father had always surrounded himself with heiresses and supermodels. Scarlet Primrose, my mother, was akin to French royalty. At nearly sixty, she is still drop-dead gorgeous, and it isn't just due to the botox and fillers she bombarded her face with nearly every other month, but I'm sure those do help.

I can't bring myself to hit the answer button. I just can't. It would break her heart if she knew I was avoiding her, and the smiles I force onto my face for her are getting harder and harder to fake—so I stay away, though it's kind of hard considering we live in the same building.

She has no idea how much Icor Tech has been mismanaged. I remember the day I found out. It wasn't long after my father died, and it wouldn't be obvious to those looking casually at the numbers.

I saw we were losing accounts, and the money going out far exceeded industry standard. Basically, we're a mess, but I've been fighting like hell to turn the tide.

And this brings me to why I'm marrying Sayo

Nguyen. Her father is one of the wealthiest men in China, and one of the best allies I could have in my corner. He's not going to want to see me fail, and my association with him alone will give Icor Tech a boost.

I bring up Remi's picture from the Organizational Chart, newly moved from the Mechanical Engineering section to Directors.

Life can be so unfair at times. It may seem arrogant for me to say this, seeing as how I've never gone without a meal and a warm bed, but now, all I have to live for is this damn Tower. The entirety of my life will be stabilizing my company and coming home to a loveless marriage. At least one day I'll have kids to look forward to. Here's hoping they actually get a say in how they live their lives.

I turn on my computer, opening up my '5 Year Plan' for how to turn the company around and create a document called the Bold Efficiency Plan, which is what I'll attach Remi to.

I'm distracted, though. The reflection on the computer screen reminds me of the reflection on Remi's glasses

And I realize, I really am hopeless.

Chapter Seven

Remi Stone...is a virgin...

"Here we are, where you'll be spending the majority of your time for the rest of your life," Analise says as she walks through the large door frame into my new oversized office.

"This...is going to be mine? Like, only mine?"

"Yes, do you like it?"

I turn, staring at the walls adorned with decadent mahogany, shelves lined with books. A window takes up a whole wall, looking out over the city. This is an office executives dream of, and here I am, Remi Stone, about to occupy it.

"Is that a bathroom?" I say, looking into an adjoining room.

"Yep."

"This is bigger than my apartment."

"That's not surprising. After all, this is New York City."

"Who did this belong to before?" I ask.

"Cregor Leskey. He's being moved downstairs."

My face flushes red, and my jaw drops. I stare at Analise wide-eyed, a wave of numbness threatening to take me to my ever-faithful friend, the floor.

"God, you should have seen the fuss he pulled. His dentures fell out, right over there." Analise points to a spot on the floor next to an oversized desk.

Cregor had been the rudest, most hateful person I've met in my short career. Not only did he refuse to glance at me, but he berated me in front of his peers. It was especially painful because I have looked up to him for so long. Because he's one of the Big 5.

"They're cleaning out his apartment upstairs right now, for when the movers come with your stuff."

I move to sit down, dizzy, and more than a little afraid.

What is Cregor capable of? I mean, losing his office and his apartment to a woman he berated during a presentation is going to be a pretty big blow. And he's old, which means he doesn't have much to lose by way of time.

No! Cregor wouldn't kill me. Stop being so silly.

"Oh my God, I didn't expect you to believe all that,"

Analise says, smirking, and I realized all at once that I've been had.

This isn't at all unusual, me not realizing when someone is joking. I am the very definition of naive.

A snortle escapes my mouth, and soon I'm giggling so hard tears are welling in my eyes.

"If ya can't laugh at yourself, you really shouldn't be laughing at anyone else, I guess."

"Oh, I'm not laughing at myself. I'm laughing at the image of old Cregor trying to poison my food or push me down a flight of stairs."

Now, Analise is laughing too, bringing redness to her white, freckled cheeks.

"Cregor's not so bad, I promise."

I roll my eyes. "Yeah, sure."

"Well, when you know him as well as I do…"

I look at Analise, stomach churning. Cregor is a rich man—richer than rich. Maxwell had been exceedingly generous with his board, and rich men were prone to marrying up attractive, younger women.

"Are you like…married to him or something?" I ask.

Analise's eyes widened, her face a look of horror.

"No!" she shouts. "Heavens, no! He's my father!"

I exhale, relieved but now regretting my every word.

"Just…don't ever say anything like that ever again!"

"Fine, daughter of Satan. Your wish is my command."

Analise is laughing, and through the chaos, I'm pretty sure I've made a friend of her.

"So, what do you do for fun?" Analise pulls a chair to face mine and takes a seat.

"Me? Fun? I…I contribute to a science YouTube

channel."

Her eyes widen. "So, are you some kind of internet celebrity?"

"Oh, no! Heavens no. I'm not even in the videos. I serve as a fact-checker."

She purses her lips, clearly disappointed.

"Ummm...I also care for a 30lb. cat."

Her face twists into a mortified grimace. "You look too young to be a crazy cat lady. Just how old are you?"

"You'd be surprised. They've been recruiting younger and younger servants these days. The greater the life expectancy, the more terror they can reign upon their human," I reply. "But, to answer your question, I'm twenty-three."

"Twenty-three? And up here? An executive office?"

"Yeah, I'm kind of a genius. And that's not me bragging."

"I'll bet. So do you have a boyfriend?"

I snicker. There's a touchy subject. I've always been curious about the dating world, but every time I try to dip my toes in, I find out the water is boiling.

"Yeah, I'm in between options too," Analise says after I offer no reply.

"In between options?"

"Yep."

"You make that sound so...lavish."

She chuckles. "Yeah, but it's not so bad. It allows me to focus on myself."

"Have you had many...options that is?" I ask.

She rolls her big, blue eyes. "Many options, you say. Do you mean to ask if I'm a slut?"

Jesus, where did I learn to be so offensive?

THE BILLIONAIRE'S BOARD

She shrugs her shoulders. "Well, the answer is yeah. I probably am."

"Oh," I reply, not knowing what to take of her admission. I'm a little anxious just thinking about it, yet very interested. How does one ask about someone's sex life without looking like a pervert?

"You?"

"Me? Oh, like...my options? Ummm, yeah. Wow."

I'm stammering, reluctant to tell her that I've never once been with a man before. Never.

Analise eyes me critically. "Wow, that question really has you riled, doesn't it?"

I look away and bare my confession. "Truth is, I'm really leaning into the whole cat lady vibe. It suits me."

She's quiet, and I glance over at her. She looks as though she's doing a complex math problem, checking and rechecking her numbers. Finally, she scowls, then the muscles in her mouth relax, and I can tell she's choosing her words carefully.

"You're gunning for the white wedding dress, aren't you?" Analise finally asks.

I nod, amused with the delicate way she asks if I'm a virgin.

"Is it a religion thing? Or a long-distance relationship?"

"It's a man repellant thing."

Analise bursts into laughter, looking almost like Julia Roberts in Pretty Woman.

"I'm not kidding. Men basically avoid me unless it's to ask for my help on a project."

"I seriously doubt you repel men."

I feel suddenly stupid for revealing something so

personal to a woman I barely know. How could Analise ever understand what it's like to repel men? She's gotta be nearly six-feet tall, with a perfect body, and apparently, she's funny too.

"Oh, you'd be surprised."

"What are you doing to meet them?"

"What am I doing?" I mulled over the question for a solid minute before saying, "I go shopping. I get coffee a couple times a week. I go to bookstores."

"Oh my gosh!" Analise exclaims. "Calm down, woman! Ya really know how to party."

She's right. I'm the most boring person ever. Seriously. I don't take risks. I go to bed by nine. I don't go out drinking. I basically exist to go to work and come home and feed my dead granny's cat.

"Have you ever tried Tinder?" Analise asks.

I arch a brow. "Isn't that for—"

"Sluts?" she arches her own brow, and we laugh.

"I created a Match profile about two years back," I confess.

Her eyes light up. "Let me see it!"

"I haven't been on in over a year. I doubt it's still up."

She pulls out her phone, her thumbs a blur. "What's your profile name?" she asks.

"S.T.E.M. Grrrl," I say, and spell it out for her.

"Seriously," she says, donning the most condescending look I think I may have ever seen on a woman before. Then she shouts, "Holy Mother of Jesus!"

"What is it?" I say, my heart pounding in my chest, wondering if someone has hacked my account and put up something raunchy.

"Do you really have a picture of yourself with an old

lady as your profile pic?"

"Yeah, I mean, I liked my hair."

"Oh, my god, this really is the most boring profile I've ever seen for someone. It's like a damn parody account."

The words sting a little, but they weren't something I didn't already know. I'm boring.

"Did you really put that you enjoy spending your evenings watching the damn Golden Girls?"

"It's what I do!"

"Naw, it's what ya did. I'm gonna tell you what you're gonna do." Analise leans back in her chair, crosses one leg over the other, and brings her hand up to rest her chin upon. "And it starts with a new wardrobe."

My phone buzzes, I pull it out to see a message from an unknown phone number. Opening it, I see it's from Tom.

> **Tom:** *Hey! Great presentation. Don't let the other members of the board scared you. You're going to do great.*

> **Remi:** *Thank you. I really appreciate your assistance in the meeting.*

> **Tom:** *No problem. So, I have a question for you.*

> **Remi:** *Okay*

> **Tom:** *Would you like to go to dinner with*

me sometime later in the week?

Chapter Eight

Gabriel is in over his head...

"You really got yourself a brain, didn't you?"

I look up from my computer, a little surprised to see Analise in the room staring at me. Her arms are crossed over the chest. She's upset.

"I know some things, I suppose."

"Oh, don't you shrug it off. You know what I'm talking about."

I sit back in my chair, jaw clenched, trying to figure out why the hell she's upset.

"You don't like Remi, I take it?"

"I didn't say that."

"Well, something about her bugs you."

Analise saunters around my desk, taking a seat next to the keyboard, looking down at me through her long, dramatic lashes.

"How well do you even know her?" she asks.

"Why does that matter?"

"Well, let me show you this." Analise turns to my computer, bringing up a web browser. She types in a few keystrokes and brings up Match, the dating site.

"Looksie."

I look at the screen at an awkwardly innocent Remi sitting next to an elderly woman holding crochet hooks.

"Jesus Christ, who the fuck puts up such a—"

"Someone who hasn't so much as been on a date before, that's who."

I blink, then give a hearty chuckle. "Wait, are you saying—"

"That Remi Stone is a bonafide between the sheet vegetarian? Yes, I am."

"Wait? What?"

"Get with the program, Gabe. It ain't just meatless Mondays for this girl."

I swallow, and to my horror, suddenly that sugary sweet picture with her dear sweet old grandma is leaving my pants tight.

"Won't be for long, though."

My stomach churns. "Boyfriend?"

"No, Tom."

"She's seeing Tom?"

"God, Gabe, how can you be so oblivious? Were we spying in on the same board meeting? Did you see how he greeted her? Did you see how he paraded her around the room like she was his damn arm candy?"

Oh shit!

I have a way of overlooking these things, especially when my mind is focused on saving Icor Tech. Tom has a reputation for being a ladies' man, but it had always been an 'off the clock' sort of thing. Dating someone from the office is just plain stupid, and fucking them—is even dumber.

"Can we keep her?" Analise pouts.

My brow raises. "Keep her?"

"She's just so adorable, Gabe. And ridiculously innocent! She would have never gotten the position without you."

The words feel like a punch in the gut. Analise is great at reading people, reading talent.

"You're saying I shouldn't have promoted her? That she's not qualified?"

She waves her hand dismissively. "Oh, no. That's not it. She's probably some kind of wunderkind, that's for sure. But she's not competitive. There's no politics going on in that big brain of hers. It's all analytical."

I breathe a sigh of relief, a slight whistle escaping my lips. "Well, that's a relief."

"Yeah, but ya better be careful. She's not going to navigate this shit storm well."

"I'm going to need you to help with that."

"Me?"

"Yeah. I'm glad she's not competitive—apolitical even. It's actually exactly what I need. Someone who's going to care about the numbers and not how Mr. Dingle-Barry feels about the hurt feelings of Charles Hackman when we drop his software."

"Dingle's not the problem."

"Yeah, but I didn't want to say—"

"My father? You didn't want to tell me my father is a problem. Trust me, Gabe, I know my father's a problem—but he's also really good at what he does!" Her face twists in pain, and I regret not choosing my words better.

Analise would make one heck of a board member, but that's an impossibility with her father still around. You see, my grandfather wrote into the bylaws that members of the board cannot be blood relatives. Oddly, an adopted son can serve on the same board as his adoptive parent, but a natural son cannot.

Because Cregor refuses to retire, Analise has been kept at arm's length from the board and anything going on behind closed doors. Because I believe she should be in there, I teleconference her in, quietly. Something that could get me in a lot of trouble, but I do it anyway because one day, I fully intend to make her a part of the board.

"Look, I like your father. Love him, actually. Icor Tech wouldn't be what it is today without him."

"You don't have to go singing his praise to me. Just be mindful."

"Yeah, mindful. You're absolutely right, and I'm sorry."

"So, you want me to babysit Ms. Brainiac?"

I look Analise dead in the eye, so she can see my intentions clearly.

"Analise, you are not a babysitter. One day, I want you to be my second. My right-hand man—or woman rather. This 'babysitting' as you call it, isn't some sort of punishment. Remi is one of the company's most precious assets at the moment. I can't afford to lose her."

"You really think this kid's going to solve all your problems."

"Well, not all my problems, but she'll be essential in streaming processes—which is exactly what we need. Without prompt, she had data compiled that I've been analyzing for months, and she was ready to present it."

"What if it's an anomaly? A one shot?"

"I have a feeling Ms. Brainiac is going to find a lot of inefficiencies, and if she doesn't, I can certainly point some out to her. The difference between her presenting them and myself is going to be what cuts through all the red tape."

"Are you sure?"

"Yeah, I mean, she has Tom charmed. As much as I hate to say it, Tom has a lot of pull with the other members of the board. If she has him, we have the numbers."

Analise chuckles. "Yeah, I'll say. He's already asked her to dinner."

A sickly feeling churns in my gut. "Dinner?"

"Yeah. Why do you look so surprised? It's Tom!"

I exhale, a small sigh escaping my lips as I imagine Remi sitting across from Tom, talking over a bottle of wine.

Now, don't get me wrong, Tom is a good guy. An intelligent man. But—putting us together is like serving Chinese at the same dinner party that's serving Italian. We don't belong on the same plate. When I'm careful, he's brazen. When I want to cut prices, he wants to raise them. Sometimes I feel like it's personal, but that would be just plain silly. After all, Icor Tech gave him his first big break, and there aren't many positions in the world better than his.

But that's not what's nagging me. As I said, Tom is a good guy, but he's also a bit of a womanizer. He'll meet a woman, lavish her with attention, take her on vacation, then lose all interest. He gets bored easily, and the last thing I need is Remi getting upset over Tom's disappearing act he likes to pull.

You're not being honest with yourself. Yes, you care about Remi's productivity, but that's not all you care about.

I swallow as I recall Remi, a disheveled mess, walking into the boardroom a whole day early and focusing so much on her presentation she didn't even realized she wasn't wearing matching shoes.

Every woman I've ever dated took hours to get ready, looking like walking perfection. It was their greatest care, how good they looked. Oh, and the size of my bank account.

Remi is different.

"This isn't a good idea," I say.

"My thoughts exactly, but there isn't much we can do about it."

Analise hops off my desk and begins her circle. It's what she does when deep in thought. Walks in circles, forgetting the world around her, focusing only on the issues. I like her dedication, her drive. If I weren't running the company, there wouldn't be more capable hands to leave Icor Tech to.

"Is it against company policy?"

Analise looks at me, glowering. "Your granddad

wasn't big on company policy. There are rules put into place about dating your superiors, but it doesn't lead to termination. We move them to positions that don't report to one another. Anyway, this wouldn't fall under that umbrella because they are in separate chains."

I think about them, laughing over cups of wine, sitting close to each other, his hand on her thigh. Soon they're back at the Tower, in Tom's suite. She'd probably spill her drink on her white dress. Tom's just so damn charming he'd probably spill some on himself to make her feel less anxious. He'd make some comment on how wine stains, pulling his shirt off, showing her how the gym's his favorite past time. She'd be impressed, of course, and she'd pull off—"

"Gabe!" Analise snaps.

"Oh, what?"

"Focus!"

"I am, I was just thinking."

"We can use this to our advantage. Tom votes against you all the time. If he thinks the idea's coming from Remi though—"

"My brain is one step ahead of you."

Is Tom thinking about Remi right now the way I am? Is he undressing her? Is he texting her?

My nostrils flare as I exhale. I shouldn't even be thinking about this? It's not like I can ever be with Remi anyway. Maybe I'll just send Tom a text, wish him luck, but also advising caution. I'll explain to him that I have no problem with him dating Remi, but to try to keep it slow due to work relations.

Damnit! What is wrong with me? I can't get involved.

"Have a suite cleared out on the forty-ninth floor for

her. I'll show it to her next week. Movers are getting scheduled."

Analise's face contorts, and for a moment, I panic, worrying she can see right through me to my turbulent emotions.

She's staring at me, critically—angrily. "The forty-ninth floor? That's with the Big 5! You can't—"

"Why can't I?"

Clearly aggravated, Analise clears her throat. Her response comes out slowly.

"Fine. I'll have it prepared right away, Mr. Icor."

Analise exits my office, and I'm left alone with my thoughts and a database full of intel showing me all the ways my company is squandering its resources—the legacy of my father's negligence.

Of course, he doesn't have to watch the ship go down, manning a bucket to throw as much water overboard as one possibly can. And he won't be blamed either. Nope. All the fingers will be pointed at me.

I can see the headlines now.

Entitled Billionaire Heir Squanders Family Fortune

-or-

Thousands of Jobs Lost after Gabriel Icor Runs Company Into Ground

No! That's not going to happen! There's still time to turn this ship around, and if anyone can do it, it's me.

Chapter Nine

Remi gets a made over by a porn star...

Exhausted, I exit Icor Tower and make my way to my apartment. It's as though I'm walking on a cloud, in a dream, some kind of fantasy.

After just four days in my position, I'm finally getting the hang of things. Sure, there's a lot of dirty glances as I'm walking down the hall, but my mind is too preoccupied with my work—among other things—to really care that much.

Just a week ago, I was a staggering mess, and now

I'm making plans to move into 'The Tower.' On top of all that, I managed to snag a date.

Tom Wellington, the Chief Finance Officer of Icor Tech, is not only smart, but he's also insanely good looking. I'm talking blond hair, baby blue eyes, suit fitting good in all the right places.

And he wants to take me out to eat.

But it's not a date. Why would Tom Wellington ever want to date you? It's almost as absurd as Gabriel Icor wanting to date you.

For once, I wish I was an optimist.

The whole week has been so crazy I've barely gotten any sleep, and it's not only because I was thinking about work.

Oh no, it's because I was reliving every moment I've been in Gabriel Icor's glorious presence. Thinking of the way his hair falls over his eyes. How his hands move when he talks. How he articulates each word.

And yes, I've undressed him in my mind—half a hundred times, and boy is he hot, though sadly, each time I get to his Under Armour boxer briefs, I chickened out, replaying the scene from the top.

I step inside my building to the maniacal laughter of Mr. Sokolov.

"You think you smart, with you tiny crevices you scurry up into. Well, Solo knows all you tricks. Pretty soon, you momma will wonder where you are. You understand?"

My smile is as inevitable as Mr. Sokolov's frustration, and as I quietly enter the stairwell, I hear his cries of victory.

Mr. Sokolov: 1; Roaches: 1,000,000.

Climbing the stairs, I'm distracted, and of course, I go past my floor, having to backtrack.

Then I fall on the landing.

Whoever says the ability to multitask is a gift doesn't have to deal with the fallout, because all at once, my ankle is hot pain and my knee may no longer function.

It takes me a minute to recover, the searing pain settling into a dull ache. I hobble through the door to my floor, pulling out my key.

My phone vibrates. It's Tom.

> **Tom:** *Score! I got reservations for us at Deco 6!*

My heart sinks, my stomach threatens to turn over.

Deco 6 can take months to get into, and Tom was able to land us reservations for tonight! I thought we'd grab something quick to eat, and listen to each other's ideas, but Deco 6 isn't a place you casually get to know each other.

> **Remi:** *Ummm...I'm sorry, but I can't.*

> **Tom:** *What's wrong? Something come up?*

> **Remi:** *It's just that I have nothing to wear. I thought we were going someplace casual.*

> **Tom:** *You can wear whatever you want.*

> *No one will deny you entrance when you're with me.*

I chuckle, but really, I'm near tears. I don't know what's going on, what Tom's intentions are. I feel stupid thinking he'd want to date me, but why would he bring a casual business acquaintance to Deco 6?

My key slides in the lock, and I open the door to a guttural growl. Kibbles.

> **Tom:** *I'm swinging by in thirty as we planned, be ready.*

My fingers hover over the keypad, wanting to cancel the dinner but too afraid of what would happen if I do.

I don't want to offend Tom. And the fact that he went ahead and booked that reservation makes me feel guilty, but before I can think on it, a 30lb. wrecking ball launches itself at me.

"Kibbles!" I shout, unable to dodge the attack.

She connects with my gut, then falls to the floor, scurrying off to get in position for another surprise attack.

I rush to my cabinet, pulling out her favorite salmon-flavored treats but bump my head on the end of a shelf.

Damnit!

The room's still dark, and I'm rummaging around for the treats, but Kibbles' growls let me know I haven't much time. She's prowling, inching closer. I can't see her, but she's really not that graceful, and she leaves chaos in her wake. I know she's close.

The can of treats is in my hand now. I'm shaking it. Buying myself precious seconds.

The growls cease, and she waddles her enormous body to my feet, knowing she has me tamed.

I scatter a handful of treats on the floor, hoping it will keep her occupied long enough for me to find something to wear.

Then, my giant brain does right by me, and I have an idea.

I dash from my apartment to the apartment next to mine and pound on the door. After a moment, Porn Star Meg answers.

"Hey, what's up?"

"I have a date!"

She smiles, clearly confused. "Well, good for you."

"No, I mean, I didn't know I was going to have a date, and now that I have one. I don't have anything to wear."

"Oh," she says, biting her lip. "Is this your way of asking me if I have something you can borrow?"

"Yes!" I exclaim. "Please! Anything."

She disappears inside, then shouts for me to follow. We stop at a closet, and she eyes me critically.

"My name's Meghan, but you can call me Meg. Your name is Rommy, right?"

"Remi, but close enough."

"Hmmm...You're about my size, but a little shorter. Rounder at the hips...you slouch."

I look down, suddenly self-conscious.

"Where are you going?" she asks.

"Deco 6."

Her mouth forms a perfect circle, her eyes lighting in

surprise.

"Does your date have a brother?" she finally says.

"I don't know. I'm still getting to know him."

"Here." She thrusts a silver, sequined dress at me and all at once I back away, hands up.

"What's wrong? You allergic to silver?"

"No, it's just so…"

"It's sexy, slinky, and in style."

"It will show too much."

"It will do the job. Now go, leave. I'm kicking you out of my apartment."

I gasp, offended, and unable to articulate my feelings.

"Oh stop, you'll thank me later," she says, pushing me towards her front door.

"But, but…"

"Oh shit, you're probably crap at doing makeup, aren't you?" she asks in a condescending tone.

"I can do my makeup."

"Let's get you dressed," she says, practically ripping my clothes off me.

I comply with her demands, and after I'm in the sequined dress, she pulls me, by my arm, into her bathroom and practically shoving me into a chair. At least a thousand cosmetics are surrounding the sink, and a ring light stands off to the side. I barely have time to register the assault before a barrage of brushes, pencils, and creams start coming at my face, and when she is done, I look in the mirror, and the face staring back to me is foreign—and beautiful.

I bring my hand up to touch my cheek.

"Ah, nope." She bats my hand away. "Give it time to set, and even once it's set, still don't touch it."

How am I supposed to not touch my face?

My eyes are dark, smokey. Lined in black pencil, they extend unnaturally outward. My lips are a bold shade of red, far different from the neutral pink tones I normally wear.

I feel like a different woman, one more suited for a magazine than corporate life.

"You have a good bone structure. Your cheeks are damn near perfect," Meghan says.

I want to tell her she's crazy, but looking at myself in the mirror, I feel a swell of pride.

"Deco 6 is literally the hardest restaurant to get into right now! How are you so unprepared?"

"I...well," I stammer, "I didn't realize until thirty minutes ago."

"Thirty minutes ago? You mean you have a date with a man that can get last-minute reservations for Deco?"

"It's just a dinner between...new friends."

Meghan laughs. "New friends? A man doesn't get reservations to Deco for a *'new friend'* honey."

I swallow, suddenly a thousand times more anxious. "I...I guess."

My phone vibrates.

Tom: *I'm downstairs, mind if I come up?*

"Who is it?" Meghan's eyes grow round with excitement.

"Oh, it's just a coworker," I say.

"A coworker, or a rich daddy?"

I snort, wondering what she thinks I do for a living.

"I need to go," I say, rising from my seat.

"Let me grab you a purse. What size shoe do you wear?"

Shoe? Damnit! My black pumps aren't going to work with this dress.

"Six-and-a-half?" I say, and she disappears from the room.

Remi: *I'll be down in ten minutes.*

I exhale, terrified of what the night will bring. What if Tom suddenly realizes what a nerd I am? What if he laughs when he sees me and drives off?

My hands are shaking. I grow suddenly hot.

"Here," Meghan holds out a pair of thigh-high boots to me. "Cram your little piggies in there."

I scrunch my brows. "You can't be serious?"

"God, you're so adorable. Now get them on—no arguing."

I pull them on, embarrassed. I'm not the kind of woman that has any business wearing something so sexy, so sultry, but when I look in the mirror, my breath catches in my throat.

"You look hot!" Meghan gasps.

I want to believe her. I want to believe the image I see in the mirror staring back at me, but my grandma's words come to me, as they often do.

You're lucky to have that brain of yours 'cause ya ain't got enough meat on yer bones for a man.

Meghan's pushing me now, through one door, then a second, and now I'm in the hall.

"Knock 'em dead!" Meghan says from her doorway, arms crossed over her chest and a smirk across her face.

Chapter Ten

Remi isn't wearing underwear...

Boxy Bessie makes a liar of me, and I finally walk from my building at twenty-five minutes after my text message only to trip over my own two feet directly into Tom's arms.

"Careful now!" Tom says, catching me.

I feel my cheeks grow red as I struggle to regain my footing, Tom's strong arms the only thing keeping me from falling.

"Oh, gosh! Wow. I'm so sorry."

Tom's eyeing me up and down. "No, it's fine, but I must say, this is the quickest."

I scrunch my brows. "Quickest what?" I ask.

"The quickest anyone has ever fallen for me."

My eyes grow wide, my mouth forming a perfect circle. I'm completely unprepared for this kind of witty banter.

"God, look at you! You're absolutely gorgeous!" Tom says, his eyes roving my body, his face displaying approval.

"Thank you," I accept the compliment, one I have never received before from a man and hope to one day get again. It feels good to feel pretty, however foreign.

"My car's coming around, fucking hall monitor threatened a ticket, which isn't a big deal, but I didn't want to be a dick."

"Oh," I say, now even more self-conscious at the amount of time it took me to get to the bottom floor.

Looking towards the street, I see a blurry haze and realize that in my hurry, I forgot to put on my glasses, but there's no way I'm going back upstairs.

A black limousine slows, coming to a stop before my apartment complex, and Tom offers his arm up. We walk to the vehicle, the driver rushing to open the door. I thank the man as I climb in, scooting over to make room for Tom.

I have never been in a limo before, and I certainly have never been in a limo with a handsome millionaire like Tom Wellington.

"Damn, executive office already—after two years! Gabriel must have a thing for you."

My brows raise. I am absolutely not prepared for a

comment like that.

"I think it has more to do with my presentation," I say, worrying I'll sweat my makeup off.

"No doubt! I'm sorry. I didn't mean to make you uncomfortable." His hand moves to my thigh, a gesture that startles me. I look up at him, and his smile leaves me breathless.

God damn, Tom Wellington is handsome.

"So you went to Cornell?" he asks. "At fifteen?"

I blush, not knowing if he means it as a compliment or to say that I'm a freak, as so many have.

"Yes, I was accepted in with conditions at fifteen years old. I graduated at nineteen, but to be honest, I could have graduated at seventeen if they had just let up on the freaking restrictions."

He nods slightly, and I realize how pompous I must sound.

"Your parents must be proud," he says.

I look down, kicking myself for allowing the conversation to go in this direction.

"Well, my mother died when I was seven. I never knew my father. My grandmother raised me."

"Oh, jeez," he says, burying his head in his hands.

"Oh, please don't. I've had over a decade to come to terms with it."

He looks at me with sincere eyes and says, "Well, I hope your grandmother knows she did one heck of a job. You're something to be proud of."

"Well, my grandmother died last Christmas. On Christmas day, actually."

Tom is pale now, his mouth open and completely at a loss for words.

"Don't worry, we weren't close."

"Weren't close? Wasn't she the one who raised you?"

"Technically, yes, but she never failed to remind me just how much she was giving up in the process. She was always mad at everything."

"Jesus, I'm sorry."

"Look, this evening didn't start off how I had intended. Is there a do-over?"

At this, he smiles genuinely. "I think we both need one."

We make small talk the rest of the way to Deco 6, and when the limousine stops, the door is immediately opened by men in suits who assist us from the vehicle. I'm bombarded with a series of flashing lights, and the confusion makes me want to climb back into the limo, but Tom's hand on my back disallows me from doing so.

I bring my hands up as a shield, but when the lights keep coming, I close my eyes—which proves to be a pretty stupid thing to do because in the moment my vision goes dark, my shoe connects with the curb, and down I go.

A roar of laughter erupts from the crowd.

I recover quickly, but not quick enough as I soon realize the flashing lights are cameras going off. Deco 6 is apparently a hotspot for celebrity date nights, which means the entrance is lined with tabloid photographers eager to catch a pricy photo of an A-lister.

Thankfully, photos of clumsy dates aren't in demand.

Tom's hands are around me, assisting me to stability.

I'm so embarrassed, I can't even make eye contact, and instead, I scuttle to the door, trying to block the laughter from reaching my ears.

Tom's left hand is pressed firmly to my back, his right is shielding me, and once we make it inside, he pulls me to a stop.

"Hey, are you okay?" he asks, going to one knee to inspect my booted leg.

I pull back, anxious, and nervous. "I'm fine. Really. If my kneecap shattered every time I fell, I'd be going through a lot of replacements."

He smirks, looking up at me, and for a moment, I get an overwhelming sensation that can only be described as lust. Seeing him down on his knee makes my blood rush to all the right places. This must be what dating feels like.

"That clumsy, eh?" Tom says.

I snap from my haze. "Yes," I reply.

I wonder if I should warn Tom and tell him that I've never dated before. He will no doubt think that I'm some kind of freak, and maybe I am, but I never really had the opportunity to.

When I was fifteen, a time when I should be learning to kiss, I enrolled in college. Sure, maybe a few creepy guys would have tried something, but I was assigned a 'mentor'—Ms. Roxwell, the retired librarian. The college knew they'd be held liable if something were to happen to me, so they made sure Ms. Rockwell was watching me all day, every day. I even roomed with her. And then, when I graduated at nineteen and started grad school, well, I really had no peers at that point. I had nothing in common with incoming college freshmen who were my age, or other graduate students. So, I became a loner.

Tom's still on his knee, his hands massaging my leg through my boot, giving me goosebumps. I find myself short of breath, caught up in a dangerously addictive feeling that I imagine could make a woman lose control. I want to lose control.

My leg lifts, almost instinctively, and Tom leans in to kiss my knee. I'm startled by my forwardness and back away. Tom, however, has the look of a starving man.

What have I done?

People are passing us, casting queer looks at Tom, who is still kneeling on the floor.

He's so handsome—a 9 out of 10. Of course, most women would give him a 10, but for me, only one man I've ever met has that honor—Gabriel Icor.

Tom rises, giving me a wink, then offers his elbow. I slide my hand into place, and we continue to the elevator.

We're brought to the top floor, which opens into a vast room with what appears to be floating lights. I blink, unable to see clearly because I don't have my glasses on.

The floor lights where we walk, illuminating aquariums built into it. I have never been to a place like this before, and the sheer decadence had me on edge.

A beautiful woman approaches, tall as a goddess with honey-blonde hair cascading down her back.

"Tom Wellington, I have your table ready."

We follow the woman to the far end of the room, which boasts a section of tables on a translucent patio. Looking down, I see the street below.

I stop before stepping onto it, scared. Tom looks over at me, clearly amused by my fear.

"If you fall, I'll catch you," he says. "Just like I did when you were exiting your building."

"What about that time we exited the limo?" I ask, brows arched.

Guilt flashes in Tom's eyes, but a wry grin soon replaces it. "Then, we'll fall together."

I step out onto the glass or whatever the balcony is made of, and it's sturdy. I still don't like it, but I'll die of a heart attack before falling through to the street below.

We sit, and I allow Tom to order me a drink. Beautiful women with mile-high legs folded elegantly in their chairs are seated across from successful men, some young, most old.

I don't belong here.

Before long, bread is put out, as well as an array of cheeses, and a beautifully crafted beet and goat cheese dish that looks better than it tastes.

Small talk pours from Tom, and I hear about his childhood, his boarding schools, and his studies abroad. It is a relief that I don't have to say much, but the more he talks, the less attractive he becomes. His dazzling smile seems not for me, but for himself and all his many accomplishments.

We eat our way through six courses, each one becoming harder to pronounce and carrying a greater risk of intestinal distress than the last, until finally, there is only a lavender créme brûlée left between us. Tom is smiling at me as he scoops the first bite into a too-small spoon, then leans in to feed me.

I accept the bite as I suppose one does on dates like this. It tastes good, but not chocolate créme brûlée good. Why people are infusing fancy flowers into sugar-laden desserts is beyond me.

"So when do you move into Icor Tower?" he asks.

"Next week, I hear. That is, if I'm still around."

"I can't imagine you'll get promoted only to get

demoted a week later. If Gabriel promoted you, he must know you and be confident in your capabilities."

"That's just it—he doesn't. You saw my presentation—that's what the promotion was based on," I answer truthfully.

He furrows his brows. "So you two didn't know each other before the meeting?"

"Not at all," I lie.

No matter what I say, it's not going to look good. If I tell him I went to the Innovation Meeting 23.7 hours earlier than I was supposed to and ended up meeting Gabriel then, it would go against what Gabriel had coached me to say. On the other hand, saying that Gabriel promoted me to director level based off of one presentation sounds just as bad.

"Well, Gabriel certainly knew what he was doing. It's one of the better decisions he's made recently."

My eyes grow round at the complement.

"I mean, yeah, it's rash, but it was a Hail Mary pass if I ever saw one."

"What do you mean?" I ask, my stomach twisting in knots.

"Well, Gabriel's lost a lot of confidence with the board, and with the directors. Part of me thinks he doesn't even want to run Icor Tech. He's never around and doesn't want to do any of the work. He'd rather just date supermodels and go on expensive vacations."

I look down, unsure of what to say. That certainly wasn't the impression I got from him, but surely Tom knows him better than myself.

"Tell ya the truth, sometimes I wonder if I should be putting my resume out," Tom says, then a startled look crosses his face. "Oh, crap. I'm so sorry. I shouldn't be sitting here telling you this, especially with your promotion. Icor Tech is fine! Great even. I guess we all just have things we'd love to change if we could."

"I guess," I say, but now I'm anxious.

Tom scoots his chair around, so we're no longer facing each other. His hand is now on my thigh, so high up, he's touching the fabric of my too-short dress.

"I want you to know that if you have any questions, any worries—you can come to me. I want you to feel welcome in the boardroom, and with your fellow directors. If anyone gives you grief, tell me. I'll set them straight."

I feel searing heat where his hand is. My heart is beating like a war drum, and my breathing grows erratic.

Tom Wellington, who can get a last-minute reservation at Deco 6, is sitting right next to me, hand on my thigh, telling me he wants to help me—offering me his protection.

"I think I need some air," I gasp.

Tom brings up his hands, glancing around, and I realize how silly that sounds when we're out on the balcony.

"I mean, I think I'd like to see more of the city from this view."

"Of course, as would I." Tom immediately gets up, assisting me from my chair, and we walk out further onto the large patio extending over the city.

It's beautiful and terrifying, and if only I had remembered my glasses, I might be able to see something more than a blur of lights and colors. How the platform extends out so far is a feat of architecture, and I force myself to take it in without running tolerance numbers through my head.

"I've never seen something like this before," I confess.

"The Heartshires constructed it, but it's nothing. You should see some of the buildings in China and Dubai, and maybe you will. There are lots of meetings to attend around the world. Eventually, you may be tapped to go."

As the night grows darker, more lights came on, and I feel as though I'm in a fairytale. And then, a familiar feeling strikes me.

I don't belong here. I wasn't born into money, and I'm certainly not beautiful. I am nothing but an intruder.

"So, what does Gabe have you doing?" Tom asks.

"Oh, I've been familiarizing myself with various systems. I've spent a lot of time reading the bylaws, what directors vote on versus what the board votes on. It's weird that so many have carried over from Maxwell's time."

"Yeah, he was a good guy, so I hear. Maybe once the Remaining 3 are gone, they'll make some updates."

The Remaining 3 is what the remaining Big 5 are now called: Lindel, Cregor, and Barry.

"Analise is forcing a new wardrobe on me, having it delivered to the Tower for when I move in. Apparently, she doesn't want to let a single article of my current clothing through the doors."

"Well, I don't know, she obviously hasn't seen you in this." Tom's eyes rove over my body,

"Oh, this is from Porn Star Meg," I say without thinking.

"Porn Star Meg?" his brows lift.

"My neighbor," I say.

"Interesting."

A slight breeze picks up, and my borrowed dress begins to flutter. It takes me a moment to realize something that should have occurred to me during my makeover, and in true Remi Stone fashion, I blurt out, "I'm not wearing underwear!"

Tom's now looking at me, jaw gaping, and I feel my face flushing red.

Oh my God! How was I born this stupid?

Tom finally recovers from the shock and leans towards my ear. "We can cut out of here if you'd like."

All words fail me. I'm standing there, red as a lobster wondering why my genius brain doesn't work. Tom now thinks I want to get laid, which is both ironic and hilarious, considering I'm a virgin.

I should run away. Definitely run away. And never come back to Icor Tech. I am in demand. I was just offered a director position from Gabriel Icor himself. I can go to any tech company I want.

Maybe heading back to his place isn't such a bad idea. Would having sex with a handsome, intelligent man be so bad?

I'd be lying if I said I haven't spend countless hours wondering what sex is like. I've dreamed of what it would be like hundreds of times, in far too great a detail. Even if it's no more than a one night stand, who better to have one with than Tom Wellington?

Gabriel Icor—that's who. As hot as Tom is, Gabriel is the only 10 I've ever met, and I'll likely not meet another. But who am I to complain? I've had zero experience, and most women never get to bed an 8, let alone a 9. Tom is more than qualified to get the job done. He's overqualified!

I think about this for far too long, confused, wishing I had a girlfriend to talk this over with. Maybe Porn Star Meg could offer her assistance. Or Analise.

I finally say, "I didn't mean to say that. I thought it, not realizing…you know."

Tom's face falls a little. He looks confused.

"Look, you did nothing wrong. I just haven't dated much before—or at all. To be honest, I don't even know what this is, a date or a business meeting."

"Well, I'll tell you one thing, I don't bring business associates to restaurants that usually take months to get into." He gives me a wink.

I melt just a little.

"I feel so stupid," I say, looking out over the patio. "I don't belong here."

"Why? Most people either have to be really smart or really beautiful to dine at a place like this. You're both."

The words hit me hard. Well, not the smart part. The word beautiful. Tom Wellington thinks I'm beautiful. I turn away, even more embarrassed than when I told him I wasn't wearing underwear.

A hand rests on my shoulder. "It's been a big week for you, and I imagine next week is going to be just as crazy. Why don't I take you home—that is unless you'd like to go back to my place."

Chapter Eleven

Gabriel is fully prepared to fall on his sword...

It's past eight o'clock, and all I can think about is Remi and Tom dining at Deco 6. I hate the feeling in my gut, the uneasy sick sensation usually reserved for when I look at company numbers.

There's nothing I can do to get Remi Stone out of my head.

Tom stopped by my office earlier, bragging about getting reservations to Deco. He was trying to throw it in my face, not the reservation because those are easy for me to get, but his date with Remi.

Oddly, it frustrates me in a way he wouldn't understand. He assumes it'll upset me because he will inevitably have more sway on the board—which isn't true. Remi is not the type that would be swayed due to a love interest.

He doesn't realize I'm sitting here jealous that he gets to be out with *her*.

I decided to call the entertainment entities with photographers that stalk the area, and they sent me pictures of the two arriving. Tom in a handsome suit, Remi splayed on the cement. Seeing the unflattering photos of her should make me lose all interest, but instead, I'm jealous. Jealous of the barrage of pictures of Tom helping her up and assisting her through the door.

Fuck, I hate feeling jealous.

I think about what they're eating, what they're talking about—the fact that Tom knows worlds more than I do about this enigma of a woman. The clumsy genius that my heart keeps tripping over.

Finally, I decide to take matters into my own hands. I pull out my phone and text Tom.

> **Gabriel:** *Hey, Tom! I think it's great that you're being so welcoming to our newest director. Just remember, she's probably nervous. Don't rush into anything.*

A minute later, my phone vibrates, and I flip it over so fast I nearly launch it across the room.

> **Tom:** *Maybe you should be telling her that. Halfway through dinner, she's telling me she's not wearing any panties. And it's all good bro, nothing against the books.*

I feel a certain numbness I've felt very few times in my life. Once when my grandfather, the person I looked up to more than anyone in my life, passed. Another time was when I looked at the financial documents for the first time after my father died. And now—I am feeling it over a woman—Remi Stone, a brainiac geek that is obviously hot for Tom.

> **Gabriel:** *Well, just checking in. Good luck.*

I wanted to tell him he better not treat her like his past conquests. That he act decent and respectful.

Maybe I should call Remi, just to make sure she's okay.

I rationalize the thought in my head, but then I have a better idea. I text Analise.

> **Gabriel:** *Could you do me a favor?*

> **Analise:** *A favor? I'm in bed in my comfy pajamas. What do you want?*

> **Gabriel:** *Can you check on Remi? Send*

her a text?

Analise: *Why?*

Gabriel: *I just want to make sure she's okay. She's important to my company, to my plans.*

Analise: *You like her.*

Gabriel: *NO!!!*

Analise: *Yes, you do, but don't worry, I'll text her. How does this sound: "How's the date? Oh, and don't go too far—Gabe wants to be your first."*

Gabriel: *Ana! You know how important she is. If she gets upset over any of Tom's usual bullshit, I could lose out big. If she quits, my plan's shot!*

Analise: *Text her yourself.*

I throw down my phone, angry. I trust Analise more than I trust most people, having known her for most of my life.

Ana was born three years after myself, a beautiful child that grew into a drop-dead gorgeous woman. Cregor was against her joining Icor Tech from the very beginning, and early on, he tried everything he could to see her gone. When she TPed his office with friends, he went so far as to bring their dismissal up for a vote. A vote! Those types of things aren't taken lightly.

The truth is, she's so much like Cregor it's scary. A better version of Cregor. Cregor 2.0. Just what I need.

One day, I fully intend to put Analise on the board, but with Cregor around, that is impossible. As well intending as my grandfather was, he ended up hindering Ana's career and my ability to initiate change—good change.

I pull up the pictures of Remi again in her silver sequined dress, boots coming midway up her thigh. It doesn't seem like something she'd wear based on the information I've gathered on her, but maybe she just wanted to impress Tom.

Her makeup is more flamboyant as well. Perhaps she went to a salon anticipating tonight. Maybe not wearing underwear was a well thought out decision.

Why am I even thinking about this woman? My company is in dire need of help—so much so I have to agree to an arranged marriage, and I'm thinking of her?

I force myself to look at Sayo's picture. Most men would be more than happy to marry into her beauty and wealth. My own mother certainly was when she married my father.

And in the end, my mom saw the error of her ways. Marrying my father might have brought her into wealth very few ever possess, but he treated her like an accessory, a pretty decoration. There was no warmth, and as she aged, he paid less attention to her, while paying the younger household staff more. It's how she grew to live for me and me alone, and now the hope of grandchildren.

Every time I'm in the same room as my mother, the subject of babies comes up. Of course, Sayo and I will have to have children, but how we will go about that is a mystery even to me. Maybe Sayo will want to go the old-fashioned route, although I think it's more likely she'll prefer a baster. That is if she even decides to carry our children herself. She could just as easily go the rent-a-womb method so many wealthy women choose nowadays.

I know this must sound strange, but as beautiful as Sayo is, I don't want to do the old fashion method. I guess some men would be perfectly fine fucking their wives that want nothing to do with them, but not me. I hope Sayo and I can form a good partnership based on mutual trust and respect, but there will never be lust. Maybe there could be love.

My mind races trying to find a way out of all this, just as it has a hundred times before, but it finds nothing. I'm trapped. I'm marrying Sayo Nguyen.

It was Sayo's father, Chenglei, that approached me. Somehow—he knew. He knew the writing on the wall, where Icor Tech was headed, and he made me an offer I couldn't refuse.

It doesn't feel good knowing that I'll probably have to be bailed out at one point by my fiancé's father, but at least the safety net is there.

After we agreed to terms, he approached my mother, pretending he had gone to her first. She arranged for us to meet at dinner. It was the first time I ever met Sayo.

We sat across the table from one another, staring at

each other throughout the night. Her dead eyes gave away part of her story, a conversation we had later told me the rest.

No matter what either of us wanted, though, by the end of the night, we were engaged.

And still are.

Formal announcements will go out in two weeks, so we can get certain documents signed first. It's the kind of thing you do when big money marries into big money.

I put Sayo's picture down and bring Remi's up again. I wonder if Sayo will care if I see Remi. I mean, once Tom is through with her and we've gotten to know each other, maybe we can pursue something casual. Sayo certainly won't want to fulfill my needs, and with Remi living in the Tower, we are afforded discretion.

Remi deserves more than being some sidepiece. There is no way a life with Remi could ever work. I'm sure I'll come to an arrangement with Sayo, but Remi will never be part of the deal.

Remi's voice haunts me. "I'm not wearing any panties," it says. I try to imagine how she would say it. Would she make her voice sultry? Or maybe she would say it in a chipper tone, excited by what they would do together. Did she give him a wink? Is he touching her now?

Just the thought of Tom touching her sends my stomach lurching.

I'm angry. Once again, life is just so unfair. Then I force myself to think of the thousands of people that would be out of a job if Icor Tech goes under, and it focuses my thoughts.

This is my job. My responsibility. If anyone has to be

a martyr, it should be me. I was born into this position, and the sword is mine to fall upon. At least, if anything, I get to make sure Remi gets the position she deserves, one that will see her doing great things. Too bad, I have to see them all.

CHAPTER TWELVE

Remi's heart-shaped pendant…

I arrive for coffee with Gabriel a full fifteen minutes early, wearing matching shoes. This is going to be the second time I've met him face to face, and I want him to see that I am indeed capable of being professional and looking like a grown-ass woman.

He bids me by text to enter the elevator that brings me up to his suite. I step out into the now-familiar luxury that I'll never be able to really get used to, and the sight of Gabriel takes the breath from my lungs.

This time, he's not dressed in casual attire. Instead, he's donning a suit so tailored to his form it's easy to tell just how muscular his body is. I have to bring my hand up to my mouth to make sure I haven't drooled all over myself.

"Cappuccino, latte, espresso? Pick your poison."

"Poison? Is that what you serve your newest directors? Is it a test to see if I'm strong enough for the position?"

He chuckles lightly, but the light is gone from his eyes. "No, I will not make you endure poison, although I'm sure you would pass all tests."

"Well, then, I'll take my coffee the same way I did before, cream and sugar."

"You're easy to please."

I follow him to the kitchen and seat myself at the island while he busies himself with various gadgets.

"I would assume you'd have someone do that for you," I say.

"It's true that I have people to do a lot of the day to day crap, like cleaning and even cooking, but I always make sure to know my way around every coffeemaker I come across. You know, in case the zombie apocalypse happens."

"We all should really fret a little more about said apocalypse. I did a research paper on it, actually."

Gabriel casts me a wink. "I know. It's available to read from your university."

I blush, completely unaware he had read any of my work. "Well, it was meant to speak to plagues in current times, but the zombie element was meant to draw—"

"No need to explain. It was brilliant."

A steaming cup is set in front of me, then one is placed on the opposite side of the island. I wish he would sit next to me again, close enough to touch, but it appears he wants a face to face chat. He takes off his blazer, and I damn near melt into a puddle on the floor seeing him in a pin-striped button-up shirt underneath a Magic Mike style vest.

And yes, I've seen Magic Mike before, though not from my own want. The retired librarian I had roomed with in college had a perchance for beefy men.

"So, how was your first week on the job?"

"Uneventful," I say.

"That will soon change."

I grow nervous, hoping that whatever drama I encounter will be with numbers and not people.

"I need to level with you, Remi. I know I bombarded you on Monday during the meeting. You weren't expecting it, but I needed you to produce a genuine reaction. The reason I'm taking you on, giving you the director position, is because Icor Tech is in desperate need of some updates. And I mean desperate. If something doesn't change soon—well, I don't even want to go there during this conversation."

Icor Tech desperate? I mean, I've seen a lot of inefficiencies, and I've wondered how on Earth they operate with some of their numbers, but for the first time I realize, maybe they're not...or they won't be for much longer.

"I need you to be an enactor of change," Gabriel says.

"But...but," I stammer, looking down at my coffee. "Why me?"

"Because you saw the first in a series of necessary changes without me having to point it out for you. And to be quite honest, how you even saw them from your program manager position is beyond me."

"All this, because I saw an inefficiency with a dated platform? You could have just pulled me and put me over some of the projects necessary to bring it up to speed."

"Well, it's not that easy. First, in order to even enact these changes, it needs to be brought up to a vote. In order for the vote to swing my way, it has to be brought up by someone other than me."

I scrunch my brows in confusion.

"My father was a pariah, and people assume I'm the same. He's the reason we're in the mess we're in. It's not that he failed to see what needed to be done, although he did. It's that he lost the trust of the board and the directors, and I've yet to recover it."

"Oh, so the only reason my proposal is coming up for a vote is because I presented it and not you?"

"Kind of. I could have forced a vote, but I could not get the votes. Coming from you, the votes may be on our side."

"I don't know. Many of them hate me."

"But Tom doesn't, and he has considerable pull. He's the one that will help you get the board and the directors on your side. And once we secure the switch to Expressions, I have other things for you to enact," he says, staring at me intensely. "Bagel, yogurt, eggs, bacon?"

"Bagel's fine," I say, mulling over his words.

He busies himself again, and I start to put together the puzzle pieces he's left scattered for me.

"So, you want me to bring up the things you cannot. And—you need my vote when it's time to cast."

He turns, pointing his finger at me. "Exactly."

"And you're positive I'll play by your rules."

"Absolutely positive."

"How can you be so sure?"

"Because you care about numbers more than politics. None of the changes I want to make are political in nature. I'm not trying to get on anyone's good side, incentivize anything, make some fucking vendor happy. I want the numbers to provoke your outcome."

"Here I thought I was promoted for my work ethic and brains," I say, slumping my shoulders.

"It's not a bad thing. I'm not saying you don't deserve the position, but there was a strategy behind it as there should be with every decision. And your work ethic is fabulous, but there are a lot of idiots with a great work ethic. You're the whole package."

"You say you don't want political decisions, but my promotion is political."

His face falls. "Yes, I made a political move, but one that I felt was necessary. And as CEO, I have to make these types of decisions, but I want you to make your choices differently."

It makes sense, and I have an enormous amount of respect for Gabriel, even more than I had after first meeting him. I was a pawn to him, but a very well chosen one.

"I think we'll work well together," I say.

"Yes, and don't worry, I plan on having a great hovercraft engineered for you. Professor X would be jealous."

A hovercraft? My face contorts in confusion.

Gabriel grabs a remote, hits a button, and the island comes to life. I'm a little shocked, though I shouldn't be. Gabe's the head of a major tech company, of course, he has all the latest technologies built into every nook and cranny.

I look on as an image forms. It's of a black limo. The door opens and out steps Tom, then myself in a silver sequined dress. I bring my hand up to my mouth, my eyes widening.

"Turn it off," I shout, shielding my eyes.

"But you're missing the best part!" Gabriel chuckles, setting a plate in front of me.

The plate's accompanied by a tray full of various cream cheeses, jellies, and butter, but I no longer feel hungry.

"Did this make the news or something?" I say, trying to keep my tears at bay.

"The news? Jesus, no. I have several entertainment reporters in my contacts."

"And they just decided to call you up and give this to you?"

"Well, not exactly. A little bird told me Tom was taking you to Deco, and I decided to see how well you clean up."

How well I clean up?

"I've taken most of the footage out of rotation. It won't see the light of day unless some obscure reporter puts it out there—but then it would really go nowhere. No one's looking for a girl falling on her ass. They might care if Angelina Jolie does, though."

"Yeah, lucky me."

I force myself to eat my food, trying not to be rude. Gabriel seems to have lost his jovial outlook from our first meeting.

"So, is it okay I went on a date with Tom?"

"It's all above board," he says, looking down at his plate.

I don't really like how he's acting. He seems full of fake smiles and random looks of forlorn despair. It's understandable though, with the state of his company and how no one listens to him.

"You know, you really should get your top Mechanical Engineer on my hovercraft pronto," I say, trying to lighten the mood.

"Should I? Do you have any recommendations?"

"Well, I'm sure you've seen my degree. My previous position."

He smiles, and my heart feels close to bursting. It's like all the world's handsome was poured into one perfect man.

"Have you always been so clumsy?"

I blush. "Well, my mind is always going in so many different directions. There's nothing wrong with me physically if that's what you're asking. I'm just always distracted."

"You know, it would probably save me a lot of money if I bought you a handler."

"A handler?"

"You know, those people that guide mascots around."

"So, I'm…a mascot?"

"Well, they are kind of cute and adorable," he says.

Cute and adorable?

I sit there confused, looking at Gabriel as a look of

horror flashes on his face.

Oh no! The only guy in my life that's a perfect 10 thinks I'm cute and adorable. Damnit! Why can't I be sexy for once? Why can't I be...more like Analise or Porn Star Meg?

"I didn't mean it to sound creepy," he says, his eyes shifting to the side.

"No, I get it. Cute and adorable is what you would call a child, and I guess I do put off a certain naive vibe. I know this."

He's fidgeting almost as though he's as anxious as I am. And for some reason, he's been avoiding my gaze.

"And now the final reason I wanted to have you over for coffee," Gabriel says.

"And what's that?"

"I don't want you to just speak for me, that's never been my ambition for you." He holds out a rather expensive looking necklace with a heart-shaped pendant. "I want you to look at the data I have on this USB and derive your thoughts based on the information—the facts. Tell me your findings. I want to see if our thoughts align. I'm not going to ever force you to agree with me, but I can't be blindsided."

I reach out, taking the necklace, analyzing it until I find the unlocking mechanism. It's clever, and probably rather pricey. I wonder if the diamonds lining the heart are real.

"I'll keep the hounds off you, or at least most of them. I'm sure nothing I can say will keep Tom away." He gives me a wink, and I'm positive I turn shades of red past the beet stage.

Not knowing what to say, I rise from my chair.

"Make sure you finish ordering the finishing touches to your office. I want you to be comfortable, and don't let Analise barrel you over. Next week, I'll show you your new home—where you will remain for eternity. I hope you don't mind, but it's already furnished. You can put in the finishing touches, of course."

"Thank you so much. I truly appreciate this opportunity," I say, turning to leave.

"Oh, and Remi," Gabriel says. "What I say stays between us."

Chapter Thirteen

Gabriel's mother wants grandbabies...

My heart sinks as I watch Remi leave. My chest feels hollow, broken. I don't know what it is exactly I feel for her, but it's damn sure more than lust.

I know I shouldn't have played the footage of her fall, but I wanted to make sure she knew that I am aware she's seeing Tom, and that I was fine with it.

But...I'm not fine with it. In fact, I'm in a sorry state. I was up all night thinking about her, her legs wrapped around Tom's waist, her back arched. It was terrible. I even played elevator footage just to make sure he went home alone, and he did, but it didn't make me feel any better.

She has the right to date whomever she chooses. If she wants to date Tom, great. Maybe she can win Tom over to my viewpoints. I should be happy about this development. Ecstatic.

I try to rationalize what's going on, to make it into some kind of benefit, but deep inside, I feel shredded.

My phone is buzzing, telling me my mother is trying to get ahold of me. It's Friday, which means I'm supposed to have breakfast with her.

But all she'll be doing is talking about the wedding, and it's slowly taking its toll on me.

I push the notification to silent and send a text to Analise, telling her to get down to Remi's office. Then I head to the elevator.

I reach my mother's floor and walk out into Old Hollywood elegance. She loved being an actress and living out in Los Angeles, and I'm sure if she were given the opportunity to do it all over again, she would have stayed there.

She greets me warmly, arms outstretched. "I was beginning to think you've been avoiding me!"

"Well, mom...I hate to tell you, but I was. That's what you get when all you talk about is flowers and babies."

Her face feigns offense, then she moves in to plant a kiss on my cheek.

My mother is gorgeous. One of the most breathtaking women of her time whose looks have extended far past what people consider the standard prime. After my father's death, I urged her to move on, but she says that being a widow suits her.

I think being with my father broke a part of her. She can never trust again.

We sit, and her servants begin setting out an array of delicacies, none of which will be consumed by myself and very few by my mother.

"We are looking at a west ceremony followed by an east ceremony. We'll fly the guests straight from here to China."

"Two ceremonies mom, I got it."

"They've sent over their own florists and decorators to assist with ours, which is rather pushy if you ask me. I mean, isn't that why they are having their own ceremony? I'm half tempted to send my own people over there."

I place my hand on hers and try to feel empathy, but all I feel is frustration.

"I know this may all seem rather trivial to you, being a man, but trust me when I say this extends beyond the wedding. This is a power play."

I almost laugh. What would my mother know about power in business? Sure, she's beautiful and was a phenomenal actress during her day, but she was never into business.

The coffee is calling to me, so I take a cup, black. I think of Remi pouring in her stream of sugar, and I wonder if she's looking at coffeemakers right now.

I think about the strands of hair falling in front of her face. Her pushing her black-framed glasses up the bridge of her nose. The way her brow arches when she's confused—something I noticed today for the first time.

"You know," my mother says in a hushed voice, glancing around the room, "I'll wager that Sayo is a virgin."

I spit my coffee out into my hand, and down the front of my suit.

"Jesus, Gabe!" My mother claps her hands, and a woman appears with a linen. The damage is done, though, and I'm going to have to change.

"I've had eyes overseas ever since the engagement," my mother says as though she runs a network of spies. "Sayo is seen out often with friends, but never with any men. My sources tell me it's been this way for years. I think her father made sure to keep her away from men to make her more appealing to businessmen like yourself."

I don't have the heart to tell my mother that no, Sayo's father didn't give a flying fuck if she dated men as long as they had the appropriate number of zeros in their bank account. She just doesn't like men.

"Isn't that smart, though?" she asks, looking for approval.

"Yeah, I guess. He may have just doomed her to a lifetime of shitty sex, but at least she won't know any better."

My mom breaks out in laughter. It's music to my ears. I may not agree with all of her ideals, but one thing is certain: she loves me more than anything, and she would never knowingly put me in the situation that I'm in. I honestly think I'm the reason she never left my father, despite his many affairs and his poor treatment of her. She didn't want to put me through that.

"Oh, Gabriel," my mother dramatically clutches her chest, "I can't believe you've grown up. I mean, you're near thirty, and it feels like just yesterday you were pulling on the hem of my dress. I can't wait for my grandbabies. I can see them now."

I picture them as well. A true light that will eventually come out of my upcoming marriage.

I think back to my grandfather Maxwell Icor and his wife, my grandma Eileen. They met before the rise of Icor Tech, and despite the fact that she never once stepped foot into business matters, they loved each other deeply. She balanced him and his eccentric tendencies. She was humble, loving, and loyal. When she died, my grandfather turned into a shell of himself until a year later, when he died. As much as I loved him and hated to see him go, there was relief in that he died with a smile on his face, the name Eileen on his lips.

"Mother, I assure you, I want children just as badly as you want to see me have them," I tell her, and it's not a lie, but the circumstance involving my procreation would be vastly different.

"Sayo is bringing with her a new chef that specializes in worldly cuisine."

"It makes sense. I'm sure she's going to crave all the dishes she had growing up."

"Yeah, but I wonder how we should handle Thanksgiving."

"I think we should keep the same menu and ask her if she'd like us to add a couple dishes."

"I suppose you're right." My mother looks nervous, like she's almost afraid to bring something up. "I'm just a little scared of change. I never imagined you'd marry a woman from China, and to be honest, I don't at all care, but I worry. What if she doesn't want to teach my grandkids about Santa? What if we can't go trick or treating?"

I place my hand over my mother's and lean in to kiss her. I see her eyes are moist and that these are very real fears for her.

"Mom, we'll deal with everything one step at a time. Us Icor's are good at negotiating, and I'm sure Sayo and her mother have a few fears of their own. I swear to you, I will take my dying breath before I allow anyone to take the rite of passage of dressing up like an idiot with my children just to consume massive amounts of pandered sugar all night long."

My mother smiles as best she can, but I can see the unknowns are weighing on her. I feel bad because she really doesn't do much, so there's nothing to take her mind off her worries. All she has is this wedding and thoughts of grandchildren.

"Have you thought of volunteering?" I ask.

She looks at me quizzically. "Volunteering?"

"Yeah. You could teach acting to a group of kids."

She looks off into the distance, clearly dismayed. "I...I left that behind...long ago."

"Think of how much you could help aspiring stars. We could set up a fund for those showing promise. You can use your industry connections."

A panicked look lights my mother's eyes. It's not that she doesn't want to do good in the world. It's just her confidence has taken a toll. When my parents first married, she was everything to my father—until she wasn't. Pregnancy and age took their toll, and my father started lavishing younger women with attention, rather flamboyantly. My mother hated leaving the Tower, out of shame. Sadly, I didn't learn how to be a man from my father. Instead, I learned how not to be a man from him.

I decide to let the topic fall away. "Well, I better get to work," I say, getting up from my seat.

My mom rises immediately, rushing towards me. I know she needs me and that I should spend more time with her, but it's hard.

"I love you, ma, and I promise you'll have rugrats running around here before you know it."

Chapter Fourteen

Remi is a master of seduction...

"This machine grinds the beans before pressing them. It assures you a fresh cup of coffee each time." Analise eyes the coffee contraption on the page as if it were a diamond necklace.

I've looked at over twenty coffeemakers this morning, and none of my mechanical engineering knowledge is coming in handy. And with Analise leading the cause, I can barely get a word in edgewise.

"I don't really care about all those special features."

Analise sighed, clearly annoyed that I'm not coveting her knowledge. "Well, what type of bean do you like?"

"Folgers."

"Are you kidding me?" Analise rolls the catalog up and beats me over the head with it.

"I have to stop looking at these catalogs." I push the stack sitting on my desk to the side and face my computer. "There's work to be done."

Analise sneers. "But are you doing the work? Or is Gabe?"

My heart skips a beat. I feel suddenly sick.

"Oh, you don't have to worry about me saying anything. I'm close with him."

Close with Gabe? How close?

I stare at her folded ever so neatly in the chair. She's both exquisitely beautiful and highly intelligent. Heck, I'm not even gay, and I'm mesmerized by her. Why wouldn't he be fucking her?

"Gabe made it clear that he wants me to come to my own conclusions," I finally say.

"Then he's probably pretty confident you'll come to the same ones he has."

I need to stop looking vulnerable. If psychology class taught me anything, it's that apex predators prey on the weak, and Analise is clearly an apex predator.

"Are you worried that maybe I'll start helping him *come* to these *conclusions*," I ask.

Her brows scrunch in confusion.

I followed it with. "It's okay, though. I'm sure he's *coming* just fine with you."

Analise's mouth opens, her head tilts. She's confused, and to be honest, I'm a little confused myself.

"Are you trying to make a sexual innuendo?"

What the hell did I just say?

"Oh my God—you really did go there! It must have been killing you! Eating you up inside."

"I don't know what you're talking about," I say, my hands shaking over my keyboard.

"There is NO getting out of this. You tried to insinuate that I'm fucking Gabe, but that's not all. You insinuated that I would care if you're fucking Gabe!"

"NO!"

"You like him," Analise says with a smirk.

"No! God, what is wrong with you?"

"What is wrong with me? Do you want to go over what you just said?"

Why am I so stupid? I haven't even been in my position a full week, and I've just given this woman all the ammo she needs to make my work life hell.

"Oh, there's no need to get embarrassed. He's Gabriel Icor, a handsome billionaire who even straight men lust after. The only reason I'm immune to his charms is because I grew up with him."

That got my attention.

"So…there's nothing there?"

"With Gabe? No. Nothing, nada, zilch."

For some reason, I'm relieved, although it's ludicrous. It's not like I would ever have a chance with a 10. It's startling enough that I had a date with a 9, and Gabriel seems quite okay with that development.

"So, how did your date with Tom go?"

"My date with Tom? It was more of a business meeting," I say, avoiding eye contact.

"A business meeting? Funny how Tom has never

taken me to Deco 6 before. I don't think I remember him taking me anywhere alone."

I look down and away. I've never had 'girl chat' like this before. Part of me wants to participate, but another part of me remains guarded.

"So, give me the deets!" Analise draws her chair closer.

"Well, if you must know—I made a fool of myself."

"Really? How so?"

"I don't know where to start, the multiple falls I had throughout the night, or the fact that I loudly proclaimed I wasn't wearing panties."

"You weren't wearing panties?"

"It's not like I planned it that way. He freaking texts me saying we're going to Deco 6, and I didn't have anything to wear. I had to borrow a dress from the 'Porn Star Next Door,' and I just kind of forgot."

"And when did the underwear confession come out?"

"I was standing out on Deco's patio…the wind was blowing."

Analise's hand rushes to cover her mouth. "So, he got a visual?"

"No! Thank God. I just kind of blurted it out."

"Oh my God, you poor thing! If any other woman had said that, I would have assumed they were just trying to play stupidly innocent when they're really just trying to screw a filthy rich man. But you…you're practically Amish."

"Amish? You realize I have a degree in Mechanical Engineering, don't you?"

"New wave Amish."

I look around to make sure no one is listening even

though the door is closed. "Do you mind if I ask you a question."

"Shoot."

"What is Tom's type? I just…can't figure out why he'd ask me out. And I wonder if he'll ever ask me out again."

Analise exhales, and I take that as a bad sign. It figures the one man I have a chance with would end up uninterested.

"I would say," she bites her lip, her head bobbing from one said to the other, then back again, "he's not a bad guy, and he certainly doesn't have bad intentions, but he's Tom, and he doesn't really know what he wants. I don't know if he'll ask you out again, but you don't have to worry about him spreading rumors or lies about you. You could end up fucking for a month, tell him you're no longer interested, and it will be business as usual."

I swallow, unsure of what to say. Fuck for a month? I don't know how I could possibly do that without developing feelings.

"Do you want him to ask you out again?" she asks.

"I don't know," I reply honestly. "I mean, he's attractive, brilliant, and respectful…but I'm just so new to this."

"Well, have you thought of asking him to keep it casual?"

"Keep it casual?"

"Yeah, late-night rendezvous, no strings attached?"

"I could never!"

"Why not? I mean, he'd even take you to dinner if you wanted. There are worse fuck buddies to be had."

Maybe having a fuck buddy wouldn't be such a bad

idea. Tom could get me through the awkward phase of losing my virginity, and I won't really have to take my mind off my work.

But you'd fuck it up. You'd call too much. You'll get too attached.

"I don't think I'm made for that type of relationship," I say, "but I would be open to at least trying it with the right man."

"That's literally the only type of relationship I'm made for."

"Oh? What's it like?"

"Harder than one might think."

"You must have so many options."

"I don't want to act like I'm not lucky—I know I am! I was born into wealth and good looks, but that doesn't mean I attract the right kind of men. Men of similar upbringing usually come at me with motives. Respectable men of lower standing in society are too afraid to approach me."

"So, you don't even try?"

"Well, I didn't say that." Analise gives me a wink.

"Do I get a picture? A story? Something to go off of?"

"His name is Diego, and he works at the Starbucks across from Icor Tower."

"Wait? You're dating a Starbucks employee?"

"I would say it's more like we are enjoying each other's company."

"Do you..." my voice trails off, but I lift my brows for emphasis.

Analise, purses her lips, snorting. "Remi, are you asking if I'm fucking a Starbucks employee?"

"Ummm, I guess."

"Yes. Yes, I am."

"I hope you get a free cappuccino out of it."

"Better. He brings me cake pops."

A knock sounds on the door, and I'm immediately anxious. I haven't been doing anything relevant all day, and the last thing I want to do is make a terrible impression with my new peers. Analise does not share in my worry, however, and she jumps up to open the door.

A parade of flower bouquets walk into my office by over a dozen delivery men. I'm confused and assume they have the wrong office.

"Guys, I don't think those belong here."

A man walks up to me with a purple vase, a stuffed monkey hugging it, and red roses arranged beautifully inside, too many to count.

"Are you Remi Stone?" the man asks.

"Yes. But I didn't order these."

He chuckles. "That's usually how it works." He turns towards his crew. "Set 'em down, boys."

I'm handed a card, and the men begin to file from the room.

"Wow," Analise says. "This cost a pretty penny."

"I don't know why I'm receiving these," I say.

"Damn, you're so adorably cute. May I remind you of your date last night?"

Tom sent me flowers?

I tear open the envelope, and sure enough, a card is inside:

Remi,

I can't wait to see you again. I got you this, so you have something more appropriate to wear next time—for most of the night, at least.

XOXO Tom

A Victoria's Secret gift card is stuck to the bottom of the card, and I feel so completely humiliated, I drop it.

Analise, swift as a cat, snatches it up, and one look at it has her reeling with laughter. I'm talking bent over, gut grabbing, red-faced, chuckles that have me worried she'll catch the attention of the whole floor.

"Will you keep it down," I hiss.

That only ticks her up a notch, and she's now booming with laughter.

"Seriously, keep it down!"

The giggles finally come to a stop, and now she's fanning herself with the card.

"So, now Tom's buying you underwear and making plans to fuck you. Do you know how many women would take decades off their life to be in your position? I was wrong about you. You're a true master of seduction."

I open my mouth to reply, but my phone buzzes, drawing my attention away.

Tom: *You must have an admirer.*

I don't know what to say.

"I can't wait to see how you're going to mess this

up," Analise says, and I cast her a glare.

"Oh, don't act like you won't land on your feet!" Analise points at my phone. "And put that thing away. You don't want to seem overeager."

I take her advice and put down my phone. After all, she has a lot more experience than myself in these matters. Then I settle back into my desk and throw the stack of catalogs at Analise.

"I have to do some work, and it appears I have slides to prepare for next week. If I have any questions, I'll give you a ring."

"See ya later! I'm gonna go get me some Starbucks," Analise says as she exits the office.

I smile inwardly, more than a little excited. It's not just that handsome Tom Wellington, the solid 9, sent me flowers, an underwear gift card, and is texting me.

It's that I now have an inside secret with a friend.

Chapter Fifteen

Remi knows it's better to just settle for the 9...

The workday flies by, and it's after six when I realize I have been looking at the USB Gabriel gave me for seven hours straight.

Pretty much, it's all discouraging and points towards gross mismanagement. Why anyone would fight these common-sense changes is beyond me, and I loathe the thought of bringing these things before the board. I know what they're going to say, what they're going to think. That I think I'm better than them—smarter than them. I am smarter. I can say this with little doubt as I read and reread the numbers.

Any idiot can see Icor Tech is bleeding money.

Then I think about the political motivations Gabriel was telling me about. It's very possible they know they're losing money, but they can't sever the political relations between themselves and the vendors. How would I fight that? How would I even be able to accuse them of it? This shouldn't be my job, it should be Gabriel's, but obviously, he's struggling with it.

My phone buzzes, and I look to see a text from Gabe.

Gabriel: *How was your day?*

Remi: *I want to believe the USB you gave me is a joke. That no one can be this stupid.*

Gabriel: *I take it you're coming to the same conclusions I have, then.*

Remi: *Just tell me how. HOW did this happen?*

Gabriel: *We can discuss it after you present your findings in a little over a week. You're going in alone, without me. You'll be bombarded—stand your ground.*

Remi: *You have me a little scared, boss.*

> **Gabriel:** *You'll do fine. Oh, and I don't want to make this awkward, but we have a company policy that states employees are not allowed to run businesses inside their office.*

> **Remi:** *Of course, why would this be an issue?*

> **Gabriel:** *Well, it seems as though you're trying your hand at becoming a florist.*

I look around at the sea of red flowers and blush. Then I remember I completely forgot to text Tom back.

But you don't want to text Tom. Not really.

How could it be remotely possible that I don't want to text Tom the 9 because I can't get Gabe the 10 out of my head? It's ludicrous and completely bonkers, and yet here I am.

I stare into my chat window with Gabriel, trying to think of something witty to say.

> **Remi:** *They're preemptive.*

> **Gabriel:** *???*

> **Remi:** *They're for my funeral. I ordered them in advance knowing I'm going into a slaughter when I present your findings… or should I say, my findings?*

> **Gabriel:** *I have a feeling we're going to work well together.*

I frown, thinking of all the things I'd rather do well with Gabriel that don't at all involve presenting before a board.

Will I ever be immune to his charms? Will I ever not want to rip his clothes off when I see him?

Probably not, and I'm suddenly jealous of Analise, who has somehow gained immunity to him.

I bring up Tom's text box, and say:

> **Remi:** *Thank you for the flowers and the gift card.*

I gather my things so I can go home to Kibbles and pack.

Remi the YouTube star...

I walk home, anxious about next week's meeting, but determined to present thorough research with common sense solutions to the problems Icor Tech faces. Tom will be on my side, and maybe a few of the other directors.

Too exhausted to walk up the five flights of stairs, I wait for Boxy Bessie, which will take up far too much of my evening, but at least it's time not spent packing.

Mr. Sokolov is cursing again, and I look down to see a roach scuttle towards my shoe, the number 8 written on it with what appears to be white out.

I take a step back, disgusted, and look over to see his friend, Number 3, scuttling nearby.

"Ah, hah!" Mr. Sokolov enthuses from the stairwell. "I see you, Number 3!"

Unable to contain my curiosity, I ask, "Why are you numbering them?"

Mr. Sokolov casts me a rather smug look, chuckling to himself like some diabolical genius.

"You see, pretty girl, in order to eradicate these fiends, we must first know more about them."

"Oh…well, what does this tell us?"

"I've numbered them up to 100, all of them in the common bathroom on the first floor. I'm tracking where they show up," he pulls out a notebook, "and recording their sightings in this."

"What will that do exactly?"

A dark look crosses his face as if he's just now realized he's been gracing an inferior with his presence. He exits the main foyer, the stairwell door slamming behind him.

Finally, Bessie opens, and a stale, musty smell assaults my senses. I step inside and take the ten-minute ride to the sixth floor and exit.

As I'm rooting for my keys, Porn Star Meg's door opens, and she jumps out, bounding towards me with entirely too much energy.

"How did it go?" she practically screams.

"How'd what go?"

"The date, silly!"

"About as well as you'd expect a date of mine to go."

"What was the food like? The atmosphere? Did you see any celebrities? How much was the meal?"

I put a hand up and blink. Meghan is going off a mile a minute and must be stopped before my head explodes.

"Who was your date? Do I know him? Is he on TV?"

"Whoa, let's slow down now. I am exhausted, and I have to pack."

"OH MY GOD YOU'RE MOVING IN WITH HIM ALREADY!" she shouts. "I mean, I would too if he could take me to Deco."

"No! No—this is for a promotion."

"Oh, where do you work?"

"Icor Towers."

I swear Meghan looks like she is about to faint, and if it weren't for that fake tan of hers, she'd be white as a sheet of paper.

"Were you on a date with…Gabriel…Icor?"

"Gabriel Icor? No! He's my boss."

"Oh my God, I had no idea you have these connections. You need to tell me everything."

I look her up and down, the opportunist in me trying to leverage the situation to my advantage. She is a lot stronger than me, with significantly more energy.

"I tell ya what, you help me pack, I give you the details. Sound good?"

"Deal!" she screeches and starts hopping in place.

Jesus, what have I gotten myself into?

I open my door, and we enter my dark hallway. I hear the familiar growl of the demon named Kibbles.

"Stand back," I say to my excitable friend as I make a

dash for the treat cupboard, but I'm not quick enough, and I feel her clawed paw batting at my leg.

"Give me just a freaking minute!" I yell, frantically searching for the small can of Pounce.

Meghan turns on the lights, a look of disdain crosses her face. "That's a fat cat," she says with a sneer.

"Meghan, meet Kibbles. Kibbles, this is Meghan."

I finally locate the Pounce and throw a bunch of treats on the floor. For just a moment, I think I can sit back and relax, but Meg has decided to do a full inspection, walking around my living room and nosing through my things.

"You don't really have much, do you?" she says.

It's true. I don't care much for decorating. I put more thought into the wallpaper on my computer than the pictures in my home. Whereas her apartment is all glitz and glam, mine is one step away from being abandoned.

"It should make for easy packing," I say as I dig for some pop tarts.

"So, where are you moving to?"

"Icor Towers."

Her head snaps towards me. "You're moving into the Tower? Where you work?"

"Yeah, executives and directors get room and board."

"Holy fucking shit. This whole time I thought you were the most uninteresting person in the world, and here you are moving into Icor Fucking Towers."

"To be honest, being uninteresting is how I got the job."

"Can ya get me a job there? Can ya?" Her eyes light with ambition.

"Well, what is it you do for a living?" I ask, feigning

ignorance.

Her brows furrow. "You don't know what I do?"

I'm a little nervous, unsure of what to say.

She's an adult. She's flamboyant about what she does. She'll be more offended if you act like what she does is shameful.

"I mean, yeah. I do. And I'm totally cool with it! I think it's great that you're comfortable with yourself and you're so confident and I hope your costars treat you with respect. Because I've heard women are sometimes —"

"I'm an influencer!" she says, a stunned look on her face. "Might Be Meghan. I have a YouTube channel, a website. I have over 100k insta followers. What the hell did you think I did for a living?"

"Oh. Well, that's cool," I say, trying to recover.

"Did you think I shot porn or something?"

"Well, I noticed the ring lights in your apartment, the nice furniture."

She walks towards me, almost seductively, a curious look on her face. "You thought I did porn?" she says.

"It was just a joke. A bad one."

"No, it wasn't. You thought I did porn. It's okay, though. I'll take it as a compliment."

I don't know if I should feel relieved or mortified.

"So, what exactly are we packing. Some books?" Meghan asks. "I've never seen a place so bare. It's like you just moved in last week. You don't even own a couch."

"Well, there's a team coming to box and take my things next week, but I want to put it all into piles, so it's not done haphazardly. I also need your help with some heavy boxes I have stored in my closet."

"So, how'd your date go?" she asks. It's clear she just couldn't wait any longer.

"Oh, great—and by great, I mean mortifying."

"That bad?"

"Well, at one point, I felt a slight breeze, freaked out, and shouted that I wasn't wearing underwear. So, yeah."

Her hand flies to her mouth, barely stifling her giggles. "Actually, you date like a pro."

My phone vibrates, it's a message from Tom:

> **Tom:** *I have business to attend to over the next couple days, but I was really hoping to see you. Would you like to do dinner on Sunday?*

I should be ecstatic, but I'm not. I know how stupid I'm being, and I don't want to ruin my chances with a good guy. But I just can't be excited.

> **Remi:** *How about coffee instead? I feel like I can get to know you better that way. There's a cute little cafe called ImPressed near my apartment.*
>
> **Tom:** *Coffee sounds great! I'll text you after I get back into the city.*

I smile, but it's forced. I wish I could be more enthusiastic, but for some reason, I'm just depressed.

It takes almost an hour to lay my things out and create some semblance of order. Then, I duck into the bathroom to pack my toiletries when I hear Meghan say, "Might Be Meghan here, and I'm in the middle of CHAOS as I'm helping a friend move! You'll see over there…"

I stare on from the doorway in horror as Meghan holds her camera at arm's length recording herself in a pile of books.

What is she doing?

I shut myself into the bathroom, my mind racing a mile a minute.

No one will know it's me, and if they do, who cares. This isn't a big deal.

I pull up Might Be Meghan on my phone. There she is, smiling all bright and beautiful for the camera in her fitness clothes. I watch clips, noting that the number of views is nearing one million.

I've been a hermit my entire life. Maybe, just maybe, it's time for me to take a step out of this shell of mine. I mean, I have the career of my dreams, but there has to be more to life than just going to work and figuring tolerances and calculating efficiencies. Maybe I should find me a Starbucks Fuck Boy too!

No amount of coaching can get me through that door, though, and when I hear a knock, I swear, if my apartment were at ground level, I would have climbed out the window.

"Remi?" Meghan calls.

"Yes," I call back.

"Care to come out?"

Sweat is pouring down my forehead, and I can't for

the life of me figure out what has me so anxious. There's no reason to hole myself in the fucking bathroom of all places, so I take a breath, exhale, and open the door.

"So…I was just wondering if you'd film a segment with me."

"Film a segment?" I say, feigning ignorance.

"Yeah, my little minions like to see what I do in my daily life, and I think many would be interested in seeing me help you move."

"So you want to film a segment…with me?"

"Yeah, if you don't mind."

"I'm a little nervous."

"Wanna crack open a bottle of wine?"

I rarely drink, but I figure there would be little harm. It's not like I'm hanging out with a guy, and I'm certainly not driving anywhere.

"Sure."

Meghan disappears from my apartment and comes back a minute later with a bottle of wine and two glasses. I drink the pink-colored liquid without hesitation, and Meghan moves in a few of her ring lights.

"Go put something cute on." Meghan points towards my bedroom.

"Something cute?"

"Oh, dear Lord, please tell me you own something other than your work attire."

Meghan pushes past me to go into my bedroom and begins rummaging through my closet and drawers. "You wear granny panties?" she says as she flings a pair of my underwear across the room. "And what's this? A muumuu?"

She holds up an orange-flowered frock that belonged

to my grandmother. I had meant to donate it to charity, but the damn thing has some kind of invisible cloak, evading me each time I thinned out my wardrobe.

"You're wearing it." She throws the muumuu at me, and I immediately toss it to the floor.

"Oh, don't be so dramatic. Audiences love seeing shit like that." Meghan shuffles the muumuu around with her foot.

I take a sip of wine and say, "I thought people liked sexy. That—is not sexy."

"Okay, then let's film in our underwear."

I cringe, the memory of last night's fumble still fresh in my mind. "You think they'll like my granny panties?"

Meghan sighs, rolling her eyes. "I get free shit all the time. I'll be right back."

She comes back a minute later with bags and bags of clothes, all holding lingerie.

We look at each of the garments, some of the things I can't even figure out how someone would wear them, let alone why.

"You really are cute, ya know," Meghan says.

I snort, taking another drink while holding up a lacy number with no crotch.

"Seriously, Remi, I never see you with a guy. With anyone. You come home and turtle in your apartment."

"Turtle in my apartment?" I feign offense.

"What the hell else do you call it? Do you have any friends?"

"I've never had many friends. My mother died when I was seven, and my grandmother hated noise. I spent most of my time mulling over books."

"Gosh, that's terrible."

"My grandma died last year and couldn't even leave me in peace beyond the grave. That monster over there was hers." I gesture to Kibbles, whose massive body is eyeing us from her cat tower.

"Were your high school years good? I mean, you could at least go out with friends, right?"

"When everyone else was enrolling in high school, I enrolled in college. Bachelor's by nineteen. Master's by twenty-two."

A look of astonishment crosses Meg's face, and I begin to feel self-conscious, so I take another sip of wine.

"You've never had any kind of fun, have you?"

"Well, last night was my first date if that tells you anything."

"Oh my gosh. You can't be serious?"

"My grandmother hated me. When I tested out of high school and into Cornell, it was the best thing that had ever happened to me."

"Why did she hate you?"

A stab of guilt swells in my gut. I look down at my glass, tracing my finger around the rim.

"She had my mother young, and she really didn't want her. She treated my mother like shit, and my mom fell for the first guy that came her way. Then she kept falling for every guy thereafter. When she was seventeen, she got pregnant with me, no man in the picture." I begin the choke, and tears travel down my face. "She was the best mom, so kind. She loved me so much, no matter how little we had."

"What happened to her?"

"She died. She grew sick when I started kindergarten. By the time cancer took her, she was a shell of herself."

Suddenly, I am wrapped in a hug, unable to escape.

"Oh, Remi. I'm so sorry! I'll be your mother!"

"Honey, I think you're younger than me," I say, maneuvering my glass around her to take another sip.

We throw on lingerie, snapping pictures of each other, then we each don our own muumuus. As it turns out, I have three stowed away.

Meghan sets the lights on us, and we begin filming, full muumuu. It's as if I get to live my childhood all over again, though this time, with a friend and terrible fashion. We talk about our favorite television shows, don fake accents, and drink way too much wine.

Sometime during the evening, pizza is ordered, and Meghan is wielding a microphone.

"Tell me, Girl Genius, what is the best part of working for Icor Tech?"

"Well, Might Be Meghan, I have to say it's the analytics."

"Did you say anal? I only got as far as anal. That's a big word."

We burst out laughing, and before I know what we're doing, Meghan pulls me up, and we're dancing, twirling, and spilling copious amounts of wine. Two empty bottles are on the floor, a third is in Meghan's hand.

"Oh! We can use your cat tower as a pole?"

"But…it's boxy?"

"Oh, girl, it'll work. We'll make it work."

Meghan drags over the cat tower, and I see that Kibble is huddled in a corner, seemingly having met her match. The cat tower extends seven feet high, and while there is a pole running its length, several boxes are running up it for the cat.

We're giggling, and Meghan begins prancing around the tower, then sits seductively on a box, bringing the muumuu up her legs that are clothed in thigh-high stockings.

She crosses and uncrosses her legs in burlesque fashion, and beckons me over.

Now, I'm prancing around the tower, rolling my hips under the tent-like muumuu. Meghan is hootin' and hollerin' me on. As I pass her, she reaches out, grabbing my muumuu, and pulls it over her head.

I'm shimmying to get away. She begins tickling me, and we're soon on the floor with our muumuus in disarray.

"I like you, Remi."

"I like you too, Meghan."

"I want to show the world what good friends we are!"

"Go ahead! Show everyone!" I say.

"Why didn't we ever talk until now?" she asks.

"I don't know," I say as I roll onto my side. She puts her head on my thigh, and I'm too tired to do anything but sleep.

Chapter Sixteen

Gabriel the stalker...

The scene of Remi stumbling out of the elevator after our first meeting is played on repeat as I stare at a spreadsheet telling me how much money we're wasting.

She's such a klutz. How could anyone be such a klutz?

I reread the texts from her, and it provides me with a measure of comfort. She's seeing exactly what I had expected her to see. What any intelligent person would see.

The picture on her Match profile stares at me from a different screen. It's ridiculous but speaks volumes. After some digging, I found out quite a bit about Ms. Remi Stone.

After her mother died at seven, she was sent to live with her grandmother, and unfortunately, Child Protective Services had been called on the woman several times.

Her grandmother was a tyrant, impressing nothing but hatred and distaste on young Remi. In the interviews conducted by CPS, she'd flat out say things like, "If it weren't for her, I could keep a man around," and, "Ain't nobody wants her. I'm doing the best I can."

Despite her hateful caregiver, though, Remi went on to achieve great things, or maybe because of her. If I were Remi, I'd do anything I could to get out of that trailer too.

She has no other relatives, meaning holidays must be lonely for her. It hurts to think of her alone, on Christmas, no one to celebrate with.

I don't care what I have to do. She'll never have to spend another holiday alone again.

I take all images of Remi off the screen and focus on the numbers, the only company I'm allowed to have right now.

My phone buzzes, and I see a text from my friend Zev pop up.

Zev: *Bad news.*

Gabriel: *What's that?*

Zev: *My father passed.*

Gabriel: *I'm sorry to hear that. Do you need anything?*

Zev: *You know what a dick he was. Now, I have to make sense of all the crap he left behind.*

Gabriel: *I know how that goes. Tell me if you need anything.*

Zev: *Will do.*

Zev is one of his oldest friends and understood all too well what it was like to have a difficult father.

He hails from a long line of architects, and they made a killing in real estate investments. I dated his sister Sari for a hot minute, but she proved to be too spoiled for my taste.

The intercom light flashes, my assistant is trying to get through to me. I hit the 'answer' button and clear my throat.

Gabriel: *Yeah, Stace?*

Stace: *Sir, you were pinged on Social Media. Instagram, to be exact.*

Gabriel: *So what? I must get pinged a thousand times a day. That's what you're for, to like, smile, and say thank you.*

Stace: *This is different, Sir. Just look on your phone.*

I pull up Instagram, and I immediately see what Stace is talking about. It's from some Instagram influencer named Might Be Meghan, and I'm tagged in it. The message reads:

What better thing to do on a Wednesday night than help my neighbor pack for her move to Icor Towers!

The video shows two women wearing god awful muumuus dancing around cat furniture, a bottle of wine in one of their hands. One sits, the other looks like she's doing some type of tribal dance.

Oh, God! Remi is doing some type of tribal dance.

Gabriel: *Thanks Stace, I'll handle it.*

Now, I see a flash of underwear, and the duo falls to the floor in a fit of laughter. I'm laughing too as I bring up my phone to text Analise. As funny as this might be, it can spell disaster with the fallout.

Gabriel: *Look at this on insta. What the hell am I supposed to do about it?*

I send her a link, and less than a minute later, my phone vibrates.

> **Analise:** *First, I'm in love. How did you find this gem? Second, turn it into lemonade.*

> **Gabriel:** *How the fuck am I going to do that? The board is going to go crazy.*

> **Analise:** *Fuck the board. They are crusty souls, even my dad. This Might Be Meghan has over 100k Instagram followers, and her YouTube platform is huge. You may run a tech company, but you're more popular among the older crowd than the millennials and younger demographic. Let people laugh and see that people in your company don't have sticks up their asses. Also, bring Meghan in.*

> **Gabriel:** *I really need you on my board. You just have this way of thinking that I need casting a vote.*

> **Analise:** *I know, and one day…if we're lucky.*

Gabriel: *I wanna hold off on bringing Meghan in. Maybe next week. I have too much to think about.*

Analise: *Fine, are we done?*

Gabriel: *Sorry, you in the middle of something?*

Analise: *Having Starbucks caramel licked out of my belly button, so I would say…YEAH!*

Gabriel: *Jeez, I'll go away now.*

I know I should put my phone down and get back to work, but the call of Instagram is strong, and I go back into the haphazardly created video done by my newest director, or rather her popular friend.

It's obvious Remi is drunk and having a good time, and getting to see this little glimpse into her life makes me like her even more. The muumuu she's wearing is ridiculous, and I want to assume it's a joke, but with a woman like Remi, you just never know. She doesn't put a lot of effort into her appearance, not that she needs to. She's enchanting just as she is.

I watch the video again. The brief glimpse I get of Remi's lacy bottom doesn't fail to send my mind racing. I can't work knowing I could be looking at a dancing Remi, so I do the only thing that might bring me relief.

Images of Remi shedding her muumuu and standing

in sexy lace come to the forefront of my imagination, and it doesn't take long until a familiar rush comes.

I'm done, and more than a little tired, but I have to go back to work—but I can't. Now that I've relieved my tension, I should be able to focus, that's how this sort of thing works.

Except this time, I can't help but stare at Remi's face, at her lips, at her cute, button nose, at her doe eyes.

Fuck! Not this again.

I'm mad at myself for letting this happen. I should be focusing on Icor Tech and my upcoming marriage, not some woman I've just met. If the parade of roses is any indication, Tom's actually really into this one. Maybe I should give him more credit. Maybe he will be good for Remi.

Without anyone else to talk to, I pull up Analise's contact info once again.

Gabriel: *Are you done fucking yet?*

Analise: *Are you kidding me?*

Gabriel: *I really need to talk.*

Analise: *Give me twenty minutes.*

Twenty minutes pass, and Analise walks through my door, coffee in hand.

"What's this about?" she asks, taking a seat in a nearby chair.

"I think I might be having a meltdown or something."

Her mouth twitches to the side as her brows shoots downward. "Why?"

"I don't really know what's causing it. Possibly marrying Sayo. Or maybe it's just financials. Before, I used to throw myself into my work for days at a time. Now, I can barely concentrate for ten minutes straight."

"Are you tired or distracted?"

"Well, I can tell you that I'm definitely getting distracted."

"What's distracting you?"

"A little chaos ball named Remi Stone."

A look of surprise lights her face. "Remi? I mean, I can tell you think she's cute, but is she really distracting you? Her?"

"Badly. I can't tell you the number of times I pull up her picture throughout the day."

"Ahem, have you thought of…you know…of taking matters into your 'own hands'?"

"It's been done. It's not enough."

"Jeez."

"Yeah, it's bad."

"Well, what is it about the girl?"

"That's what I'm trying to figure out. There are so many things I like about her. I like how smart she is. I like how she doesn't wear a lot of makeup. I like how damn clumsy she is. I think I really fell, though, when I learned her history. She's had it rough, yet she's doing amazing things."

Analise brings her cup to her mouth, takes a sip, and shrugs her shoulders. "Tell her how you feel."

My gut twists with anxiety. "Are you mad?"

"This may be exactly what she needs. Offer to relieve her tension, if ya know what I mean."

"That would be highly improper and insulting."

"Why do you assume she'd be insulted? She's a career woman. From what I gather, she probably doesn't have the time or energy to dedicate to proper dating. Lay out some ground rules."

"This is all crazy talk."

"Is it, though? Would you rather she fall head over heels for Tom only to be dumped when he gets bored of her? At least with this, she knows what she's getting in for."

"But I'm getting married."

"To a lesbian. A lesbian that does not, I repeat, does not want to fuck you. You managed to get engaged to one of the .009% of women that does not want to rip off your clothes and rub against your junk. I also happen to be a member of that club."

"Do you really think this is a good idea?"

"She's a twenty-three-year-old virgin—she's got to be frustrated. We actually talked about friends with benefits situations today. She seemed conflicted."

It's getting hot in my office, and I unbutton the top button of my shirt.

"Are you sure…she's a virgin?"

"Pretty damn sure."

"Then I can't! What if she gets attached?"

"Good. I mean, you're going to need someone consistent that's not into muff diving. It's not like Remi's out searching for a husband. This thing can last for decades if you're discreet enough. It could be perfect for her. Better you than some creep she meets at a bar because she's fucking tired of being a virgin."

The thought of Remi meeting up with a man at a bar fills me with dread.

"I just don't know," I finally say.

"Get out your damn phone."

"Get out my phone?"

"Yeah, you're going to invite her to dinner."

"No—"

"Save it. Now, you're going to do what I say so you can save the damn company. Pull out your phone."

I pull it out.

"Bring up her contact and text message box."

I pull it up, excited butterflies aflutter in my stomach.

"Invite her to dinner."

"But it's 1:30. She'll be asleep."

"If you don't do it now, you'll never do it. Invite her to dinner. You can feel out the situation over carbs."

I suck in a breath and let my thumbs do the work.

Chapter SEVENTEEN

Remi did a bad bad thing...

"What the hell is going on?" I mumble, my body against the hard floor.

I look down at a weight on my leg and see Meghan sleeping.

Bright lights hurt my eyes. I blink and see ring lights set up in the corner of the room.

I pull my leg out from under Meg, and her head drops to the floor, but she doesn't wake. I look around and find Kibbles' cat tower in the middle of the room, and three empty bottles of wine cluttered nearby. My phone is buzzing.

It's 1:58, and there are more notifications on my phone than I've ever had before.

I turn it on to possibly the worst thing that's ever happened to me, save my mother dying.

Meghan had posted a video of us dancing around the cat tower. It's been viewed over fifty-thousand times over the course of two hours.

My hands are shaking, and I grow dizzy. I want to yell for Meghan to take it down, but I'm unable to say a word.

I see notifications of text messages from Tom, Analise, and Gabriel, and I don't know if I should just turn off my phone and give myself a few hours before I 'face the music' or dive right in.

Can I get fired? Oh, God—I'm going to be fired.

I cringe inwardly as I pull up Tom's message, not knowing exactly what I have gotten myself into.

> **Tom:** *OMG! What am I watching? You are super sexy girl, and I'm glad you made good use of that gift card. I can't wait to see more.*

A small wave of relief washes over me. After all, he is in a high position within the company, and he hasn't admonished the action or screamed for me to have it taken down. Next, I move to Analise's message.

> **Analise:** *Girl, you're probably gonna wake to some crazy shit and feelings, but*

> *just know—it's all good. Gabe loves it! He thinks you're going to draw in a younger crowd. If anyone asks you any questions, say nothing.*

An even larger wave of relief washes over me. My fears subside, but I still feel an unhealthy amount of anxiety. I mean, what's the board going to think? What's Cregor going to think?

Finally, I open Gabriel's.

> **Gabriel:** *Your apartment should be ready Monday. Would you care to join me for dinner before I show it to you?*

Apartment? Dinner? He sent the text at 1:30, about a half-hour after I received Analise's text, which means he knows about the video and said nothing about it.

> **Remi:** *Sure*

I'm immediately greeted by a text bubble. He's busy typing, which means he's still awake.

> **Gabriel:** *Good, bring something to the office to wear, we'll leave straight from work.*

My heart stops. No—the world stops. Gabriel Icor, the 10, wants to have dinner with me! Of course, it's for work-related reasons, but still, I can dream.

What am I supposed to wear? Is he going to take me to a place like Deco? Or will it be more like an Olive Garden dinner? Endless breadsticks do sound good.

> **Remi:** *What are you wearing?*
>
> **Gabriel:** *I'm still in my work suit, but three buttons of my shirt are undone. I shed my belt hours ago. Please tell me you're still in that muumuu. It really brings out the color in your eyes.*

Oh, God! That's not what I meant.

> **Remi:** *I meant Monday! Will you be wearing something casual? Or dressy?*
>
> **Gabriel:** *Whatever it is, I'll be wearing underwear at least.*

I throw down my phone.
What the fuck just happened! Fucking Analise must have told him what I blurted out to Tom!
Kibbles is breathing heavily in a corner, but she's not being aggressive. I think whatever happened last night scared the living daylights out of her. Brought her to God.
I go to my bathroom to splash my face with water.
Was he trying to sext me? Or was he making a joke? Why would he want to sext me? He's Gabriel Icor the 10!
I rush to Meghan, shaking her until she shows signs

of life.

"Meghan! I need you. Meghan! Wake up!"

I continue to shake her frantically until she grunts and rolls over.

"Meghan! It's Gabriel Icor!"

That got her attention.

In a moment, she's sitting up, hands on head, blinking.

"What the hell is going on with Gabriel?"

"I need you to look at this." I hand her my phone.

"Oh my God! Gabriel Icor's asking you to dinner!"

"Well, it has to be a work meeting, right?"

"Then why wouldn't he schedule a work meeting? This is dinner! You're not some special client. He's taking you out to eat."

"I'm sure this is just what fancy businessmen do."

"God, you really are stupid. Your brainy and hot, and that might just be what Gabriel Icor, Tech Genius likes."

Gabriel Icor the Tech Genius, that's what they had called him on the cover of Investor Today. He was supposed to make a big splash in the tech world, but instead, headlines died shortly after the issue was released. And now I know why—his board wouldn't let him get anything done.

"Oh my God! He just told you what he's wearing, and you fucking clarified?"

"He's my boss!"

"He was flirting!"

"I didn't know what to do!" I plead.

"Get me a cup of coffee. It's time for you to go back to school."

I open my mouth to protest.

"Nope! Get your ass in the kitchen. It's going to be a long night."

I make two cups of coffee and bring them to my table where Meghan is now seated.

"Give me your phone."

"No!"

"Remi, do you want to go the rest of your life receiving promotions and watching everyone else live their lives while you invent whatever you invent?"

"First of all, I've invented nothing. Second, no. I want a life too."

"Then trust me. I have more experience than you do. You can do all the shit you need to do career-wise, I'll be like your PR rep."

I hand over my phone, and she pulls up the text box.

Remi: *Boxers or briefs?*

What did she just type!?! Oh my God, this was a mistake!

I reach to grab the phone from her, but she pulls it away.

"Damnit, Meghan, he's my boss!"

"Yeah, and he just told you in explicit detail how he was dressed. And then he mentioned underwear. This is warranted."

"Look, you're probably right. Right about everything —this just isn't me."

"You're shaking," Meghan says, placing her hand over mine.

My phone buzzes and bile fills my throat. Meghan looks, but I turn away.

"Oh, my God—you need to see this."

She turns the phone towards me, and I gasp.

Gabriel sent a picture of the lower half of his body. His button-up shirt is completely undone, his white undershirt is pulled up, showing his taut abs. His pants are unbuttoned, revealing skin-tight boxer briefs, a large bulge underneath.

"Does this mean he's interested in me?" I ask.

"At the very least, it means he wants to fuck you."

I feel myself stir, a sensation that always catches me off guard. There is no denying I want to fuck Gabriel Icor, and now there's no denying he wants to fuck me as well. But, he is my boss, and by pursuing something with Gabriel, I could be excluding the possibility of Tom—who may want more than just to fuck me.

"What do I do?"

"There's only one thing to do," Meghan says with way too much confidence. "Take a picture."

My first reaction is to slap her.

"Oh, don't look so fucking prude. You're going around telling guys you're not wearing underwear and asking them what they're wearing."

She's right.

"So, how should I pose?" I ask.

"Well, he mentioned the muumuu, so I think you should keep it on, but bring it up around your waist and look over your shoulder. Here, sit on this stool."

Meghan moves a stool into position, then repositions the ring lights.

"Are you kidding me? You have to be kidding me."

"Absolutely not," she says.

I sit on the stool just as she instructs, and she has me

grab the hem of the horrid, orange-flowered gown.

"Now look over your shoulder, smiling confidently," she says.

I comply, and she moves into position to get a picture. After taking a few shots, she shows them to me, and against all odds, I do not die from embarrassment.

My hair is disheveled but in a sexy kind of way. The muumuu is up around my waist, my black lace underwear on display. It's not a model-worthy shot, but there's no denying that it's cute.

"Can I send it?" Meghan asks.

"If you think I should."

A big smile spreads across Meghan's face, and she begins typing.

Snakes of dread and butterflies of desire start waging war in my gut, each claiming the territory as their own. I wait anxiously for a return text, which is taking way longer than it should.

Finally, my phone buzzes.

> **Gabriel:** *You look unbelievable sexy in that. I'd love a view from the other side.*

I damn near smack the phone from Meghan's hand, completely mortified.

"Oh, stop! What the hell did you think he was going to say, *'I love the floral print.'* He's a man, and men are visual creatures."

"So, you think I should?"

"No! Absolutely not! You need to keep him wanting—needing."

"I don't understand."

"Gabriel Icor can fuck anyone he wants, and he wants to fuck you. Chances are, women don't hold his attention for long. Once he sees the goods, the mystery is gone. We're going to tell him that the view is better in person."

Meghan starts typing, and I turn, unable to even look at her as she texts my new obsession.

> **Remi:** *A picture would never do justice. I'd love to show you in person...*
>
> **Gabriel:** *Should I send a car to come get you?*

"Fuck! No! Tell him no!"

"Don't worry, girl. That's exactly what I intend to do. We don't want Gabriel to think you're overeager."

> **Remi:** *I'd love to, but I'm a bit tired.*
>
> **Gabriel:** *That's fair. What about tomorrow, are you busy?*
>
> **Remi:** *I am. Sorry. You'll have to wait until Monday.*
>
> **Gabriel:** *One last request?*

"One last request? What the fuck is he going to want?"

"He's a guy. It'll be something perverted like, 'Don't forget to think of me when you masturbate tonight.' Guys like thinking that shit."

Remi: *What would that be?*

Gabriel: *I'm sending over a driver. I'd like you to give him your panties.*

I feel like I'm about to throw up. Gabriel Icor is asking for my panties.

Remi: *Sure thing!*

"Hot fuckin' damn, you have one of America's sexiest billionaires sexting you. I fucking spend all my time on the web wearing short shorts and flashing my tits, and Little Miss Introvert is sexy posing in a fucking muumuu with Gabriel Fucking Icor."

"How could you have agreed to that?" I gasp.

"Oh, chill. It's no big deal. We'll just throw them in a sandwich bag and tape them to the door."

A swell of heat blooms inwardly. I'm smiling, excited. I went from having zero dating prospects to having two men ask me to dinner in one week—each of them brilliant and sexy.

"That fucking bulge. That FUCKING bulge." Meghan is enlarging the picture Gabriel sent to me.

His member is fully clothed, but I can see a hint of a ridge, and for a moment, I regret not grabbing the phone and telling him to send a car.

I need that fucking bulge.

Chapter Eighteen

Remi has coffee with Tom the 9...

The smell of coffee grounds invigorates me as I walk into the quaint café I'm meeting Tom at. I'm seven minutes and thirty-eight seconds early, and I'm unsure if it would be rude for me to grab a cup before he arrives.

I decide to utilize my on-call backup, Meghan.

> **Remi:** *I'm early. Should I grab a coffee before he arrives?*

> **Meghan:** *No. Part of getting to know each other is figuring out what kind of coffee they like. And let him pay.*

I don't need Tom to pay for my coffee, but Meghan knows more about this kind of thing than I do, so I take her advice and wait.

A couple is sitting by a window arguing. It looks like the woman has been crying. The man is leaned back, glancing around the room as though he is embarrassed.

The barista behind the counter with frizzy red hair yells out a name, and a man with converse sneakers and wireless Apple earbuds in his ear grabs it and walks off.

The jingle of the door bells rings, and I turn to see Tom walking in wearing a baby blue polo and khaki shorts.

His face lights when his gaze finds me, and I smile in return.

He pulls me into an embrace, kissing my cheek.

"How was your trip?" I ask.

"Boring! You know what got me through it, though?" He's looking at me with a droll expression on his handsome face.

I have a feeling I know what he's going to say, and I divert my eyes.

"Well, what will it be?" he asks, nodding to the menu.

"Something sweet, with lots of sugar."

"Any syrups?"

"I like caramel."

"What about that Toffee Coffee Crunch?" he asks.

"That sounds perfect."

We get in line, and I stare at the pastries behind the glass, too scared to even look at Tom.

His hand is on my shoulder, playing with my hair. It's an unfamiliar sensation, but a nice one—something I could get used to.

Tom orders for us, and it doesn't take long for our drinks to come up. We take a seat and blow the steam off our drinks.

"Cute place," he says, glancing around the café.

"Yeah, I try to frequent mom and pop businesses, though this may be more hippie and bro."

He laughs as he stirs his drink, glancing up at me from across the table. I can tell he wants to say something, and I have a good idea of what he wants to ask. I brace for impact.

"So, you have a cat," he asks with the face of an angel. "A very large one."

He must have seen Kibbles in my cat tower video. Wonderful.

"I do. I'm gunning for crazy cat lady, but instead of having several cats, I chose to have one very large cat."

"And that porn star you live next to?"

"Might be Meghan. Yeah…I was off on that one."

"Just a little."

"Well, she always looks so perfect. And she has a shit ton of ring lights in her living room. And her furniture is very nice for our shitty apartment complex. It was a logical conclusion, although a wrong one."

His phone buzzes. He takes a moment to respond to someone, then his attention is on me again.

"Sorry about that. I have some side ventures. It's actually why I had to go out of town."

"Oh?"

"I'm investing in a bourbon company and a private airline."

"Wow, what got you into that?"

"I'm trying to build a brand outside of Icor Tech. My aim is quality and luxury."

"Maybe you could let me sample it sometime, although I'm not sure I'd have any good input."

"Definitely."

We talk for the next half hour, or rather Tom talks. I get to hear about his life, his many accomplishments, and his plans for all his money. So much money, apparently.

I have very little to tell him in return, not that I could have gotten a word in with how much he likes to talk about himself.

What is wrong with you? You have a handsome man wanting to spend time with you, and you're sitting here judging him.

But I know exactly what's wrong with me. I can't get my mind off of Gabriel the 10, who is in possession of my panties.

I dread seeing him, yet he's all I think about. He's the most handsome man I've ever seen, and he made it clear on Friday he was interested in me.

"So, what do you say?" Tom says, staring at me.

Holy shit, why wasn't I listening!

I glance downward, wondering how I should tell him I wasn't paying attention.

"I mean, I know it's a bit forward, and I mean you no disrespect. I'd love to lavish you with attention. I think you'll find me very attentive."

Oh…that… It sounds like he's wanting some alone

time. I wonder if he cares how inexperienced I am. And what exactly does he mean by very attentive?

"You know, I don't think it's a good idea. I'm going to be moving soon, and there's still packing to be done. And I'm getting ready for my first meeting as a director."

"Oh, so what are you preparing?"

"Gabriel told me to do whatever I did that got me into that meeting. So, I found some inefficiencies with international shipping and the ports we utilize."

Tom clears his throat, leaning back, a critical look on his face.

"I tell ya what. Let me have a look at it first. I'd love to see if I can help you out before the meeting. I'll be able to tell you who's going to object and what they're going to say. We'll go in there prepared."

"Wow. That would be great. Thank you."

"I'll try to stop in Monday, but Mondays are busy, so it might end up being Tuesday."

"Awesome. I look forward to your criticism."

We get up to leave, but Tom grabs me by the arm, catching me off guard.

His lips press to mine, a short kiss, just a peck.

"Care to pose for a picture?" he asks.

A picture? No one's ever wanted to take a picture with me before.

I nod, and we pose, Tom extending his long arm out.

"Say cheese," he says.

"Cheese!"

Gabriel can't outrun his heart…

Sunday is my cardio day. I lift three days during the week, meditate and stretch on another, and Sunday, it's all cardio.

I've already run five miles and sprinted several laps. I'm tired, but there's still a lot left in me, so I crank up Prodigy and begin to sprint again.

What am I doing? I need to get back to work.

But I'm avoiding work.

Every time I sit down to get something done, I think of her. I pull up her pictures. I watch her videos.

And quite frankly, after Friday, I feel like a filthy pervert. I asked an employee—a director—for her panties when I knew she had been drinking.

I run faster, but there's no outrunning my mistake.

Nothing I can do will undo my overstep. On Saturday, I composed half a hundred text messages trying to apologize, but I deleted each of them. Terrified.

It doesn't take long before I slow, exhausted. I grab my water bottle and towel the sweat from my face.

Get back to work. There's a lot to be done.

My phone buzzes. I pick it up to see a message from Tom. It's an image of Tom and Remi together, smiling.

At least I don't have to worry about breaking her heart.

My heart is racing, and not just from my workout. Just seeing Remi wrapped in someone else's arms does something to me I can't quite explain.

This is one of the best things that could have happened. If she can win him over to my cause, it will be that much easier to save Icor Tech.

No amount of rationale makes me feel at all good about what I'm seeing, though.

I put down my phone and go back to my treadmill, setting it to eight out of ten, determined to outrun my problems.

Chapter Nineteen

Remi has a choice to make...

I enter Icor Tower at quarter after seven and step into the elevator absolutely terrified. My arms ache from all the crap I'm lugging in at Meghan's behest, but at least I won't have to bring it back to my old apartment again.

It takes an insane amount of effort not to rip off the fake eyelashes Meghan insisted I wear, and it's a constant struggle not to touch my face and smear my makeup.

Stepping off the elevator takes an act of courage I

don't often have to muster, and as I walk the thirty plus feet to my office, I'm met with blatant stares from others in the hall.

Everyone knows.

I hold my breath as I complete my walk of shame. I've spent most of my life trying to make the right decisions, and everything I've gained could be taken from me in an instant because of one stupid night.

I walk through the door to my office and turn on the lights. I'm relieved to be away from judging eyes, and I just want to bury myself in my work.

After I take a seat at my desk, I begin to log into the mainframe when my door opens.

"Looks like you had quite a weekend," a voice echoes from the doorway.

I look up to see Cregor Leskey, his face full of contempt.

"I'm sorry. I don't understand what you are talking about," I say as I bring up the system.

"Six-hundred thousand views and climbing. I can't recall the last time we've fired a director so quickly. This may be a record."

"You're saying I'm going to get fired?"

"You doubt it?"

"Well, judging from the texts I've received from both your daughter and Gabriel Icor, CEO to Icor Tech, I would say no."

A dour look crosses his face, his lip pulling into a sneer.

"Move along, Creg," a voice says. "She just spent all weekend packing. I'm sure whatever you need you can get from her tomorrow."

Tom appears behind Cregor, a megawatt grin on his face.

Cregor huffs loudly, turning and hobbling back to his office.

"Yeah," Tom looks to me warmly, "you're going to get a lot of that."

"I guess I should have expected it." I bury my head in my hands, overwhelmed by the few short minutes I've been at work.

"I talked with Gabe this morning. You have nothing to worry about. I made sure to tell him if you come under any scrutiny, he's going to have to face me."

I muster a smile, more than a little anxious.

Tom pulls a seat over to the side of my desk, facing me, sitting very close.

"So, how do you like it?"

"The office or the job?"

"Both."

"Ehhh, I'm getting used to it."

"You look amazing, by the way. Did your friend make you over?"

I blush. "Yeah, she's pretty persuasive."

"Do you want me to look at the inefficiencies you've found?" he asks. "I have a sliver of time this morning."

I pull up the spreadsheet I made last week showing the research I've been doing.

"We're using outdated shipping methods and inefficient ports."

"Really?" Tom says, leaning in.

"Yes, if you look at this row, it shows what we currently spend, the row to the right shows the range of what I believe we can get it down to. Conservative estimates, of course."

Tom squints at my screen, so close to me, I can smell the scent of pine.

My phone vibrates. I pull it out to see a message from Gabriel.

I grow a little tense. We haven't communicated since the night of my debauchery, when I sent him the panties I had been wearing. Meghan assured me his silence was fine, that it was normal for men to do this, but I can't help but feel his distance might be due to regret.

> **Gabriel:** *You smell abso-fucking-lutely amazing!*

My jaw drops. I'm at a loss for words.

I don't think Gabriel Icor is feeling regret.

"What's up?" Tom asks.

"It's just...It's just Meghan. I guess the video's getting a lot of traffic."

"As it should. You were adorable—and by adorable, I mean sexy, and adorable."

I should be flattered. Tom is hot, respectful, and absolutely interested in me, and yet I can't stop thinking about Gabriel the 10.

Tom's hand moves to my thigh, his touch so warm it feels scorching.

"I was hoping I could take you out to dinner tonight," he says.

It suddenly occurs to me how stupid I've been behaving. With Gabriel, I don't stand a chance. Maybe he'll *allow* me to fuck him tonight if I'm lucky. He dates supermodels—there's just no future.

With Tom, well, if his actions are giving me any indication, he could be my first real boyfriend. Like a walking hand in hand through parks, sitting next to each other at the movie theater kinda thing that I've never had before.

Then there's the matter of my virginity--both seem eager to relieve me of.

Tom has this good-natured appeal that's easy to fall for. The 'boy next door' if there ever was one. Blond hair, blue eyes, dimpled smile, and a muscular physique. Nothing wrong with that.

Gabriel, on the other hand, is all dark and mystery. He smirks, and has a look that will melt you. His hair is styled ruggedly, always a five o'clock shadow. His eyes, God, they kill me every time. He's a little leaner than Tom, but damn, his suits fit well.

"I'm sorry, I already have plans for tonight."

He frowns, and my heart sinks a little.

"So, have you made use of that gift card?" he asks.

"I haven't had time to go shopping yet."

"Well, judging by that video, it seems as though you have that covered."

"Actually, my neighbor has bags and bags of stuff sent to her for free. We went through them while I was packing."

"So, she has muumuus sent to her?"

"Oh, not those. Those are mine."

Tom leans back in his chair, a grin on his face, and I realize how that sounds.

"It's not that I wear them! They belonged to my grandmother."

"Well, what is it you wear to bed then?"

I don't know what to say. I have Gabriel Fucking Icor the 10 sexting me. And, I have Tom Wellington in my office talking dirty. How the heck did I get myself into this mess?

"Something you'd likely consider uninspiring, and I'm sorry, but I'm really anxious about this presentation, especially because I know the room's gonna have it out for me."

"Well, by what I saw, you certainly seem to know what you're doing."

I smile, relishing the compliment.

"If you don't mind me saying so, those figures might make you some enemies."

"How so?" I ask.

"Barry's cousin runs that port there," he points to a map I have on one of my monitors, "the one you're suggesting we cut. There's also additional inland travel from the new port."

"That port extends us out a day, and if we travel just a little further, our docking fee is cut by a third. I've also been given access to a few documents that are not yet released, and it looks like we have pop-up shops in development for the area around that port. It's a new business strategy that's gaining ground and will make the additional inland travel from that port worth it."

"Yeah, I hear what you're saying, but numbers aren't the only determining factor of how people cast their votes."

"So we're supposed to pay a third more and deal with a 72-hour turnaround versus and 48-hour turnaround so Barry's cousin can have our business."

"Look, I'm not trying to—"

"Does Icor ever make any decisions that make sense?"

Tom puts up his hands defensively. "Hey, now—"

"With the amount of money we are saving in one year alone, we could retire Barry's fucking cousin and a handful more people if we wanted, or are we also concerned about his pride."

Tom's face grows stoic, and I realize how inappropriate my lashing out at him is.

"I'm so sorry," I say.

He smiles. "It's okay, and I understand your reasons behind this. It's just better that you go in armed with the knowledge. I'll back you up in there. I promise."

Point: Tom.

Tom gets up from the chair, patting my shoulder. "Well, I better get back to work myself."

"Thanks! For the flowers and letting me vent."

"Don't worry about it."

Tom leaves, closing the door behind him, and I can't help but pull out my phone to look again at Gabriel's text.

What do I say to this? What does someone say to this?

I stare at the words on the screen, unsure of what to do.

What would Might Be Meghan say?

I decide to say the opposite.

> **Remi:** *I'm sorry for acting like a nut the other day. I hope I didn't put you in an awkward position.*

Gabriel: *It's fine. Do you regret our conversation?*

Remi: *Not really....*

Gabriel: *Would you like it to continue?*

Remi: *Kind of.*

Gabriel: *All I can think about is tasting you.*

Remi: *Oh?*

Gabriel: *Down on my knees, under your desk.*

Remi: *Oh...*

Gabriel: *Is that a good oh? Or a bad oh? Is it the big O?*

The room suddenly feels ten degrees hotter. I'm unsure of what to say but very interested in what he's telling me.

Remi: *It's a 'new at this' kind of oh.*

Gabriel: *Am I going too fast?*

> **Remi:** *I don't know. Where is this supposed to lead?*
>
> **Gabriel:** *Hopefully, to you touching yourself.*

Touching myself? Am I supposed to tell him I'm touching myself? How am I supposed to touch myself and continue whatever it is we're doing on the phone? I'm such an amateur.

> **Remi:** *Maybe we can discuss this more tonight?*
>
> **Gabriel:** *Definitely. I think you'll find I'm pretty convincing with my words. It's due to my skillful tongue.*

I toss my phone down, utterly unprepared for the torrent of emotions suddenly coursing through me.

God, please let this be real and happening.

Curious, I pick my phone back up and read and reread Gabriel's text. The feelings they're provoking are highly addicting.

Is this what it's like to feel wanted? To feel desired?

Before I can think on it any further my office door opens again, this time it's Analise.

"I worried you wouldn't show!" she says as she hops over to my desk.

"I damn near didn't after that video. God, how

embarrassing!"

"It's funny. The board is going to go nuts, but it's hilarious. There's nothing they can do about it."

"Oh, and thanks!" I say glaring.

Her face contorts in confusion. "For what?"

"For telling Gabriel I told Tom I wasn't wearing underwear on my date!"

Her lips shoot out like a ducks, her eyes shift from side to side. "I didn't tell him that."

"Yes, you did."

"No…I didn't. We have talked about you, but I never told him that."

"Oh…"

"So, how do you know he knows?" she asks.

I go to show her the text messages, then remember how fucking stupid that would be considering everything that was said between us—and the pictures.

"You told him what I said to Tom. That I blurted out I wasn't wearing any underwear."

"No, I didn't. I promise you."

Then how does he know?

After a minute of thinking, I decide I believe her. I barely know Analise, and she's Cregor's spawn, but something tells me she wouldn't lie.

"Hey, if you don't mind, I could really use some help. I'm in uncharted territory."

Analise sits down, crosses her long legs, and says, "Your therapy session has started. I charge more for boring stories than fun ones."

"It's just, I don't know what to do about Tom," I say.

"What about Tom?"

"He's asked me out to dinner tonight. I said, 'no.'

Maybe I shouldn't have."

Analise dons a smirk. "So, you're playing hard to get?"

"No, it's just I'm going to dinner with someone else."

"Oh? Well, you must tell me who."

"There's this guy, very different from Tom, but hot. Super hot. I like him, but there's no way he would ever date me, and Tom, well, he just might want to date me."

"So what you're trying to tell me is you can't decide whether to lose your virginity to Tom Wellington or Gabriel Icor."

My cheeks flush every shade of pink in existence, and I jump up to cover Analise's mouth with my hands like a damn toddler.

She chuckles. "Like—you didn't think I'd guess?"

"How?"

"Me and Gabe are close. Real close."

"Oh, my God, so you know?"

"Know what?"

"What a fool I made of myself the other night."

"Is this aside from the cat tower video?"

"So, you don't know about the texts?"

"I was in his office pretty late on Friday. The last thing I told him to do before I left was to text you and invite you to dinner."

The words feel like a punch in the gut.

"So…he didn't want to take me to dinner?"

"No, he did. I just had to nudge him in that direction."

"I'm confused."

"Yep, I would be too, but it's Gabriel that's going to have to straighten it all out for you."

"So, you're not going to help me at all?"

She exhales an annoyed breath. I can tell she wants to discontinue the conversation.

Finally, she says, "I can't tell you what to do about Tom or Gabe, all I can say is you need to go into whatever situation knowing what you're going to get out of it. At a minimum, both of them will fuck you. Without a doubt. But beyond that…well…that's a conversation you're going to have to have with each of them."

I look down at my keyboard, frustrated.

"So, what exactly is it you want?" Analise asks.

"What do I want?"

"Yeah, I mean, it's not just about them. You get a say in where everything goes."

"I…I don't know."

"Well, do you want a relationship? Do you want a boyfriend? Do you dream of a husband and kids in your future?"

"Sometimes. I want all the good things in life without having to work for them."

"Then why the hell are you working for Icor Tech?"

"No, that's not what I meant. I just don't want to have to guess and worry, and put years into a guy hoping for a proposal just to have him dump me."

"I guess a lot of us feel that way."

What Analise said sounds so ridiculous, I snort. "Yeah, like you ever have to worry about that."

"You think I don't have to?"

"You're rich, smart, and beautiful. You're the whole damn package."

"My fiancé left me for my cousin. I had to go to their wedding to keep up appearances. Wouldn't want a scandal."

"Oh, gosh."

"Another ex sent nude pictures of me to a host of tabloids after we broke up. My father spent almost a million dollars keeping them off the internet."

"I had no idea."

"Of course. You wouldn't. My problems may not be the same as yours, but I promise you, I have just as many."

"I hear ya, and thanks for setting me straight," I say. "And I want love and a career. It doesn't have to be in that order."

"The good news is, there's nothing wrong with you dating Tom since he's not a direct superior."

"And Gabe?" I ask.

"That gets tricky. When Icor employees date, there's usually no drama unless it's kept hidden. As long as you report it with HR, you're above board. If one of you reports to the other, they do their best to reassign one of you. Maxwell never wanted to have to deal with disciplining employees because of what their hearts want. With Gabe? I can't say. I've honestly never thought about it before."

"So, with Tom, I can have romance, sex, love, and keep my job. With Gabriel, I can have…sex?"

"You'll have to talk that out with him."

"Thanks," I say, though very little was cleared up for me. "So, how's your sexy barista?" I ask.

Analise closes her eyes and gives the cutest '*humph.*'

"If you're asking whether I came into work fifteen minutes late because I was being worshipped by a man who may be related to the Energizer Bunny, then I would say you're crazy."

She gives me an exaggerated double wink, and I snicker, more than a little jealous.

"I need to get back to these reports." I wiggle my mouse to wake my computer. "Maybe we can chat later."

"Sure thing," Analise says, and gets up to leave. "Catch ya later."

Chapter Twenty

Gabriel won't give up without a fight...

Fuck me! How did I get myself into this mess? And why do I keep fanning the flames?

The delivery guys arrive on time, and I tell them where to put Remi's boxes. They're all marked well, what few she has.

I spent all Sunday telling myself it's over. That I'm going to act completely professional around Remi and hope she could forgive my overstep, but then Tom had to threaten me this morning, telling me if Remi got in trouble for the video, he'd pull some legal bullshit.

And then I had to see him stepping into her office.

All men have a competitive drive. It's the most basic qualifier of success, and Tom certainly ticked up the rivalry this morning.

With Remi, I almost feel territorial. Partially because I don't want to see her get hurt, but also because she plays the starring role in all my most recent fantasies.

Remi has three large boxes of books, two large boxes of clothes, a desk in dire disrepair, an assortment of other medium-sized boxes, and a morbidly obese cat that clawed its way through two of the delivery men.

How can one person have so little? I ask myself while staring at her household wares.

Growing up in abundance leaves you oblivious to the lives of those with less. I know that what she has doesn't mean she's poor. It's just so foreign to me. Every woman I've ever known, ever dated, ever spent time with, was a ravenous consumer.

Tonight, I will take her here, to her own apartment. Hopefully, she'll react well when she gets to the master suite, which I spent an hour putting the finishing touches on. If not, well, that will make for an awkward workplace.

My alarm buzzes, alerting me to my upcoming meeting.

I leave the suite, providing the decorator and delivery men with strict instructions, and as I'm walking down the hall, I see Analise coming towards me.

"Figured I'd find you here," she says.

"How do you figure?"

"I haven't seen you this hung up on a woman in… like ever. I've never seen you this hung up on a woman."

"God, Analise, you make it sound so serious."

"Isn't it, though?"

"No, it's not. It's this whole marriage thing. I think I'm feeling the weight of…of—"

"Marrying China's most eligible lesbian?"

"Don't say that so loud!"

"Oh, don't be so sensitive. How are you going to react when you hear rumors that she's diddling the maid?"

"Fuck, Ana, can't you show a little tact?"

"Well, you should know that Remi's having major anxiety over this."

"Anxiety? Why?"

"Jeez, Gabe, you can't be this oblivious. The girl's a virgin with two men romancing the fuck out of her. She wants to make sure she makes the right choice."

"What does she assume her choices are?" I ask.

"Well, she knows whatever she has with you will be driven by lust—she probably assumes you fuck a bunch of supermodels."

"Really? Is that the vibe I put out?"

"Gabe, you have fucked a bunch of supermodels."

"It was a phase. A fun phase, but not one I'm eager to go back to."

"The other option she thinks she has is a possible relationship with Tom."

"Oh, fuck."

"I know. I didn't want to be the one to break it to her."

"Who knows, maybe he's finally ready to settle down. I mean, he's 30. Isn't that around the time men start looking for life partners?"

"Gabe, you're an idiot. I honestly think he's been looking for a life partner for a while, but he gets bored. Easily. Do you remember that woman he met when he was finishing up the paperwork on his car? He bought her a damn Hummer and lost interest in three weeks. Three weeks!"

"So, what do we do?"

"Easy—you have to be the one to romance her."

"I don't know. I mean, I'm up against her hopes of a relationship."

"Gabe, just lay your cards on the table. She may decide on her own that she doesn't want to date anyone she works with. After all, she is analytical. You could become the appealing option by way of her not wanting to fuck up her work life."

"Yeah, because screwing your boss never complicates things."

"I never said that, but with you, she knows what she's going to get."

Analise's logic is actually pretty good, but I don't know if I'm simply telling myself this so I have a reason to fuck Remi.

"Well, I'm out," Analise says, bringing her phone up to her ear and walking a little way down the hall.

"Later, Ana."

I step into the elevator and push the number eight, bringing me to the meeting rooms. I've received at least twenty emails from high up people at Icor regarding Remi's video from the other night. There have been some scandals at Icor, and some of those same people involved in said scandals are calling for me to dismiss Remi, which makes it all the more fun when I tell them she's sticking around. I didn't spell out the word hypocrite, but I let my words show my feelings more subtly.

Exiting the elevator I see Lindel, her face brightening when she sees me.

"You've been busy," Lindel says, and I give the woman a hug.

"I have been."

"Something's up with you."

Lindel knows me better than my own mother. As soon as I told her about my engagement, she knew I wasn't happy about it.

"Things will start going better soon," I say.

"That new girl you promoted."

"Remi."

"Yeah, her. How you feelin' about that?"

"I feel just fine, actually. It was the right decision."

She looks at me critically, and I can tell there are things she wants to say on the matter. Lindel is rather conservative, which is hilarious because her daughter Keisha is absolutely wild—too wild for even me during my own wild years.

"Look, I have to get to a meeting, but we can pencil in some time tomorrow if you feel there are things we need to discuss."

"A talk's coming, but maybe not tomorrow. These things take time."

I smile, drawing Lindel into another embrace and make my way to my meeting.

The presentation has already started, and I slide into my chair, facing the screen.

Of course, the meeting is entirely unnecessary, and my mind begins to wander almost immediately—to

Remi.

I pull out my phone and enter the chat thread I have with her, bringing up her picture in the lacy black underwear. The underwear I keep in my desk.

Her friend must have taken the picture, Might be Whatever, or is it Amy? I don't know, but Remi couldn't have taken the picture herself. She has a playful smile on her face, and I try to envision her smiling at me like that. Playful…coy.

She deserves someone that will appreciate her. That will laugh at her clumsiness, and possibly cover all the doorframe and hard edges with padding. All I can give her is fleeting moments of pleasure.

What if Analise is right? What if casual is what she wants? She's twenty-three and hasn't pursued any serious relationships, and she's so hot that if she wanted a man, she could easily find one.

My mind conjures images of Remi without the muumuu, wearing a matching lace bra, sitting on the conference table, legs spread.

Damnit! The last thing I want is to be 'standing at attention' in a room with six other people. Baseball, basketball…hockey. Dentist, oh shit, there was that hot one. Wait, are they looking at me?

"What are your thoughts, Gabriel?" Kelsey, a corporate lawyer, asks.

I exhale, knowing I've been caught not paying attention.

"My apologies," I say. "I've just had a lot on my mind."

Kelsey dons a smug look. She's hated me ever since I rebuffed her advances several months back, but she does damn good at her job, so we deal with each other as best we can.

"We want to offer the features listed to clients, but it seems like you've had them in beta testing forever."

"Well, I can assure you, I will check on this personally."

I make some notes on the matter, and tell them to proceed.

The meeting wraps up rather quickly, and I hurry to my office to resolve some things before my dinner with Remi tonight.

Unfortunately, when I enter my office, Tom is waiting for me.

Chapter Twenty-One

Remi goes to the top floor...

It's almost five o'clock, and lucky for me, my work is done for the day, and I have nothing hanging over my shoulder to mess up my evening.

I shut down my system and enter the bathroom attached to my office, so I can change into my evening attire.

I pull up Meghan's contact info and hit the FaceTime button, a moment later, her face pops on the screen.

"Let me look at you!" she barks.

I hold my phone up to my face.

"Your lashes stayed on, good. Your hair needs some work, though."

I plug in two curlers because Meghan was clear this morning that my bottom layer required a softer curl that the top, and I spread out the array of cosmetics she gave to me.

For thirty minutes, Meghan issues orders like a drill sergeant, walking me through a process most women have down before they enter college. In the end, I look like a different woman entirely.

I've never felt so sexy before.

My eyes are dark and dramatic, my cheeks well defined. My lips are a shade of bright red that you see on a sports car, not at all the dramatic crimson she put me in for my date with Tom. My blonde hair is set in loose curls, flirty Meghan calls them. And the dress I'm wearing—well let's just say I'm nervous about leaving the office in it.

It's black and made of thin cotton. A metal ring holds the fabric together at my breasts, creating a peephole effect that has me blushing. It feels rather appropriate, considering the text last sent by Gabriel. The dress is short, and the shoes Meghan lent me are open toe ankle booties that elongate my legs, and give me a different, more brazen posture.

In other words—I look good.

Meghan squeals when she sees me, jumping up and down so that her head bobs out of the frame of the screen.

"I swear, it's like an ugly duckling makeover!"

I scowl at her.

"Except you were never ugly! And you're not a duck."

We both laugh, and I disconnect from FaceTime after saying goodbye.

I don't have to wait long until a soft knock echoes from my office door. I freeze, and my brain stops working entirely for a full minute before I finally say, "Come in."

Gabriel enters my office, and oh my God, does he look hot! Like beyond perfect 10 hot. Godly levels of hot that not many can ever hope to aspire to.

His dark, rugged hair hangs over his intense blue eyes that are staring at me, taking me in. He looks pleased.

Suddenly, he frowns, hands on hips, exhaling loudly.

"What is it?" I ask, more than a little nervous.

"It's just that, well I was excited to see you in that muumuu of yours."

I smile and pick up the purse Meghan lent to me from my desk. Then I slip off my glasses and tuck them inside.

"I kinda like those on you," Gabriel says.

"Well, I've been advised by my beauty benefactor not to wear them."

His hands are busy, they're toying with something.

"You're wearing a top hat?" I say, a small chuckle escaping my lips.

"Well, something like that. You'll see." He offers me his elbow, and I tuck my hand in its nook. For a moment, I feel light-headed, like the physical contact is too much for me to bear.

He puts the top hat on, and I notice he also has a cane, which I find very peculiar. In all the pictures I've seen of him, he's never dressed like this before.

"And, we're off," he says, pulling me through the door and to the most anticipated night of my life.

Gabriel the Magician...

Remi Stone is the sexiest woman I've ever laid eyes on, of that I am positive. Escorting her down the hall to the elevator should be a source of joy, and yet, I only feel sorrow.

We step into the elevator, and I push the button that brings us to the top floor, or rather, the roof.

"Oh, do you have some kind of super-secret restaurant up there?" Remi asks.

"Something like that," I say, avoiding her eyes.

The door opens, and we exit, my helicopter is in plain view, the pilot waiting for our arrival.

Remi turns to me. "I didn't expect this," she says, stopping in her tracks.

I lean down and say, "You have no reason to be scared. The helicopter is top of the line, the pilot, Diger, flew missions in Iraq. Diger is the most qualified man I could find. There is no better."

"I believe you." She looks at me with a smile that breaks my heart, and I walk her the rest of the way to the launch pad.

After we're seated, I give her a headset to wear, and

the pilot takes off. Remi looks out the window hesitantly, a mix of anxiety and excitement. I can't stop myself from putting my arm around her, no matter how ill-advised it is.

"I've never been in a helicopter before," she says, fumbling for her glasses so she can get a better view.

Diger flies around the city so Remi can take in the scenery, then touches down at our next destination.

"Where are we?" Remi asks.

"You'll see."

We exit the helicopter to a sea of beaming faces greeting us.

"We're at a hospital," Remi says, a look of astonishment on her face.

"Yes, Mother of Mercy Children's Hospital. Every Monday, I come here to spend time with the patients."

The look on Remi's face damn near melts my heart. It's a mixture of surprise and devotion that can only be genuine. I want to say I'm not shocked, but I am. If I had brought any other woman here, they'd act gracious but be livid.

"Take 'em out!" I shout to Diger, and a nurse brings two children out to the helicopter.

"The ones that are well enough get a short ride. They take turns, getting to see a couple sights."

"That's amazing!" Remi's eyes light, and I can see they're moist with tears.

I give some high-fives as I pass the children waiting their turn for the helicopter, then we enter the hospital, taking the elevator to one of the many common areas.

I don my top hat as we enter the room and twirl my cane to the delight of the crowd.

For the next hour, I do haphazardly concocted magic tricks, many of which I fail miserably at, but the kids don't seem to mind.

Remi goes around to each of the little girls and talks, colors, and plays dress-up. At one point, I overhear a child tell her she wishes she were as beautiful as Remi. Remi immediately wraps her in a hug and tells her, "You are!"

A nurse approaches as the children are being brought to bed, tablet in hand.

"We have three children this week whose parents cannot afford care," she says.

I look at the numbers, frowning. "I'll tell you what, I'll pay half if Mercy agrees to discount the rest."

"That's what I figured," the nurse says as I sign the tablet. "I already have the discounts approved."

It's the same dance it always is. I agree to pay half, they write off the rest. Once, they tried to go after the patient's family for the rest, and I showed them quickly what a shrewd negotiator I am—that never happened again.

"Dinner time," I say to Remi, and I bring her back to the elevator and to the ground floor.

We sit next to each other in the cafeteria, dressed in our finest, as the hospital chef brings us our plates.

Marcel is a damn good cook. I should know because I hired him. When I saw what they were feeding the children here, I was disgusted. Children recovering from illness need proper nutrition, and Marcel knows his way around restrictive diets.

"You do this every Monday?" Remi asks.

"Yeah, it's been my tradition for about five years."

"This is amazing. I mean, I don't know how you do it."

"Well, being my own boss means I can make the time."

"No, I mean, it's heartbreaking."

"It's also miraculous, in ways. These children are so strong, stronger than I'll ever be. They've changed me. This is the least I can do in return."

Her hand covers mine, and the physical contact sending a jolt through my system. I want her, badly, but she's just so far beyond my reach, and just within grasp of Tom's.

We finish eating, my heart weighing heavy with each bite. I don't know how to undo the damage I've done, the stupid situation I've gotten myself into. I should tell her now that this can go no further, but I look at her, and I feel this indescribable joy I've never felt with anyone else before. I'm hopeless against her wiles.

"I don't know what I'm doing," she says, looking up at me with fear in her eyes.

"Well, you're eating. Asparagus and a rather delightful—"

"No, I mean, I don't know what to do next. What comes next. How to act."

"You know what? I'm kind of in the same boat."

She looks at me critically. "Are you? I mean, how is that possible?"

I ask her the million-dollar question, unable to hold off any longer. "What is it you want?"

She stares forward, mouth gaping, and finally says, "I don't know."

"Then I'll start," I say, clearing my throat. "Since the

moment you walked into the boardroom, I've wanted you —sexually. Then, there was this connection—it extended beyond lust. I've never met another woman like you, I mean, even the smart ones are so different. I sit here next to you and feel inadequate."

"Inadequate?" Remi says with a skewed brow.

"Is that so hard to believe?"

"Why would you feel inadequate?"

"Because everything about you is inspiring, you're smart, and you weren't born into this. You worked your ass off to get where you are and everything I have to offer you is fleeting. Nothing we have together can last. It can't even be a footnote in the fucking biography that will one day come out about my life."

She takes a deep breath, then exhales slowly. "Oh."

"And Tom, well, he is certainly in a position to offer you more."

We sit in silence as heavy as a shroud, both of us staring forward, not daring to look at one another. It's cruel. Remi is the only woman I have ever thought I could fall in love with, and she's sitting right next to me, yet she's so far away.

I turn to her and say, "Tom came into my office today. He told me he wants to take a relationship with you on books."

"What does that mean?" Remi asks.

"It means that your relationship will be reported to HR, and special care will be taken to ensure we always follow proper protocols and practices that will make sure everyone stays out of trouble. Trust me, with what you guys handle, it's necessary."

"So, he just decided that without me?"

I snicker. "I'm sure he was waiting for your next date to ask you. He just wanted to clear it with me first. Truthfully, he knows what he's doing is above board. I just think he wanted to rub it in my face."

"Why would he do that?"

I debate going into detail about how Tom has more control in the boardroom, easily getting a majority of the votes on his side, but I don't want to stress her out or taint her image of him.

"My life is just kind of complicated is all," I say and leave it at that.

"So, my choices are: enter a sexual relationship with your or a real relationship with Tom?"

"Well, when you put it like that, it makes the choice rather obvious."

"I choose you," she says.

I feel the color draining from my face.

Why would she ever choose me?

She turns to me, biting her lower lip. "I like the way you think. I like how you spend your Mondays. Tom is attractive, but he talks too much about himself. It's hard to stomach sitting through a whole meal with him. I'll find someone else eventually, to suit my long term needs, but for now, you'll do."

For now, I'll do.

"So...let me get this straight. You are completely okay with just fucking and friendship. No one knowing about us?"

"Yeah, I mean, one day I do want to start a family, but it doesn't have to be now."

Part of me is thrilled; another part is terrified. After all, Remi Stone is shaping up to be the girl of my dreams.

"Well, I guess we should go check out that new apartment of yours." I stand, offering my hand, which she takes. I notice hers is trembling. She's scared too, and that comes as a relief to me.

As we make our way up to the launchpad, I wonder just how the night is going to go.

Chapter Twenty-Two

Remi gets laid…

Gabriel hands me the keycard to my new apartment while we are in the elevator. It's metal, a chip inlaid with the information necessary to allow me access inside.

My phone has been buzzing all night with messages from Meghan wanting updates. I never knew how enjoyable girl talk was until she and Analise came into my life, and I find myself wanting more. I want the girl squad I never got to have during my formative years.

We exit the elevator and walk to my apartment. I'm

in shock when I first see it, a massive, archaic door in the middle of the hall.

"My grandfather Maxwell had a flare for the dramatic," Gabriel says.

"I'll say."

I swipe my card and enter a suite fit for magazines. White, plush couches are laid out in a vast living room. The back wall is a window looking out over the city.

"Holy Jesus," I say, knowing I look like a gawking idiot.

Gabriel takes a remote, pushes a button, and a fireplace roars to life.

I hear a familiar growl from across the room—Kibbles. She doesn't approach, though. It appears the week has traumatized her.

I see bookcases spanning from floor to ceiling, some of my books already in it mingling with others I've never seen before.

"If you need anything, all you need to do is ask."

"Well, I can tell you right now, I already have enough. This room is bigger than my whole apartment."

"Just wait until you see the rest."

The kitchen appliances are massive and more aligned for a family of eight than myself.

"This is all wasted on me," I insist.

"You say that, but if you ever get that family of yours, you'll be glad you have it."

I smile forlornly, knowing that the man I want to start my family with is right next to me, but he doesn't want a serious relationship. He made that very clear.

The second we entered the children's ward, my mind was made up. Tom may have treated me to a nice dinner and later a coffee, but the whole time he talked about himself. Tom is family connections and accomplishments that he's all too thrilled to share with anyone that will listen.

Gabriel, on the other hand, runs deep. He's kind, generous, and honest. He let me know upfront we could never be truly together. I'm fine with that. If I had the choice of picking anyone in the world to have my first time with, it would be with Gabriel—no regrets.

We enter the bedroom, and my breath catches in my throat. The furnishings are white and incredibly costly, but that's not what has me caught off guard.

The room is lit softly with beautifully scented candles, and it's covered in flower petals, from the floor to the bed. Purple, pink, cream-colored petals that must have cost a fortune.

"Is this how you decorate every new apartment?" I ask when my voice finally returns to me.

"Yeah, you should have seen the look on Jim's face when he finally made the board."

So, as if I needed any further indication, I guess I'm going to lose my virginity tonight. Here, in a bed of flowers, with a perfect 10.

"We're not done yet, follow me," Gabriel says, leading me to a door on the opposite side of the room.

We enter a cave, or rather my bathroom. It's cream-colored elegance, a lesson in decadence. There is a double sink with enough counter space for ten, a giant cove that leads to a walk-in shower, a door that leads to a commode, and a heart-shaped jacuzzi already filled with giant bubble.

"Wouldn't the water have cooled by now?" I ask.

"I have it programmed on a remote. I had it start filling when we finished dinner, and it keeps the temperature warm."

"Oh, well, I guess you are the head of a tech company."

He presents me with a monogrammed robe so soft it's like a cloud, there are matching slippers on top.

"Shall we?" he says with a sultry smirk.

I turn away, anxious. "I've never been naked with a man before."

A hand grips my shoulder. "If you'd like, I can leave, and you can have this all to yourself."

I place my hand over his. "No, I think I'm ready."

Gabriel goes to his knees, unzipping one of my ankle booties, and I slide my foot out. We repeat the process with my other foot, then I feel his hands on my thighs, slowly inching upward.

I get this crazy rush. My head is spinning.

Oh, my God! I'm about to climb in a tub with Gabriel Icor. I mean, I met him a week ago, and now, we're about to climb into a giant bathtub.

His hands continue to slide up my body, and now he's cupping my ass, kneading it with his large hands. He begins to slide my panties down my legs. I suddenly feel self-conscious. Meghan insisted I go bare for the occasion, and I must admit, the thought of it gave me a rush, but now I feel so much more naked.

I decide he's taking too long and grab the hem of my dress, bring it up over my head. He sits back on his heels and whistles his appreciation. It's silly, really it is. I mean, he's dated supermodels. Women six inches taller than myself with bodies designed to model underwear.

Why would he ever be interested in me?

But there he is, gazing at me like a hungry animal, and I'm all too eager to find out what happens next.

"Can we get in the water now?" I ask.

I'm anxious, and my hands begin to shake. I don't want him to realize how big a deal this is for me. I don't want to ruin the moment.

He rises, his hand moving to his collar to undo a button. "Of course."

I watch him undress with a fascination many would expect from a virgin, though maybe one far younger. At twenty-three, I should be well versed in the art of lovemaking—should be.

He makes his way down the column of buttons, pulling off his dress shirt. Then he takes off his undershirt, my eyes growing wide. It's as though he were sculpted in the likes of a Greek God: taut muscles, tawny complexion, sweet smile, dangerous eyes.

With his shirts now on the floor, he begins unbuttoning his pants, and for a moment, I almost shield my eyes. I don't know if I should stare brazenly or look away. What exactly are good manners when you're getting naked with somebody? From the limited number of pornos I've watched, I feel like I should go find a peephole to look through.

His pants are down around his ankles in a flash, his thumbs are hitched in the elastic of his boxer briefs.

"Are you sure?" he asks, head tilted to the side.

Am I sure? Should I really be doing this?

"Absolutely."

I try to don a grin to match my enthusiasm, but I'm positive I look goofy.

He's lowering his underwear now, and when I see his member, I can't help myself. I gasp, my hand flying to my mouth.

Is it supposed to be that big?

"I hope that was a good gasp," he says, feigning concern.

"It was the best kind of gasp I could possibly have."

We climb in the tub and lower ourselves into the bubbly water. He takes a bottle of champagne sitting in ice from the side of the tub and begins to pour two glasses.

"You know, I'm kind of a cheap date," I say. "It barely took me any alcohol to make that stupid video the other day."

"Then, I have this." He pulls out another bottle close by. It's Sprite.

I furrow my brows.

"I don't want to get you drunk, but I still want to celebrate. So, I'll give you half this, half that."

"Sounds good," I say, smiling.

He really has thought of everything.

I sit in one half of the heart, a curve, Gabriel sits in the other, between us is a small platform for drinks, but our legs are touching. I can easily turn a little and face him squarely, and if I wanted to cuddle, I could go over to his curve.

Gabriel takes a sip of champagne, and I take a sip of my drink as well, thankful there isn't much alcohol in it. I want to remember this night.

"So, how is this going to work out between us?" Gabriel has settled into his nook, getting right down to business.

"I was hoping you'd take the driver's seat on that."

"Well, we can do as little or as much as you'd like."

He's staring at me, and I'm thankful for the bubbles covering my breasts. It's not that I don't feel safe with him, I've just never been so utterly naked with a man before.

"What does company policy say?" I ask.

"Company policy says I shouldn't be doing this, but there's nothing they can do about it. I'm the CEO. If they try to go after you—well, let's just say they're not that stupid. Still, we'd keep it discreet."

"I can be discreet," I say.

"Analise will know, but no one else. Even casual friends outside of work shouldn't be let in on what happens between us behind closed doors."

It hurts that I have to keep this a secret from Meghan, but I completely understand. I work for him, and he probably wants to keep his options open and reputation intact. I can't blame him.

"I have access to your suite through a hidden passageway my grandfather built in that connects many of the apartments. Not even the Big 5 knows about that."

"So...how often?"

"Well, I guess we can figure that out as we go. If you're ever in the mood, send me a text telling me you disagree with a report."

"What if I really do disagree with a report?"

"Well, then whenever I receive your texts, it will be quite the guessing game. I'll show up here naked, you'll be scowling behind a computer."

I giggle, taking another sip of my drink. I have a million questions for him, but I don't want to ruin the mood.

Finally, I muster, "So, what is it you like when you're...um..." I cast my eyes downward, unable to finish the sentence.

"What do I like? Well, I can tell you right now the thing I'm most eager for is you. It's not any one thing I want to do in particular. It's just you that I want."

My heart feels damn close to melting in my chest, and it takes all of my willpower to remain on my side of the tub.

"Is there anything in particular that you like? Something you've wanted to try?" Gabriel asks. "Analise has told me you're...new to this sort of thing."

Of course, she did. But it's good that he knows. This isn't a bad thing.

I run through the various fantasies I've had over the years—so many fantasies. I don't want to seem boring and say nothing, but I've also never talked dirty before. Now, I wish my drink had just a tad bit more alcohol.

"You're going to think this is so stupid," I say. "That I've never done it before."

"Try me."

"Oral sex?"

His face lights up, and I feel instant relief. That must mean he doesn't think I'm stupid.

After a moment, he says, "Giving or receiving?"

"Receiving. But also giving. But very much receiving."

Gabriel moves our glasses to the opposite side of the tub.

"Well, take a seat, my lady." He gestures to the platform between the two heart halves.

Oh my God, is this really happening?

My heart is pounding in my chest, and blood rushes to my loins. I feel dizzy with want and burdened with fear.

Gabriel has a devilish look on his face, as though he were up to mischief. He pats the platform, and once again, I wish I had been given a stronger drink.

What if he doesn't like my body?

Gabriel is staring at me, eager look on his face.

There's no reason to think that. Stop being shy! Gabriel wants to please me. Just look at him. He's excited.

I sit on the platform, legs pressed tightly together, absolutely terrified.

The platform is perfectly comfortable, and I wonder if it was made for this reason. My back fits against it nicely. It's the perfect height.

Gabriel shifts his body and positions himself in front of me, hands on my knees, kissing my thighs. He wipes the suds from my breasts, cupping one in his hand.

My nipple grows tight under his fingers. With his other hand, he's now parting my legs. My body complies with his demands, far bolder than my brain.

"God, you're sexy," Gabriel says as he starts kissing up my body. My legs are trembling, and I pull them around his waist.

He takes a cup, rinsing my body of soap, and starts to kiss, lick, and suck my breasts. My loins begin to radiate heat, it's pleasant, but there's an edge to it—an urgency.

He finally makes it to my mouth, and as we begin to kiss. I feel his fully erect cock against my core. I consider bidding him to enter, eager to feel him breach me. But

I'm terrified.

Our tongues dance. His hands massage my sides. He pulls back a little, his blue eyes staring intensely into my brown.

"Are you ready?" he asks.

I unwrap my legs, spreading them as far apart as they will go. Then I close my eyes.

A moment later, I feel his stubble as he's kissing my inner thighs, a part of me no man has ever touched before. I don't know how it's possible, but every touch feels amplified. My legs begin to shake volatility, pushing him away, but Gabriel throws them over his shoulders roughly, scooting my butt closer to him.

Looking down, I see him, hungry—no, starving as he moves towards the junction between my thighs.

His first lick takes my breath away, a slight moan escaping my lips.

Oh my God! How does this feel so good?

My back arches. It's as if I've lost control of my body.

His tongue's now lavishing me with attention, moving in, out, and around the delicate folds of my sex.

I expected him to show some interest in pleasing me. I never expected him to do so with such enthusiasm. His face is now buried in my pussy, and I'm finding it harder and harder to maintain what little control I have over my body. His pace increases, and I find myself wanting—no needing release.

My hands are in his hair, pushing his head to me. My hips gyrate, and a pleasant warmth begins to radiate from my loins.

"Please…oh…God…Gabriel…just do it."

"Do what," he says between licks.

"M-m-make me come."

"Are you sure? I really like what I'm doing and want to stay down here a good while longer."

"Just fucking do it!"

"As you wish."

His tongue accelerates, and I feel my body begin to surge.

I'm dizzy. Desperate. So fucking hot, I think I might be going into heatstroke.

My hips jerk, and Gabriel has to bring his arms up over my legs to keep me from bucking him off.

Pleasure courses through my enter body, radiating from my core.

Holy fucking hell, how could it possibly feel this good?

His tongue doesn't relent, and as my body calms, he speeds up again.

I nearly scream, and I try to push him off, but he is firm in his position.

"It's too much…Oh, God…It's too much."

But Gabriel knows what he's doing, and it's as though he knows my own body better than I do.

A familiar rush threatens to release. I try to breathe, try to gain some semblance of control, but I fail utterly, and now I'm pressing his head against my core, begging for release again.

And it comes. Oh, God, does it come.

This time, I'm screaming, my thighs pressing against his stubbled cheek. Gabriel is mission-focused, keeping his tongue strokes steady and on course.

It's amazing, and I never want to go without it. I

swear, I could get addicted.

My body finally stops, and I realize I have no feeling in my extremities. It's as though my release used every last drop of blood in my body to fuel its fire.

Gabriel's rising now, moving in to kiss me, and tasting myself on his lips feels so erotic, so primal, that I can't help myself from returning his kiss with fervor. A deep need has manifested in my loins, and I feel an urgency unlike any I've felt before—the need for him deep inside me.

His cock presses against me, at the apogee of my thighs. My blood rushes with a want only he can satisfy.

"We can stop here," Gabriel says between kisses.

"No, I need you."

"What is it you need from me?"

"I need you inside of me."

He smirks like he knows what he's done to me.

"Let's move this party into the bedroom," he says.

"No!" I reach down, grabbing his member. It feels so big in my hand, so thick. I run the numbers through my analytical brain, and I realize—he is indeed massive.

Now, it's his turn to gasp as I slide my hand down his silky-smooth flesh, exploring the unknown territory.

"Take me," I beg. "Now!"

Gabriel obliges, cradling my head in his right hand, and my hips in his left.

"Thank you," he whispers. Then I feel sheer and blinding pain for but a moment as he penetrates me.

The pain is replaced by pleasure so intense it sends my whole body into spasms.

"Are you okay?" he pants.

"Yes," I rasp. "Please, more."

He begins to thrust, filling me entirely. He kisses me the whole time, his tongue darting in and out of my mouth.

It doesn't take him long, and in truth, I don't think I could have handled much more. As he nears completion, he brings a hand down to massage my clit, and I feel a now-familiar stir.

"Please, come with me," he says, and the words alone send me over the edge.

Chapter Twenty-Three

Gabriel...devoured...

Waking up, I look down at my heart's desire, disbelieving she's curled in my nook, sleeping contently.

Going into yesterday's dinner, I felt despair bordering on terror, thinking I would have to live my life watching the woman of my dreams enter into a relationship with my CFO while I endure my loveless marriage. It was crushing, but I was perfectly willing to accept my fate for the good of everyone.

And then something miraculous happened.

As it turns out, Remi chose me, even if she couldn't have me—and I did make that clear. I told her there would be no future for us, but that Tom would like to date her. Apparently, she's not as fond of Tom as most of his dates are, even though he brought her to the most elusive new restaurant in town and lavished her with an epic shit ton of flowers.

It's 5:30 am, and she's not due into her office until 8:30. There's plenty of time for me to ogle her while she sleeps.

Remi is the perfect mix of shy and desire. She knows what she wants, but she's a little intimidated by it—and I'm hooked.

Most of the women I've been with try to be ultra-sexy, dropping sexual innuendos in every sentence—practically deep throating bananas in my presence. Most men would revel in it. Heck, I did, for a time.

The truth is, though, it's all a lie. All they care about is the financial incentives, doing whatever they can to gain girlfriend status, or at least a credit card with their name on it with me footing the bill.

I'd take Remi over any one of them. Shy Remi that actually has sexual desires of her own. Who wants me to be the one to fulfill them. I was afraid of disappointing her, being unable to pleasure her, but that didn't turn out to be an issue at all. And now that I've had her, I'm not sure I can settle for anything less. Whatever this is, I know it's more than lust. Remi Stone has somehow found a way to imprint herself onto my heart.

I shift, letting her head slide to the pillow. She purrs, and I kiss her forehead and pull the blanket up over her.

Then, I get out of bed, throw on a robe I had put in the wardrobe for me, hoping for such an occasion as this, and go to work on breakfast.

I'm fully aware that I am not a master chef or culinary genius, but I can make my way around some breakfast potatoes, bacon, and eggs, and that's just what I do. I slave for my lady love for twenty minutes, finishing it off with a cup of fresh coffee.

When I walk back into the bedroom, tray in hand, I find her lying where I left her, eyes open.

I'm more than a little nervous. What if she regrets last night? What if she hurts? What if it wasn't as good for her as it seemed? But when she sits up in bed, blanket covering her body, beaming at me, I know I'm once again overthinking.

I set the tray down on the nightstand and sit on the edge of the bed.

I need to tell her about Sayo, but now's not the time. As soon as everything's settled, we'll have a long talk about my obligations and what we could possibly be. What I can offer her.

"Can we cuddle?" Remi asks.

"Of course, we can cuddle. You have an hour before you should start getting ready. If you want, I can give you a back rub."

"I want you to lay down."

I oblige, and once I'm lying flat, she lets the blanket fall, and I'm lost in the lush curves of her flesh.

I watch her breasts sway as she climbs into position atop my body. She's giddy, a mix of sexy and sweet that not many can pull off.

Once she's straddling me, she leans down, pressing

her lips to mind. I can feel her breasts fall against me, so soft, so fucking sexy.

I want her all to myself. The thought of her being with another man makes me sick. I push the image from my head, focusing on the goddess sitting atop my cock.

"Thank you, for last night," she says, her eyes avoiding mine. She's being shy again. I love it. It's so genuine.

"It's I who should be thanking you," I say, cupping her face in my hands, forcing her to look me in the eyes. "It was amazing. Every moment of it."

"I didn't want it to end," she says, and I believe her.

"I didn't want it to either."

"There are things left…that we didn't get to do."

I frown, sorry to have disappointed her. "Well, women are able to keep at it a lot longer than men. I'm sorry if we'll have to explore all your wants over time."

"I look forward to it." She lifts her bottom from my cock, and I immediately want to feel her against me again, pressing, rubbing. She's on all fours, scooting down, pulling at the knot on my robe.

"What are you doing, Remi?" I ask, my interest piqued.

She says nothing. She merely continues to pull at the knot, looking me in the eyes the entire time. It's intoxicating, watching her. Her sweet innocence being rebelled against by her lust.

The knot is soon undone, and my robe is open, my cock standing at attention. I smile, thinking that she's craving sex again and wants to try riding me, but instead, she brings her hand to its base, lowering her lips to my head.

"You don't have to do that," I say.

The truth is, as sexy as it may seem, I don't want to spoil her. And I certainly don't want her to feel like she owes me anything. She's the sexiest woman I've ever encountered, a goddess in her own right. She shouldn't have to do a damn thing.

She says nothing, letting her actions do the talking.

The heat from her mouth makes me shudder, and as her tongue circles the ridge of my head, I moan, a guttural sound I cannot stifle.

I can tell she's unsure, more than a little anxious, so I reach down and run my fingers through her hair.

"You're doing amazing," I say, and it's the God's honest truth. It feels pretty fucking amazing.

Her hand works its way up and down my shaft as she gets used to sucking the head. It's perfect. She's perfect. It's the kind of head you get when you're still a virgin, scared shitless, unsure of what to do but eager to try things.

I feel the familiar rush I get when I'm about to come, and I pull her head back a bit.

"I'm close. You better stop," I say.

She bats my hand away and precedes to devour me.

Holy fucking shit!

The gesture may have been small, but her take-charge attitude is all it takes to push me over the finish line. I explode, and she's so fucking hot as she's sucking and moaning, and practically begging me for more.

She swallows it all, and when she withdraws, she's smiling. Delighted in whatever the fuck it was we just did. I'd call it head, but it felt like so much more than a fucking blowjob.

"God, Remi, what a way to greet a man."

"It's the least I can do for the man that made me breakfast," she chirps as she grabs a slice of bacon.

I grab her arm, maybe too hard.

"Remi, I don't want you to ever feel like you owe me anything. Not for the job, for the apartment, for the exorbitant amount of money I'm going to spend on you, for the millions of orgasms I will bestow. Or for breakfast."

"Trust me," she gives me a wink, "I've been wanting to do that."

"Well, give me a moment to recover and game on."

"Sorry, can't. I want to head in early, check out the slides again, look at some of the other things on the drive."

"I've looked at the slides. They're great."

"Friday's a big day for me. I have to look over it a hundred more times."

"Remi, I have a business meeting tonight. Are you really going to make me wait?" I roll onto my side, tracing my fingers on her thigh. "What if I want you now? What if I crave your taste?"

"Wednesday?" she asks.

"I have a busy week. I don't think Wednesday will be good. And Thursday I have to do an interview with a magazine. There will be a photo shoot, and it will take way too long."

"You'll just have to wait until after the meeting then."

"You're cruel."

"I tell you what: if the meeting goes my way, you can have me all weekend."

"And if it doesn't?" I ask.

"Well, then you still have my panties."

Chapter Twenty-Four

Remi and Tom are just friends...

I'm giddy as I take a seat at my desk, replaying the events of last night in my head for the tenth time this morning.

Gabriel Icor, the 10, took my virginity last night, and it was AWESOME!

Before our coupling, I had been blissfully unaware such pleasure existed in this Earthly realm. Now I know how sex addicts are made.

I want to text Meghan, but Gabriel made it clear I

couldn't share any details with her, so I pull up my contact for Analise.

Remi: *Guess what!!!*

Analise: *What?*

Remi: *Come to my office!*

Analise: *Girl, some people aren't as ambitious as you. I'm still rolling out of bed.*

Remi: *It's nearly 9?*

Analise: *Yeah, and some of us grew up the privileged daughters of the Big 5. So what?*

I guess I'll just dive straight into work, then.

The data on my slides checks out every time I pull the numbers, and I start looking at another inefficiency. It's hard to believe that millions of dollars are mismanaged each year, but here I am, staring the evidence in the face. Icor Tech isn't the only company with issues, but one thing's for sure, it's not in a hurry to fix them.

My coffeemaker has been delivered, and of course, there are too many buttons. As I'm trying to figure them out, a knock sounds from my door.

"Come in," I yell.

Tom steps into my office, a smile on his face.

"Oh, hey," I say anxiously, a stab of guilt threatening to murder me.

Be cool. Act professional. He has plenty of options. It's not like he's going to care that much if you want to focus on work.

"Let me help you with that," he says.

He comes over, pushes a bunch of buttons, and before I know it, my magical morning elixir is being poured.

"Thank you."

"So, how was dinner?" he asks.

I swallow, trying to keep my breathing normal. "It was great."

"That's good to hear. I have to go out of town again, but I wanted to take one last look at your slides."

"Ummm...yeah, let me pull them up."

I pull up the slides for Friday's meeting, hoping Tom will respond well to them. Having him on my side will be a huge boon, seeing as how he's established with the company and has gained respect over his tenure. If he pushes the board and those who have a vote to pass my proposal, I can have a real effect on a billion-dollar company.

"Wow," he says, squinting at the screen. "You've really put a lot of time into calculations."

"Yeah, I've quadruple checked them. Actually, like ten times that."

"And you think you're prepared for Barry?"

"As prepared as I can be."

"You can't back down. You can't let him intimidate you. Go in there with these numbers, and don't let them make you second guess yourself."

"Do you think he's going to pose an issue?" I ask.

"Hell, yeah. This is family pride he has on the line here. Don't worry, though. I'll have your back. Lindel will too. She doesn't give two shits who she's pissing off when it comes to money."

"But he's Barry. One of the Big 5."

"Remi, to the rest of the world, they're the Big 5, to us, they're dated board members."

I smile weakly, unable to shake the terrible guilt I feel.

What if I made the wrong choice?

"Well, you're gonna knock it out of the park—and that's a fact," Tom says as he rises from the chair to leave.

"Thanks, Tom. It's good to know you're there for me."

He turns to leave, then slowly turns back around, a tight look on his face.

"Remi," he says.

"Yes."

"I'm sorry if I was pushing too hard to make something happen. I feel like an ass. We're going to be working together, so I think we better keep things strictly professional."

I smile, trying not to show my elation.

"Thanks, Tom. To tell you the truth, it's been weighing on me. I just don't want to make my work life awkward in that way."

"I'm glad we're on the same page," he says and leaves me to my slides.

I could not have planned this better myself.

Remi has girl talk...

Making my way through the USB is going to take me months, but I've already found the next item to sink my teeth into, and it has to deal with pricing.

One of the invoices I was reading led me down a path that not even Gabriel himself has walked before.

If we price our base product of enCor 30% cheaper, we can capture about 55% of the market based on current market trends. That would be an increase of 15%. The increase in the volume of sales quickly makes up for the discount, but we can also bump up the price of the add-ons 20% to show a positive cash flow.

I send a quick memo to Gabriel regarding my findings, even though I haven't completed all the research. If it's a path he's already tried to go down and couldn't make it work, I don't want to be redundant.

Damn it! it's already four o'clock. I've been so involved in my research, I've completely forgotten to eat lunch, and now it's almost time for dinner.

My phone vibrates, and I look down to see a text from Analise.

Analise: *I'll pop in soon.*

Butterflies explode in my stomach. I'm dying to tell someone about my night with Gabriel, and he made it clear, Analise is my only option. So I wait.

What if he's already talked to her about it? What if it was terrible for him?

I pull up the slides again, trying to pry my mind off my insecurities.

Analise walks in with two venti Starbucks in hand.

"So, what you're telling me is that you were not indeed sleeping. You were fucking the Starbucks barista," I say.

"Hush now," she says with a wink, setting a drink down for me. "You said you liked mocha caramel, right?"

"I live for mocha caramels, and I live for the details. Now tell me how are things with your coffee maker."

"Don't call him that. I don't want anyone to catch on to who he is. We can call him…Mr. Drip."

"Why do you want me to call him that?"

"Because he has so much precum."

A fountain of latte spews from my mouth and nose, Analise squeals a response, grabbing napkins to blot my desk.

"Okay, so now that we've ventured into TMI territory, do you care to guess what I did last night?"

"Well, I hate to go with the obvious, but my guess is Gabriel Icor."

"Ding, ding, ding, we have a winner."

"Is it everything you hoped it would be?"

"That and more. Oh my God—that and more."

She scrunches her nose in distaste. "I don't know if I wanna hear all this."

"Well, you're the only one Gabe will allow me to tell, so deal."

"Fine. Go ahead. Make me vomit."

"So, you've never been curious?"

"About Gabriel? No! But I've heard details from my friends."

"Oh..."

"Look, don't be upset. He's the heir to Icor Tech. There's been a revolving door of women since he was sixteen. If he's had all that and then he wants you—that's something special. You're special."

"I wish that were the case. However, he's made it clear it's an *'off the record'* kinda thing."

Analise looks down. I can tell she has something to say on the matter.

"You knew, didn't you?"

"Knew what?" she asks, a tight look on her face.

"That he wasn't looking for anything serious."

Analise exhales, then bring her feet up and sets them on my desk.

"Remi, whatever goes on between you and Gabriel, is between you two, and it will never make it past my lips. I promise not to betray your trust, not even to Gabe. I like you. Whatever you have to say, say it without fear, but just know, I extend the same courtesy to him."

"So you know things. Things he's not telling me."

"His life is complicated—and it's also unfair. I'm here to listen, but that's all I can do."

"I understand," I say, but I don't. There's something Gabriel hasn't told me. Something that has Analise tense.

"So, I know you want to tell me all the dirty details. Spill it. I'll bathe in acid afterward."

"Oh my God! I swear, I came so hard, it's like he launched me to another planet!"

Analise's face contorts in horror. "Holy fuck, maybe

not all that."

Analise is laughing. I'm laughing. This is girl talk.

"It started in my tub. It's heart-shaped. It also ended in the tub."

"I'm familiar with said tub."

"He had me sit on the little platform, between the two heart halves, and holy shit, what he did to me—"

"Does it involve his mouth traveling south of the border?"

I feel my cheeks redden, I want to scream out yes, but all at once, I feel shy. "It was amazing. Everything about him is amazing."

"And is it a one-time thing, or will it be ongoing?"

"With how he was talking, I think he wants it to be ongoing. He treated me so sweetly, like I was his girlfriend. I slept in his arms. He made me breakfast."

"That's good. No, that's great. Just…be careful. I don't want to see you hurt."

"Yeah, you're right."

"So, there's nothing with Tom?" she asks.

"Well, Gabe told me at the beginning of the evening that Tom was interested in dating me on the books. He wanted to go to HR with it."

Analise's brows rise in clear surprise.

"On the books?"

"Yeah, why?"

"That's just…unlike Tom. He's always been a bit of a player. He must really like you."

"Oh, well, he came in this morning, and I guess he rethought things. He doesn't want to mix work and personal life."

Probably because you refused to go to dinner with

him.

I immediately fill with regret.

What if I made the wrong decision? If Tom was a player, but he's settling down, maybe he would have changed. Not been so self-involved. What if I just ruined my chance with someone that I could be happy with, forever, and not just right now?

"Okay, enough of this chat, come look at this," I say.

I show Analise the slides, and she's impressed. When I show her my thoughts on lowering the price point of enCor, she says it's a bold move that none of the board will agree with because they're old and dumb, but give it a shot anyway.

She leaves, and overwhelming loneliness threatens to consume me.

I'm conflicted by my decision, but as soon as I look at my phone, all worry washes away. I'm in a good place.

> **Gabriel:** *I want you to know how amazing you are and how you make me feel. You're gorgeous, beautiful, and I'm completely unworthy of your charms. I can't wait to hold you again!*

I smile as I grab my things to go to my new apartment. Gabriel made sure my refrigerator was well stocked, and I'm glad I have no reason to leave the suite tonight. It will be just me and Kibbles.

Chapter Twenty-Five

Remi shows the numbers...

Why is this week going by so slow?

To put it simply, nothing has been going my way, and I'm about ready to say screw it all and beg for my job as a program manager back.

I know I'm being dramatic, but this week has been about people management, which I hate, and now I'm sitting in a meeting with a team that has absolutely no confidence in me. And it sucks!

My phone has been buzzing for ten minutes now, but

it's clear that the team assigned to me needs guidance on a few projects that have gone stale.

The lead, Ernest Feltmore, is at least two decades older than I am, and it's clear he doesn't like reporting to me. I imagine it must sting to see me as a director, a position he no doubt once dreamed that he would be in, but I make it clear, he'll either work with me or work for another company.

It takes about twenty minutes to set directives and drill in the importance of their timeline, then I send them on their way. Analise, who was asked by Gabriel to sit through the meeting, says farewell, and I'm left to my own work.

Tomorrow is Friday, the day of my big meeting, where two things are going to happen.

The first is that I'm going to give another presentation. This one is regarding the shipping route. The second is that the switch to Expressions is being put up to a vote.

This is terrifying. Voting is not taken lightly, and it's not done often. Not only are we voting on my proposal tomorrow, but Gabriel wants to set up another vote scheduled two weeks from now for the port shift.

In other words, in a very little amount of time, I'm having an enormous impact.

The door opens, and Gabriel pops his head in.

I swear, I cease functioning when I see him. The last time we were together was Tuesday morning, or as my biography will read, the day I gave my first blowjob. It was such an intense experience, so primal. I never understood why any woman would ever want to do such a thing, but I've found myself thinking about it several times since.

Craving him.

Some acts are meant to be savored.

"You busy?" he asks.

Oh, God, how is he so hot?

"Yes, I'm always busy."

He comes in, closing the door behind him.

Oh, God! I cannot be trusted alone with this man.

"I'll have to work around you working."

"Work around me working?"

He comes around to my side of the desk, repositioning my chair to face him and goes to his knees.

"What are you—"

There's a devilish look in his eyes. He's licking his lips and waggling his eyebrows.

His hands are traveling up my skirt, along my thighs, and I suddenly realize why he came here.

"It's the workday!" I gasp.

"All work and little play makes Remi a—"

"Seriously, though! We can't do this!"

He withdraws his hands from my skirt, a frown on his face.

"But I want to taste you," he says with such longing I find my resolve weakening.

"I thought you had that interview?"

"They're lucky to get an interview. I am running late so I can see you."

I glance at the door.

"It's locked. I pressed the button when I closed it."

"Are you sure?"

"I own the company—the building even. I'm sure."

I part my legs slightly, inviting him to explore.

"We'll call this a working lunch. You'll work, I'll lunch. There's an email sent to the directors, one that you need to respond to. You must send the reply before I am through."

"What?"

But he says nothing more. Instead, he positions himself under my desk, pulls down my pantyhose and panties, and brings my chair towards him. I feel his hand slide into place, then he scoots me closer. When his tongue connects with my core, I melt.

Holy fucking shit—it feels so good!

"You have roughly fifteen minutes to reply," he says.

I pull up my email, trying to stifle my moans. Below my waist, Gabriel is licking, stroking, and sucking me into a frenzy. I don't know how I'm ever going to get this email done.

"Is it up?" he asks.

"Y-y-yes," I stammer.

"Read it out loud."

Fuck me!

"F-f-for the a-a-attention of t-the—"

"That's fine, carry on."

His tongue is on my inner thighs, my labia, the bundle of nerves that he uses to send me into bliss. It's everywhere, all at once, and through it all, I have a mission to complete.

He wants numbers from the last two quarters. All I have to do is pull up the slides from the quarterly meetings and report the numbers for the teams that have been assigned to me.

I hit reply all, as required, but I don't get much further.

His tongue is a tornado, and I can't last much longer. My leg is shaking. I feel lightheaded. I'm close.

Then—his tongue withdraws.

"How are you doing?" he asks.

"Please-don't-stop!" I scream as my body threatened to recede back into work mode.

I feel a long lick, then another.

"You have a job to do, Remi."

He gives me another slow lick.

"You like this?" he asks.

"Faster."

"Then I better hear you typing."

I pull up the slides I need to enter the numbers. He's licking faster now, rewarding me for complying.

I type my opening, having to correct it half a dozen times before getting it right.

Meanwhile, Gabriel is moaning while he licks, and rubbing his stubble on my inner thighs in such a sexy way, it's setting my body up for one hell of an explosion. This man will ruin me.

"You almost done?" he asks.

Oh, God! How does he expect me to concentrate?

"Yes!" I blurt out, worried he'll stop.

"Good."

He focuses his attention now, licking me so fast I can barely get the numbers typed as my fingers tremble.

It takes just a minute longer to get the data input, then I hit send, sit back in my chair, and allow Gabriel to release me from my torment.

He rewards me, and soon I'm shaking violently, screaming out in pleasure. He's pressing his arm across my abdomen, trying to lessen the bucking of my hips.

When I come, I see a thousand stars, all of them pulsing with lust, singing the name Gabriel.

He's scoots my chair back and gazes up at me, his mouth moist and grinning.

Fuck me! It doesn't get much better than this.

Chapter Twenty-Six

Cregor hates board meetings...

Gods, if I have to suffer through many more insufferable meetings run by people who just want to hear themselves talk, I'm going to just up and retire. Gabe would like that, I imagine. Analise would be rather pleased as well.

I cast Lindel a stoic look. A look she knows too well. We've seen the highs and lows of Icor Tech. We know how to weather a storm.

Insufferable Tom is seated, glowering. It's not like

him to don a dour face.

Jim takes a seat, followed by Essie. The board is now present, except for Gabriel—which surprises no one.

One minute to go now, and Remi is making her way into the room, walking with entirely too much confidence.

Her name has been on everyone's lips for all the wrong reasons. First, there were her bold assumptions during the so-called 'Innovation Meeting.' Then, there was her sudden promotion that caused all kinds of chaos. People mad they've worked well and faithfully for the Icor's for decades without such a promotion. And finally —the release of that YouTube video.

So erratic, it's hard to tell whether or not it was planned, though why anyone would want a video of them dancing around a cat tower in that god-awful frock is beyond me. Analise insisted it was just her having a fun night with a girlfriend, that the upload was done by the friend unintentionally, and when it took off, they just decided to go with it. To that, I responded: to what end?

It's a rather poor representation of the whole of Icor Tech, if you ask me. Analise says it will appeal to a younger crowd, and we'll get an influx of resumes from young professionals that think Icor will be fun to work at, but do we want to look like a 'fun place to work?' That all sounds rather dangerous. We'd never get anything done.

Remi takes a seat, and I can't help but notice Tom casting her an icy gaze.

I approve.

The meeting begins, and we cover a few issues that had been previously tabled. Gabriel is nowhere in sight, which is no surprise. He'll come in at the last minute to cast his vote, telling us he's already reviewed the slides.

Remi is due to present in the second half of the meeting, and although I'm sure what she's presenting is rubbish, I am interested in what she has to say.

Barry breaks to go to the bathroom, no doubt his IBS has been acting up again.

I turn to Lindel, who is checking her phone. "Can you believe it, Lindel? That we're forced to sit through so many damn meetings?"

"Well, it's how we get shit done," she says, not bothering to look up at me.

"You can't mean that," I say.

"Creg, how do you think we got Icor Tech up off the ground? We sat in a room, much smaller than this, with folding chairs, around a table that needed a brick to hold it level, and we talked and brainstormed. This is no different."

"But it is! Back then we had six minds working together, all of us—"

"Underqualified. Underpaid. Scraping to get by. Yeah, we did that, but climbing our way to the top is very different from staying up there. If we aren't careful, this will all go away just as quickly as it came. Scratch that, it took decades to get up here, and it can take a matter of days to send us crashing."

"This Remi woman—"

"Deserves to be heard," she snaps at me. "Did you have a chance to look at her slides from last week?"

"No, why would I?"

"Because it's part of your job. We are set to vote on that this evening. Get with it, Cregor."

"There's no way—"

"I sure do hope you are voting to pass it."

"Voting to pass it—"

"Yeah, Remi hit that shit home. I didn't even realize until I looked late yesterday afternoon, at the behest of Analise. We might as well just be burning our money."

I straighten up in my chair, one part insulted, another part confused.

"This Remi girl may not be who you like to see in our boardroom, heck at one time I wasn't either, but she knows her shit. And so help me, if we go under and it's because of your refusal to bend even the slightest and admit when someone you deem inferior has a good idea—Analise will never forgive you."

If anyone else had said what Lindel just said, Barry included, I would be seeing them out of the boardroom and demanding a formal apology. The last thing I need is for Analise to have another piece of ammo in her arsenal against me.

It's time for the meeting to resume, and I force myself to look at Remi as she makes her way to the front of the room, smile on her face.

Well, I might as well listen to what the mouse has to say. After all, if Lindel is willing to hear her out, I suppose I should as well.

The door opens, and Gabriel sneaks in. Taking his seat without a word.

"Good morning, everyone, I'm pleased to stand here before you today presenting some research I've been looking at over the last couple weeks. It's regarding shipments and ports, and our practices regarding importing into other countries."

"We're excited to hear what you have to say, Remi," Tom says, staring at Gabriel rather oddly.

There's an edge to his voice. It certainly wasn't there when the mouse presented previously. There was a rumor that he was seeing Ms. Stone, and a parade of flowers entering her office all but confirmed it. But this edge, well, that's new.

Remi brings up a visual of our shipping routes, and we go through our current practices. She is very knowledgeable, answering questions from both Jim and Essie. She brings up the costs and how much we're spending along with turnaround times. Nothing too surprising, until she goes into her *'Bold Efficiency Plan.'*

Or at least that's what Gabriel calls it. After last week's meeting, Gabriel announced she would be looking at our processes and focusing on updating outdated systems. It's not something we've approached with vigor in quite some time, because a simple change in one system can affect so much. One mistake, and you're burning money.

"Now, I'd like you to look at what we could accomplish by changing our current route into Asia," Remi says as we stare at the figures on the screen.

I exhale, waiting for the next slide, and when it comes up, even I am taken aback.

"By simply using Port 5486 instead of 2987, we can cut a day from our travels and save roughly 20%. Furthermore…"

Remi keeps talking, but her voice is now a murmur as all I can see are the numbers before me. How could we be wasting so much money from shipping alone?

When Remi is done, everyone looks to each other,

talking in hushed murmurs.

Lindel is looking to me, grimly, and I don't know what to say.

Barry begins to speak. "I have a cousin at Port 2987—" he begins, but Remi cuts him off.

"Mr. Casteel," she addresses Barry, "I'm aware that your cousin manages at Port 2987, but I'm sure you can agree that our losing three-million from utilizing that port alone is a justified reason for the switch."

It's not many that would dare to interrupt one of the Big 5, or rather now the Remaining 3. We are all but revered around Icor Tech, and for good reason.

Barry is white-faced, his eyes lit with anger. He's clearly unsure of what to say.

A small smirk plays on Lindel's lips. She's enjoying this. She likes Remi.

Barry's stammering, about to speak, but then a bold clap sounds at the head of the room, coming from Tom.

What has me on edge is the thunderous applause sounds more menacing than congratulatory. I should be happy—thrilled the upstart mouse will be put in her place.

But I'm not.

"Bravo, Remi. Good work. I can see you've done your homework."

"Why, thank you, Tom," she says uneasily.

"Oh, don't thank me yet. I've done my homework as well."

All eyes are on Tom now, and I feel a sinking sensation in my gut.

"It appears that the port you want to use, Port 5486, is controlled by people associated with Gabriel Icor's future father-in-law."

Gabriel's head jerks up, a look of surprise on his face.

Remi's brows draws inward as she glances at Gabriel.

Why is he saying this? Very few are supposed to know about Gabriel's upcoming nuptials. I don't even think Tom is supposed to know at this point. The directors sure don't.

"So you can shame Barry all you want, but don't act like there isn't a similar political agenda in the works."

Remi looks confused, her hand clutching her chest. "I...I—"

Gabriel rises, his jaw shifting, but Tom cuts him off.

"Furthermore, Port 5486 brings us further away from our eventual destination by taking us inland. We would have to account for land travel, which can be just as tedious and even more costly than shipping by sea."

People are looking between Tom and Remi, talking amongst themselves. When Remi fails to respond, the whispers grow to murmurs, and soon it's hard to even hear myself think.

Tom turns to Remi. "I think we can all agree that the nature of your relationship with Mr. Icor has hampered your judgment, or at the very least, your research skills."

"Tom," Gabriel cuts in, "we need to take this into my office—now!"

"Why, Gabe? You don't want people finding out you're diddling a director? Feeding her ideas? Does the rest of the board know she'll do everything you ask of her."

"No!" Remi blurts out, eyes wide with fear. "That's not it at all. Just look at the numbers. Everything is accounted for."

"Ladies and Gentlemen, I think we've heard enough. Along with tabling this proposal, I think we should call off today's vote and see beyond the information presented on these slides, thrown together by a woman lovesick under the influence of a megalomaniac."

Gabriel is seething, glaring at Tom, but it's of little use. Tom has the room's attention. Their trust.

Remi is standing by the podium, openly sobbing. Tom stands opposite her, a look of hard hatred in his eyes, and I immediately realize this whole debacle isn't about shipping routes.

Lindel is standing now. "This meeting is adjourned. Voting is postponed. Tom, I expect to see you in my office, stat. Remi, I will be meeting with you—"

"No," Remi says, walking to the door. "I'm done here."

Remi exits the room in a fit of tears, Tom smiling, reveling in his win.

Gabriel seats himself again, burying his head in his hands.

I realize now the balance Tom had been to Gabriel was never out of necessity. It was because Tom was never a friend of Icor Tech.

He's most certainly an enemy.

Chapter Twenty-Seven

Gabriel phones a friend...

I spend the afternoon with my phone off, computer shut down. No one knows where I am or how to reach me. I should be trying to undo the clusterfuck from this morning's meeting, but instead, I'm drinking scotch and trying to figure out how the fuck Tom Wellington knows I'm getting married. How the fuck he knows what ports my future father-in-law is associated with. And how the fuck he knows I'm fucking Remi Stone. Or was fucking Remi Stone. Chances are, I won't be seeing her again.

Remi left straight after she exited the meeting, not even stopping at her office. She's probably back at her vacant apartment by now, which will have no furniture.

It makes me sick knowing that I caused her any strife, and I'm fully planning on making it up to her. I'll issue out a huge severance, and now that everyone knows I was screwing her, HR can't really say no. Unless they want Icor Tech to get sued. I can also put in a good word for her with several other companies. She can have her pick. This doesn't have to be a low-point in her career.

I know I should be thinking about the future of my company—but I'm not.

All I can think about is Remi. Two weeks ago, she stumbled into my heart, causing chaos only she could create. Now, I've lost her. She's humiliated, and it's all my fault. I can't say I blame her for walking out. The CFO of Icor Tech practically interrogated her in front of the board, accusing her of fucking the CEO, which she did, and then accused her of making decisions based on politics, which she wasn't.

I wanted desperately to come to her aid, but I knew how that would look. I knew it would only fan the flames.

She's probably furious I never told her about my engagement to Sayo. But—I couldn't. Details are being hammered out, and all parties involved are practicing discretion. Only a handful of people at Icor Tech knew about the upcoming union. Tom was not one of them.

I think about the way Remi felt in my arms, her soft skin, her warm affections. I had toyed with the idea of giving this all up, running away, and being with only her, but that would be selfish.

Thousands of people would lose their jobs. My happiness is nothing compared to the meals my company puts on the tables of its employees.

Why didn't Tom come to me? Why did he pull this shit at a board meeting? He wants to shame me—to shame Remi. He's never cared this much about a girl before. Somehow he found out about us. Somehow, he knows about Sayo. But how?

I turn on my phone and dial a number I very rarely contact. The phone picks up on the third ring.

Sayo: *Hello, Gabriel.*

Gabriel: *Hey.*

Sayo: *I heard what happened at your morning meeting.*

Gabriel: *Holy shit, is it on the news or something?*

Sayo: *No, but we have ears over there.*

So, Sayo's family knows what goes on in my meetings, great.

Sayo: *Do you like her?*

Gabriel: *Pardon.*

Sayo: *This Remi girl. I'm looking at her*

picture now. Certainly not who I would have chosen.

I laugh, remembering once again that Sayo is a lesbian in addition to my fiancé, and she's looking at a picture of my lover.

Gabriel: *She's wonderful, but I'm not going to discuss her.*

Sayo: *That's fair.*

Gabriel: *I can't figure out for the life of me what the fuck happened.*

Sayo: *Would you like me to tell you?*

Gabriel: *So, you know?*

Sayo: *You haven't been present enough at your board meetings. You've mismanaged.*

Gabriel: *Wow, well, good thing I have you to tell me what I'm doing wrong.*

Sayo: *Well, just think, soon I'll have a place on your board, and you won't have to worry so much.*

Her words catch me off guard, and for a moment, I

wonder if I heard her right, so I clarify.

> **Gabriel:** *Excuse me? A place on my board?*
>
> **Sayo:** *Yes, the original three you have left are aging, and the rules state two of the same blood cannot be on the board serving, but we are not of the same blood. Who better to appoint than me? Cregor is the oldest and most likely to retire soon. When he does, I will take his place. It says in your bylaws that when any of the original five leaves, you can pick their replacement. You have three picks left.*
>
> **Gabriel:** *His daughter Ana will be taking his place.*
>
> **Sayo:** *We'll see.*

In that moment, I'm so angry I'm scared of what I might say next. I take deep breaths, reminding myself of just who I am talking to. It takes me a full minute before I can talk again.

> **Gabriel:** *Well, Sayo, I have to go, but I look forward to seeing you.*

I disconnect before she has a chance to reply, not wanting to cause the first fight in our relationship.

First, Tom blindsides me during a board meeting, and now Sayo's gunning for a place on the board. None of this makes any sense.

I see a message from Analise, and I open it.

Analise: *You okay?*

I'm not okay. I am in no way okay. I'm angry, hurt, depressed, and now I've inadvertently created a shit storm that I'm going to have to deal with over the next several weeks. Nothing is okay.

There's no use replying to Ana. I'm sure she has already heard all the details, and there's nothing she can say to make it better.

I turn on my system, not looking forward to the barrage of emails I will have to suffer. I've been putting them off all day, but it's evening now, and they aren't just going to disappear.

A message with an attachment catches my attention. The sender's handle reads: *A Concerned Board Member*

I open the message, scanning the attached documents.

Suddenly, the events at the board meeting make total sense.

Holy fucking shit!

Chapter Twenty-Eight

*Meghan doesn't let **Remi** stay down...*

"I'm so sorry this happened to you," Meghan says, arms wrapped around my shaking body.

"I just can't believe he did this to me. He seemed so genuine. Everything about him was perfect. He volunteers at a fucking children's hospitals and pays their medical bills. And what he did to me—oh my God." I erupt into another bout of uncontrollable sobs.

I've been like this for two days, shaking, crying, a complete and utter mess. I don't know how Meghan tolerates me, but she's somehow become my rock.

"Maybe he wasn't really that great in bed after all. I mean, it's not like you have much to compare him to."

"I was fucking numb, Meghan. Fucking numb. It was damn good."

"Okay, okay."

"I didn't care if he just wanted to be a bachelor, but to have a fiancé? What a fucking scum bag."

"I know. I hate him for you."

"And to have me of all people present a plan that will give his father-in-law business? I mean, that's tacky, right? Tell me it's tacky."

"Super fucking tacky. The tackiest."

"How stupid am I to think a fucking hot, sexy, smart, billionaire would ever really want me? I was manipulated the whole time. So he could get a fucking shipping route for his father-in-law. He fucked me for a shipping route!"

Meghan smooths my hair from my face and plants a kiss on my forehead.

"Remi, he may be a scumbag, but he also may have really liked you. He knew what you were going to present, and he knew you'd do it without sex. He wanted you, if at least for that."

"And then there's Tom. I feel bad. So fucking bad. Tom wanted to take me out. He wanted to fucking date me. And look at what happened."

Meghan pulls away, eyeing me critically. "I wouldn't feel so badly for Tom. I mean, look at how he went about things."

"He took me out to the hottest new restaurant. Bought me a ton of flowers. Gave me a gift card. Asked his fucking boss if he could date me."

"And yet you say he never mentioned his criticisms when viewing your presentation."

"Just little things, nothing major. It's weird. And, something doesn't make sense."

"What?"

"What really has me angry is that I couldn't even properly respond to his criticism. Some of the plans, like for the pop-up shops, aren't released yet. They're 'need to know.' I built my argument around other aspects of the plan, but he tore them apart."

"And he knew about the pop-up shops?" Meghan asked.

"Yeah."

"And you absolutely couldn't brief them in the meeting?"

"I couldn't. If it had been just board members, then maybe. The directors can be opportunists. They will often go from company to company, trying to elevate their position. They could use information like that to get a foot in the door somewhere else. Or even just sell the information to the highest bidder. If the locations for all the pop-up shops get bought up, they could charge Icor Tech twice the price."

"So, he took advantage of your discretion. What criticism did he mention?"

"He mentioned a conflict of interest with Dingle."

"Dingle?"

"Yeah, Dingle Barry. One of the Big 5 that can't let go. He encouraged me to present boldly, essentially shutting Dingle down."

"So he created a wedge between you and Dingle, then went on an affront against you, knowing you were making enemies with the Big 5."

"Oh…"

"Something more is going on here. You're just too involved to see it clearly."

"What do you mean?"

"Let's start from the beginning: The first meeting you presented two weeks ago, you went into some fancy meeting, gave a presentation, shook a few souls, and got a promotion. He's nice to you and invites you to dinner, which you go to."

"Yes."

"You go to get coffee. He decides on his own he wants to take a relationship with you to HR."

"Yes."

"At some point before the second meeting, he sees your plans and says they're fine. Warns you about Dingle."

"Actually, he saw them twice, but yeah."

"Exactly, he had two opportunities to point out the flaw, and instead, he encouraged you to present. This isn't a heartbroken, lovesick guy—he's a conniving manipulator."

"You think?"

"God, you are the stupidest smart person I know. You're just too close to see it. Another thing you fail to see, he's not out for you, he's out for Gabriel."

My brows scrunches in confusion.

"Based on what you're saying, these are things that Gabriel has been trying to approach for some time, with little luck."

"Yeah, he's given up on even presenting his findings because he knows they will get vetoed. Which is why

Gabriel asked me to present them as my own findings."

"So, being the CFO, Tom should know more than anyone about the financial state of Icor Tech, and he's smacking down a plan he knows will lead to saving a shit ton of money. He knows about those whatever they are shops that are going to solve the issue, an important detail you weren't allowed to brief, and he exploited it."

"I guess."

"He also exploited Gabriel's engagement—weaponizing it against him."

"Stop!" I gasp, bile filling my throat.

Meghan exhales. "Too soon? I get it."

It will always be too soon.

Meghan gets up and disappears into the bathroom, coming out again with containers full of makeup.

"What are you doing?" I ask.

"First, we are going to make you look cute. Then, we're making plans for a video."

"A video? Oh, hell—"

"Yes. Hell, yes. Trust me."

"I can't!"

"You can. You're going to be looking for a new job, and we have over two million views on the last video we did together. I owe you big! My audience is dying to see you in real life. This one won't be like the last. We are going to have you looking professional. We will talk about what it's like being a woman in business. We will casually allude that you will be looking for employment soon, while not making you look thirsty."

"Why would we do that?"

"Because I can guarantee you, you're going to get offers."

"Based on a fucking video?"

"Based on the fact that you were promoted to a director position at Icor Tech at the age of twenty-three, and you decided to leave the position to explore your options. We'll put some spin on it."

As stupid as it sounds, it might not be a bad idea. In a single video, I could reach thousands of potential employers, and it may balance the video of me in the muumuu galavanting around a cat tower.

This may be my best shot at finding a new job.

Chapter Twenty-Nine

Cregor gets his groove back...

After Barry enters my office, I bid him to close the door and take a seat.

A familiar rush courses through my veins, one I haven't felt in decades. The Big 5 are back together again, or rather, the Remaining 3.

It's Sunday, but I've been working all weekend trying to make sense of things—trying to figure out how Friday's meeting could have gone so wrong.

"Barry, Lindel, I've gathered you here for an urgent

matter I'd like to discuss."

Lindel is already seated. Barry is navigating the chair I have out for him.

"What happened at that meeting—is reprehensible!"

Lindel glowers, as though I'm wasting her time. "Creg, she's already quit. She's gone. She left right after the meeting and won't be back. You should be happy."

"I'm not talking about the little upstart mouse. I'm talking about Tom Wellington and Gabriel Icor himself."

There it is. I said it. The elephant in the room. I know what Tom did isn't lost on the other Remaining 3, but for some reason, it's something hard to address. To even put into words. Probably because we bought into it for so long.

Gabriel Icor, however, well, I'm sure we all expected that.

"Ever since Tom was named CFO by Gabriel's dolt of a father, he's held an enormous amount of sway at Icor Tech. Maybe too much." I look at the two of them, hoping they see the very obvious writing on the wall.

"Are you saying you liked Remi's proposal?" Lindel said, a look of surprise on her face.

"It wasn't bad," Barry cut in. "I saw where the numbers made sense. I was even going to tell her as much, that is until she popped off about my cousin. It was like—"

"She was prepared for it. It's obvious Gabriel coached her into saying that. After all, Gabriel had been feeding her ideas," I say with distaste.

"Actually, it wasn't Gabriel," Lindel snaps.

Barry and I look at her, confused.

"I talked with Analise yesterday. I found out that even

though Gabriel gave Remi some information, her initial presentation was all her own. And Gabe never told her about Barry's cousin."

Barry's chubby fingers fidget on his lap. I've had to deal with his fidgeting fingers for upward forty years now, and I'm quite tired of it.

Finally, he says, "So who told Remi about my cousin?"

"We don't have concrete confirmation, but the only person that makes sense is Tom, who Analise said viewed it ahead of time."

So I'm right. Tom is not to be trusted. He never was.

Lindel clears her throat, and I can tell she's angry.

"We brought this on ourselves. Gabriel worked his ass off when his father died, trying to undo all the damn bullshit his flashy-ass father left him, and we never gave him a chance. It was never enough for us. We took everything out on him and disallowed him from getting anything done."

Barry and I stare at Lindel, knowing what we're in for. Lindel is not shy, and she knows when to make her points—perhaps this one should have been made years ago, though.

"So, don't you go bringing up Gabriel this or Gabriel that. If we go under, there's no one to point the finger at but ourselves."

"We've weathered the storm now for—"

Lindel cuts me off. "Oh, Cregor, shut your mouth. Look what happened to companies like Compaq and Blockbuster. Did they 'weather the storm?' If we don't adapt, we will eventually go under. It's only a matter of time."

"So, you suppose we should let Gabriel go all willy nilly and make whatever changes he wants?" I say.

"Did I say that? No, I did not. What I'm saying is we should allow him to present his ideas without our negative comments. The Big 5 still hold a lot of weight in that boardroom, and every time you make a snide remark, Cregor, he loses ground."

Damn, she's right.

I have been an obstacle to Gabriel for quite some time, but I always reasoned it to be for the good of the company. After hearing Lindel talk, though, I'm not so sure.

"Well, now what?" Barry asks.

"We see if we can undo the damage," Lindel replies. "I'm not a numbers woman. I've always figured that to be the CFO's job, but I've been talking with Analise a lot lately, and she's confirmed some suspicions of mine. To say it plainly, we are running this company ass-backwards into the ground, and it's gonna catch up with us real soon. We are in for a world of hurt if we don't change our ways."

We look at each other, solemn, ashamed. Each of us has played a role in the shenanigans, no one more than myself.

"So, what do you suppose we do?" I ask. "To undo whatever damage we've caused."

Lindel looks satisfied that she has our agreement.

"First, we need to figure out what Tom's end game is. Analise knows what went on inside that meeting, and she clued me into something. Tom failed to mention the pop-up shops on Friday, even though he damn well knew about them. It would have solved that little inland travel problem, making it more viable. This means he wanted a good idea to fail."

"So, one of the main flaws in her plan wasn't a flaw at all?" Barry says, a critical look on his face.

"Not at all, and Remi couldn't speak to it because the deals still going through."

"I knew something wasn't right!" I say, scratching my chin.

"That's not all, and this has to stay here. It appears there was a little love triangle going on between Gabriel, Tom, and Remi. Now, I'm only telling you this to show you just how manipulative Tom is being."

"We knew about Tom because of the flower shenanigans," I say, "but this speaks to Gabriel's and Remi's character."

"Look, I puzzled this out with Analise, and let me tell you, it all happened rather unexpectedly. We know Tom's seen with a revolving door of women, but Gabriel has been wholly focused on the company for the last four years."

"And he's about to be married," Barry interjects. "Making his role worse."

"Yeah, but he's marrying to save the company. I didn't really know why until Ana clued me in. It's Gabriel's safety net if he can't turn us around. Work out a deal, a possible merger. Save the company—save jobs. The woman he's engaged to is a damn lesbian for crying out loud!"

My eyes grow wide. *A lesbian?*

"Very few knew of the engagement. The Remaining 3 were told, but we keep our traps shut. Apparently, Tom was left in the dark. Somehow, he found out, and he released the information at just the right time to have the greatest negative impact. We all saw what we thought was a shady business practice, but it was just Gabriel doing whatever he could to save our damn jobs. And, from what Ana says, it just about broke Remi's heart."

"I don't understand what Tom's motive is," Barry says. "He's just over 30 and the CFO of Icor Tech. Why bite the hand that feeds you?"

Lindel sighs, relinquishing her control of the conversation, and we sit there in silence, mulling over our mistakes.

I had not expected Lindel to hijack my meeting, but the woman's done good work, and as our meeting draws to a close, I realize I have to do something I've been avoiding for a long time now.

I have to meet with my daughter, Ana, and find out what's really going on.

Chapter Thirty

Remi gets a severance...

"So, I see you graduated from Cornell at age nineteen. That's quite an accomplishment," Meghan says.

We are seated on her white, leather couch, putting together a women's empowerment video.

I smile for the camera, my hands fidgeting on my thighs. "Yeah, it's definitely not what I would recommend for many, but it was the right path for me."

"And from there you went on to get your Masters?"

"Yes. I could have received it in half the time if they had just let me take more classes."

"What was it like when you started your first job at Icor Tech?"

"It was amazing. I interned with them before I graduated and then went on to become the youngest person to hold a program manager position with them at twenty-three."

"But that's not all. You went on to become a director too."

"That's right. Gabriel Icor himself offered me a director position."

We talk for thirty minutes about women in the workplace, the push for S.T.E.M., and even dating. Finally, the interview needs to close.

"With such an amazing position held at such a young age, why are you out looking for a job now?"

"You know, Meghan, I just hadn't realized what I was missing out on. Working for Icor Tech had been a dream of mine, but it's all I know. I don't feel like I can properly assume a director position without gaining more industry experience."

Meghan casts me a secret wink, and I know I'm killing it.

Meghan gives her closing remarks, shuts off the cameras, and I slouch back on the couch.

"Would you be offended if I just lay pantless?" I say, unbuttoning my top button.

"You do you," Meghan says as she puts the ring lights back against the wall.

Leaving Icor so quickly after receiving my promotion is a detriment to my career. It reeks of scandal. When

Meghan suggested we get ahead of the gossip, I was initially fearful, but after thinking on it, it's the only way to spin the situation to my advantage.

Yes, I was a complete idiot for getting involved with Gabriel Icor, but it did not affect how I did my job. I deserve to land on my feet, and with this interview, it will give the appearance that I'm not hiding anything.

I've been sleeping on Meghan's couch for a week now, helping her with a few projects and creating databases and spreadsheets to help her run things more efficiently.

Unfortunately, I had already surrendered my key to Mr. Sokolov, so I'm technically homeless. With any luck, though, I'll be gainfully employed soon.

"It's going to take me some time to edit, then we can throw this up." Meghan gives me a hopeful smile.

"I can do the editing if you'd like?"

"If you would be so kind."

This video is going to be the first in a series of videos by Might Be Meghan interviewing inspirational women. She got the idea when I was destitute, crying on her couch. A way to help me out without seeming too obvious. Soon after this one releases, we will release one with Meghan interviewing the woman who founded Style-Rex Salon. A salon specializing in unique looks highlighting cultural heritage.

The founder, Ishi Rue, wears her own hair in an exaggerated anime style she says speaks to her ancestry while allowing her to have fun and be an individual.

I've edited two videos in the week I've been with Meghan. It helps to pass the time and take my mind off my worries, not that it helps too much.

A knock sounds on the door, and Meghan goes to answer it. A minute later, she comes back into the room, a manilla envelope in hand.

"It's for you," she says, setting it beside me.

In the upper left-hand corner, Gabriel Icor's name is stamped.

"I can't," I say, pushing it in the trash.

Meghan is quick to retrieve it. "It could be work crap."

"I don't work there anymore."

"But they still have your stuff. They still have Kibbles."

I chuckle, imagine the havoc the monster cat is wreaking.

"Let them have Kibbles."

"I'm opening it."

"Don't you dare!"

"You can legally take people's trash, and you canned it."

"I'm not sure that's how the law works."

But Meghan doesn't seem to care, and as she tears the manilla envelope open, I can't help but look on, eyes wide with horror.

Meghan's pretty blue eyes widen. She blinks, shaking her head slightly.

"Do I want to know?" I ask.

"Well, it appears Mr. Asshole Billionaire left you a parting gift in the tune of $200,000, and he says he'll hold your stuff for up to six months, the monster cat will have his room and board paid for at a vet of your choosing."

She thumbs through the documents, pulling out one

in particular.

"He's also included glowing letters of recommendations and a list of places that would be happy to hire you on."

My lip shoots up in a sneer. I push the documents away.

"Like, you do realize he could have given you nothing—no money, no help."

"You do understand that to him, this is nothing. A drop in a Hoover Dam sized bucket is what it is. Wonder how he plans on making it up to his fiancé, that is, if he'll even tell her."

"Don't you think it's curious she's never seen with him? I mean, you know nothing about her. Not even her name."

It does bother me, but not enough to think about it too hard. Billionaires play by their own rules, and maybe they wanted to keep things quiet, with only their families attending. With what Tom had said, she is probably an heiress of some sort.

"Please, I don't—"

"Well, you're going to have to talk about it eventually."

"No, I don't."

"Do you think you're going to get better just wallowing in my apartment, editing videos, eating carbs, and...did I mention the wallowing?"

"I just don't fucking understand. Why did he act all sweet? Like he was a good guy. He's just an asshole cheater."

"I really feel like there's more to this. Like you should maybe pick up the phone and call him."

As if Meghan had some kind of sixth sense, my phone starts vibrating, but it's not Gabriel—it's Analise. She has tried to call me four times since I left I Friday, each time I let it go to voicemail.

"Pick it up!" Meghan says.

"No, I can't."

Meghan grabs my phone, hits answer, smirks, then handing the phone back to me.

"Damn you!"

Analise: *Remi!*

I want to hit end, but when I hear her voice, I get a rush of emotions. I remember what it was like, sitting in my office, gossiping. It may have only been for a few days, but my time with Analise was precious, as I've had so few friends throughout my life.

Analise: *Remi, I know you must be furious. You have every right to be. Please, just let me explain.*

Fresh tears come as I hold the phone, a million thoughts rushing through my head. If anything, Analise was worse than Gabriel. She could have at least warned me. But no, she played the role of fake friend too well.

The line eventually goes dead, and I feel relief.

"Don't you ever do that again," I say, glaring at Meghan.

She pouts, and I find it hard to stay mad at her. She has good intentions but very poor execution.

"Just throw it all away."

Meghan hikes a brow. "Throw it all away? Throw away this check, which you so richly deserve? Throw away your household goods? Throw away…your giant cat?"

"Everything is replaceable, and if anyone deserves that cat—it's Gabriel."

Chapter Thirty-One

Gabriel courts Kibbles...

"How the hell is this thing even real?" Sayo says, staring at the massive cat named Kibbles with disgust.

"Just don't move too quickly!" I hold up a hand to advise caution. "You wouldn't believe how fast she is."

"What the hell did that girl feed it?"

"Actually, I called the vet, and it's not Remi's fault. She inherited the cat from her grandmother last year. She's actually down five pounds. Maybe that's why she has such a temperament."

Sayo takes a step toward the beast, but a guttural hiss stopped her in her tracks.

"Are you sure you want to take care of this thing?" she asks.

"She'll eventually go to a vet, but for now, it's my... last connection to..."

All at once, we are silent. Sayo, Kibbles, and I stand staring at each other, not sure how to proceed.

Remi has no idea that I'm standing here thinking about her right now. That she hasn't left my head. That I can't sleep, and I'm clinging to her obese cat like a security blanket.

Last night, in the desperate throws of sleeplessness, I decided I would try to cuddle the terrifying creature named Kibbles. I lured her to my apartment with Pounce treats, then nearly threw my back out lifting her, bringing her to my room, and hoisting her onto my bed. I work out pretty regularly, so the weight itself wasn't an issue. It was how she jerked her solid mass of flesh that did me in.

It was a fight I couldn't win, but I tried nonetheless. Now, my arms are covered in scratches, and a traumatized cat now stalks my apartment.

Sayo's flew into town earlier this week, coming to live in Icor Tower sooner than expected. In a few days, a press release will go out, and over the next couple months, Sayo and I will be the talk of the town. Our schedule is packed, seeing us at all the hotspots, not just in New York City but across the entire US.

We will be a dream couple, two attractive people in their primes, hailing from prominent families, with more money than anyone could hope to spend in a lifetime. But none of that matters to me.

A lot of problems came out of that meeting. Tom harboring a huge, life-changing secret being one. Remi should be the last person I'm thinking about, but she hasn't left my mind. Not for a minute.

"Call her," Sayo says from across the room in a tone that makes it sound so easy.

Sayo knows I don't want her in my business, so I say nothing.

The board meeting lost me what little trust the board had in me, as well as the woman of my dreams. Needless to say, it was a bad day.

It is stupid to think that there is only one woman for any one man, but if that is the case, Remi would be mine. She's the perfect mix of smart, sexy, and sweet.

And I can't believe I lost her.

"While you are clearly engaged in your personal life, I've been thinking about the future of Icor Tech. Your upcoming meeting tomorrow should be a big one. I want to be present." Sayo crosses her arms over her chest but doesn't take her eyes off Kibbled. It's simply too great a risk.

"Really?" I reply sarcastically. "A press release is set to go out in two days. We'll be on the cover of magazines across North America, China, and Europe. Now's not the time to come marching into my board room."

Sayo says nothing. Instead, she stares at me, making me feel as though I'm being judged, no. I honestly don't know how I'm going to get through the next few months and make it to our wedding, let alone having to spend years like this with her.

Sayo turns to leave the room, though every two steps she glances over her shoulder to make sure Kibbles isn't stalking her.

When Sayo shuts the door behind her, I let out a huge sigh of relief.

She's an ambitious woman. Demanding to be fully engaged in the family business. Whenever we spend any time together, it always goes to numbers and my poor management.

There's nothing wrong with Sayo, but she displays so little emotion, it leaves me ill at ease around her. She's quiet but brazen with her stares. Heck, Kibbles might be just the thing I need to keep her from staring at me with those judgmental eyes.

I have to remind myself, she doesn't want to be here just as much as I don't want her here.

But there's nothing either of us can do about it.

Gabriel discovers a secret...

You've Received 83 New Messages

Not bad. I've been averaging 75 an hour, so receiving 83 over two means I get a little reprieve.

I open my Messenger to see the damage. Six from my mother, four from HR, seven from lawyers, two from Analise, three from board members, and an epic ton from entertainment reporters.

Zero from Tom.

Tom Wellington, the snake in the grass. The unaccounted for factor I had underestimated. So much more than just a board member who votes against me.

How had I never seen it before? It was staring me in the face all along. And now, I've lost the one woman I could actually see myself growing old with.

I know how crazy that sounds. That it's crazy I'm imagining myself growing old with someone I've only known for two weeks, but when you meet the one, I guess you just know.

Remi Stone is the whole package, and one day she's going to make some lucky fool the happiest man alive. I know it. That is if I didn't break her too badly.

By now, she should have received my parting gift. The one Analise helped me put together.

I wanted to give her so much more, but Analise insisted that I keep it professional. Be generous, but not over the top. Basically, don't make her feel like a damn hooker.

My phone buzzes—it's the board. An email was sent reminding me of tomorrow's meeting, as though I could forget.

> **Cregor:** *The board meeting will be held tomorrow at noon. Your presence is expected to discuss urgent matters we will be voting on.*

Urgent matters we will be voting on? Fuck me! They're planning a coup!

I'm angry for a lot of good reasons. For four years, I've barely been able to get a word in edgewise during company meetings. They've undermined my position and allowed Icor Tech to continue using prehistoric platforms that are both costly and inefficient. And now, they want to oust me.

Fuck them! I'm surrendering myself to a loveless marriage so they can keep their lofty positions and their pride. The last thing I need is them telling me how 'I've let the company down.' If they want to offer me a buyout tomorrow, I'll be happy to show them what's going to happen when I leave, and when I'm no longer set to marry Ms. Sayo Nguyen, Grand Lesbian of China, maybe I'll get to explore my option with Remi.

Except you can't do that. They need you, and it's going to slap them in the face real soon. There is no escaping your marriage. Not for you. Not for Sayo.

I toss back a drink—cheers to my new life. Then I bring up a new video of Remi posted by Might Be Meghan, and I swear, I fall in love all over again.

Chapter Thirty-Two

Remi is in demand...

"Oh my God! I can't keep up with all these messages!" Meghan says while scrolling through her phone. "I don't even know how to filter through them all."

"I'm a little swamped too. I'm getting 50 messages an hour, at least a quarter of them appear to be legit."

"You are the most wanted woman alive!"

"Yeah, I just wish it were for my body."

Meghan sits down on the couch next to me, entirely

too close, but it's her couch. What can I say?

"So, what do you think you're going to do?" she asks.

"I don't know. I had been planning to stick around New York City—but why? I can go anywhere it seems."

"You just want to get away from him, don't you?"

It's true. Staying here, I would be forced to relive the whirlwind romance I shared with Gabriel Icor, if that's what you would call it. I guess it was more of a one night stand.

A knock sounds on the door and Meghan jumps to get it. A moment later, she's calling to me.

My heart stops.

What if it's him? That would be foolish, though. Gabriel Icor's thoughts are not on little old me.

"Remi, hurry your ass up!"

I finally rise from the couch and shuffle to the door, not caring that I look bedraggled.

When I get there, I see one of the most beautiful women I've ever seen before staring at me, two giant men flanking her.

Her black hair hangs like a silk, black curtain. Her lips are ruby red, contrasting her milk-white skin. She's clearly Asian, as are the men accompanying her.

Are they bodyguards?

She's wearing an expensive-looking white dress with a black flower pattern, the hem sitting midway up her thigh with bright-red ankle booties. Her whole body seems to sparkle from the various jewels strewn across her.

Is she a headhunter for some tech company?

The woman's mouth forms a sneer, clearly finding

me distasteful, which is rather insulting considering the shit I've been through.

"I don't give a fuck what you think about me," I say.

Her eyes widen, she brings a hand to her mouth as if she's deep in thought.

"I do not know what he sees in you," she says.

"He sees what in who?" I ask.

"God, you can't be the genius he raves about."

"Listen, lady. You knocked on MY door!"

"Actually, the door belongs to me," Meghan interjects.

I glare at her, and she slinks back, giving me and the woman some privacy.

"I need you to come with me. It's very important," the woman says.

I place my hands on my hips. "I'm not going anywhere with you."

"Damnit! I was hoping I wouldn't have to do this," she says. "Boys."

One of the men bends down, sliding a large chest from the side of the door and undoing the latch.

"What's in there?" I ask, more than a little anxious.

"Nothing, but you will be if you don't come with me."

My jaw drops as the second man steps towards me, arms outstretched. My body goes numb, unable to move. I try to scream, but I can't find my voice.

A burst of laughter explodes from the woman. Both men crack wide grins.

"Down boys. You've had your fun."

I blink, confused. The men are withdrawing, giggling softly.

"What…what the fuck is going on?" I shout.

"Oh, I was just having a little fun."

"Well, that's pretty fucking sick threatening to kidnap someone, ya know."

She shrugs, taking a casual stance.

"Who are you?"

"My name is Sayo Nguyen. In just two months, I will be marrying Gabriel Icor."

My hand covers my mouth as a knot forms in my gut. "I'm so sorry. I'm so terribly sorry. I never meant any harm. I had no idea!"

She's grinning, not at all how a woman looking at the bitch that fucked her man should look.

"I'm not even working there anymore. I quit when I found out."

"I know. If you had been smart, you'd have looked for a way to sue the company. After all, you were grossly mistreated."

"Look, lady—I'm a genius."

"So Gabriel says."

"I don't need to sue Icor Tech to make ends meet."

"I'm sure you don't."

"Then don't worry about my life choices," I snap. "Are we done? Now that you've seen your romantic rival, are we done?"

"I've had the misfortune of encountering your cat," she says.

"Kibbles?"

"Whatever you call that thing. It's vile."

"I guess that's something we can agree on. Now, do you mind telling me why you're here? Is it to rub it in my face that you're with Gabe? To size me up? To lecture me on pet health?"

"As I said earlier, I need you to come with me."

"Oh, hell no!"

"Well, you did sleep with my fiancé." Sayo is frowning now, her shoulders slumping. "It's the least you could do for me."

Is she really using the worst night of my life against me? Well, technically, it was the best—but it was followed a couple days later by the worst day of my life, so the point's still valid.

"Do me the pleasure of joining me for lunch. Well, I'm not really sure if pleasure is the word I would choose. Chances are, I'm going to want to stab my eyeballs out after just a brief conversation with you."

I've had enough. "God, you're terrible. What could Gabriel possibly see in you? He must be blind."

"Follow me. We're going to brunch. Don't make me throw you in that box."

If she's made the effort to track me down, I should probably hear what she has to say. If only to spite Gabriel.

"Wait! Can I at least get dressed first?" I ask, looking down at my shirt that I now realize is stained with mustard and my poor life decisions.

Sayo looks at me, amused, but then something catches her eye, and her face contorts from arrogance to sheer horror.

I follow the direction of her gaze and see what has her so riled.

"Oh, say hello to Number 11."

"11?"

"Yeah, he's actually pretty well-traveled. I saw him in

the lobby just three days ago. How he made it to the sixth floor is beyond me, but I think we can both agree it's rather impressive."

"What on Earth could Gabriel possibly ever see in you?"

Chapter Thirty-Three

__Gabriel__ is ousted from the board...

I walk into an already full boardroom, six sets of eyes staring at me and waiting to get started.

Tom's wearing a megawatt grin, and I can tell that in his mind, he's already won. That may be the case, but I'm not going down without a fight.

"I guess we should begin," I say, taking the place left for me at the head of the table.

"Actually," Tom says, spinning his chair to face mine. "We're still waiting for someone to arrive."

"This is a board meeting," Cregor snaps. "The directors won't—"

"Oh, trust me, Creg. You're gonna wanna hear what they have to say."

I know Lindel won't vote me off the board, and I'm fairly certain Barry won't either, but Cregor has never been a proponent of mine. He absolutely hated my father, from what I heard, and when my father passed, he let it be known he'd rather not have me on the board at all.

Jim and Essie are looking down towards their laps. This isn't a good sign, and I begin to wonder just how much my board has been plotting against me. I'm literally in a room full of sharks, circling, trying to catch the scent of blood.

The door opens, and my heart sinks to the pit of my stomach.

In walks Sayo, who Tom is much too happy to see, but trailing her is what surprises me.

Remi Stone walks in, chin up, wearing a tee-shirt and jeans.

What is she doing here?

"How nice of you to make it, Sayo," Tom says smugly, "and it's good to see you again, Remi."

Tom shoots Remi a wink that makes me want to stab him in the eye with my pen. After what Tom put Remi through, he should feel ashamed. Instead, he's arranged some crazy fucking shenanigans to make some power play to oust me from the board.

At least now, I know why.

"Get them out of here!" Cregor shouts. "This is a board meeting."

"Yes, but you'll see that their inclusion is necessary."

Cregor looks ready to shout again, but Lindel places a hand on his arm, and he is silenced. She has that effect on people.

"Whatever it is you have planned, Tom, you can do it without them. I have nothing to hide, and I wouldn't want an ex-employee or my fiancé going through undue stress."

Sayo smiles brightly, taking a seat next to Remi in a chair against the wall. "I assure you, we are fine," she says.

Seeing that smile and knowing that Tom was expecting her lets me know the situation is far worse than I had thought.

"Let's get this over with," I say.

Cregor rises to take the floor, no doubt intent on going through a laundry list of things I've neglected as CEO of the company.

He opens his mouth to speak, but Tom cuts him off, saying. "Cregor, I know you think this is your meeting, but take a seat."

A stunned look crosses Cregor's face, and when no one moves to question Tom, I know for sure he has the board in the bag.

I rise.

"There's no need for a dog and pony show, Tom. I know you want me off the board. Everyone else knows you want me off the board. But, does everyone know just why you want me off?"

I look around at the sitting members, their eyes shift to Tom.

"Well, I was going to tell them, but I guess I'll let you."

I take a few steps, circling Tom, then stop to look at the board members. "You see, there's a very specific reason why Tom has put so much effort into turning you all against me."

I turn, making sure to draw out the suspense.

"There's a bylaw written into company policy stating that two blood relatives cannot serve on the board at any one time. The wording is unique. It means a husband and a wife can serve together, but not brother and sister, or rather—brother and brother."

The board members now look confused, whispering to each other.

"I'd like you all to take a look at these documents." I pass around copies to each of the board members.

"Large payouts my father made using a fake name over time. It appears he sponsored your private schools and ivy league education. Yours and your mother's living expenses as well."

The board members flip through the documents, surprised looks on their faces.

"Was it your idea he appoint you to the board? Bringing it from six to seven? Or his? My guess, it was probably his. He wanted to keep you a secret, so he could go one living his 'picture perfect' life. The only way he could ensure you wouldn't go public with the information and embarrass him, was if you were on the board because no two blood relatives can serve together. You'd lose your job."

"I earned my position on this board! I had to take what was owed to me!" Tom's red with rage now that everyone knows his secret.

Sayo clears her throat and takes a position alongside

us.

"Enough of this confrontation. I'll tell you flat out what's going on. Tom and Gabriel are blood relatives, and cannot serve on the board at the same time despite doing so for four years, and Tom also serving with his father. Since this is being brought to the board's attention today, this is what we will be voting on."

"You do not give us orders—" Cregor starts, but Sayo cuts him off.

"I will give whatever order I want because if you don't listen to me, you will not be getting any of my father's money to help bail you out."

The room is silent now, Sayo commanding the floor.

"For the last several years, Icor Tech has grossly mismanaged their money. You're in need of some help."

"Well, if the CFO had been doing his job, then maybe we wouldn't be in this situation," I say. "But no, from the sound of it, Tom knew exactly what he was doing. You knew too."

"You must be mistaken," Sayo says, now walking around the table as she speaks.

"I'm surprised, Sayo. I thought it was only your father with these ambitions. Turns out, you're a bit of a player yourself."

Sayo smiles at me, a smile showing she thinks I'm already defeated.

"Well, since we're airing all the dirty laundry, after I found out that Tom was my brother, I dug a little deeper. Tried to figure out what else is going on, and wouldn't you know, the same platforms Tom had insisted we stick with, are having their shares bought up by Sayo's father."

Sayo's neck snaps in my direction, clearly caught off

guard.

"Yeah, I suppose you thought that during the meeting, you'd tell them I was being negligent, you'd parade Remi around, telling everyone I was trying to manipulate votes and fucking employees—when it had been Tom all along."

The board's staring, slack-jawed, looking to each other confused.

"It doesn't matter what Tom has done," Sayo says, scanning the room. "My father's the only one who can help you out now. You're a sinking vessel. Once you vote Gabriel out, Tom will become CEO, as he is of Icor blood. Then, we can go about rebuilding."

"Actually, there's still hope. I made some calls to Telwire and some of the other companies we've been doing business with, and I found out some interesting things. First, your father owns shares, but he's not a majority owner. He can't force decisions. And second, Tom has initiated a few handshake deals. You see, after the wedding, which I realize now is supposed to be between Sayo and Tom instead of Sayo and myself, a buyout is in the works. We are set to purchase Telwire, but that's not all. They've been working on a new system, a better system and, even if Tom's gone, the deal's still on the table."

"If you think getting rid of me is a good idea, just remember, this all happened on Gabriel's watch," Tom says, his voice thick with menace. "In a year, under me, we'll be showing record sales."

"I brought Remi here, for you," Sayo says. "Go with her now. We'll put together a buyout package. You'll never have to want for anything the rest of your life."

"Enough of this!" Cregor is on his feet, taking command of the meeting. "It's time we vote."

Each board member takes the stone they use to cast their vote out, a tradition that was carried over from my grandfather's days. One side of the stone is black, the other white, each side has a pan scale balance etched into it.

Cregor looks to me. "Today, we were not intent on voting Gabriel out. As a matter of fact, we were going to vote on the many proposals he's pitched over the years. But instead, we must vote on whether to keep Tom or Gabriel."

A silence settles over the room as we take in the information. I went into the meeting expecting to be voted out of power, but it seems Cregor had other plans in mind. Now—I really might be voted out of power.

"If you vote white, we keep Gabriel. If you vote black, we keep Tom. You have ten minutes to make your decision."

I turn my stone white side up as Tom sets his to black, and we wait. Lindel is the only other person with their stone turned up in front of her, white side up. The others hold their stones in their hands, not wanting to put it down until the last moment.

Barry needs to use the bathroom, but it's a rule that no one can leave the boardroom during voting, so I pray he can hold it.

At nine minutes and thirty seconds, the stones begin to get placed on the table.

Cregor, Lindel, and I vote white. Barry, Tom, Essie, and Jim vote black.

I have lost my position as CEO of my grandfather's

company.

Tom smiles, rising from his chair and extends his hand out to me.

I don't want my last moments on the board to be of me acting like a petulant child, so I raise my hand to meet his—to meet my brother's.

"Wait!" Remi shouts, and all eyes turn towards her.

"I need to speak to Cregor!"

"Well, it will have to wait," Tom snaps.

"It can't wait! It's a matter of urgency."

"Well, take it outside then."

"I can't! Vote's not over yet!"

Remi gets up, walks over to Cregor, and whispers something into his ear. A dour look crosses his face, and he nods. Remi begins typing furiously into her phone.

Tom scans the room and grins. "Well, now that Gabriel has been removed as CEO—"

"Actually, he's still CEO until the end of the day. You should read your bylaws," Remi says, not looking up from her phone.

Tom's jaw clenches. He forces his smile wider.

"Enjoy your last day. I have things to do now."

Cregor rises. "I would like to announce my retirement," he says.

What the hell is going on?

The room looks at Cregor, stunned.

An anxious look crosses Tom's handsome face. "Well, that's great. We'll get to announcing our newest board member—"

"It's Analise," I say, understanding exactly what Remi is trying to pull here.

Whenever one of the Big 5 leaves the board, the CEO

is allowed to choose their successor. If any other board member leaves, it goes before a vote—another one of my grandfather's odd bylaws.

An angry look crosses Sayo's face. She was fully expecting to be the next new member of the board.

"Fine," Tom says. "Analise will be joining the board."

The door swings open, and Analise steps in.

"I'm here to cast my vote."

"Actually, you can't. We've already voted on the matter, and we can't have eight votes."

Remi takes a position at the head of the room to address the board.

"I've read your bylaws, and admittedly, they're dated and worded oddly. You see, Cregor will serve on the board until the end of the day, but Analise started immediately after Gabriel named her. Maxwell Icor was insistent that every board member not only be present to vote for items voted on during the whole of the day, but be allowed to cast a vote. Since we don't have another stone, Analise, could you please tell the room your vote."

"I vote we keep Gabriel and ditch Tom," she says without a second thought.

Now, there are four votes for me, and four votes for Tom. And I realize this last-minute play will only lead to my eventual oust, but it will at least be delayed by a day, and Analise will now have her position on the board. I'm fairly certain she'll give them hell.

"This is all fine," Tom says. "I call for an emergency meeting to take place tomorrow. Tomorrow, we'll vote again, with seven. And we can assume no one will change their votes in the next twenty-four hours, and I'll win again."

"Not so fast," Lindel says. "This retired life sounds like a good gig. I think I might be throwing in the towel too."

Oh no! Not Lindel. Anyone but Lindel.

I know what she's doing. She's sacrificing her position for me, so I can get the last vote.

"Gee, if only there were some mousy woman qualified to be on the board. One with an ivy league education. A young program manager type. Someone who wears a muumuu to bed."

There's no other choice, and my hand is forced.

"I appoint Remi Stone to Icor Tech's board. Now please, cast your stone."

And so I manage to remain CEO of Icor Tech after a coup staged by the half-brother I never knew I had and my fiancé I never wanted to marry.

Chapter Thirty-Four

__Gabriel__ makes sure Barry doesn't shit himself...

Tom leaves immediately after the vote, and I call security to tail him.

Sayo approaches. "Well, this should make for an interesting wedding," she says.

"You're still marrying Tom?" I ask.

"No, my father is insistent I marry Icor's CEO."

"Then you're out of luck."

"Don't be so stupid."

"Yeah, I'm trying to break that habit. Leave now, or

else I'll call security. Your stuff will be sent back home."

Sayo shoots me a look of poison, but obeys, leaving me to my board.

"Congratulations, Barry. You're now the Remaining 1. Now get to the bathroom before you shit yourself."

He complies, avoiding my gaze, and Jim and Essie follow him out the door.

I look to those remaining, Remi, Analise, Cregor, and Lindel.

"Thanks, you guys. You really came through for me today," I say, tears welling in my eyes.

"I'm not so sure you owe us a thanks as much as we owe you an apology," Cregor says.

The weight of his words is not lost on me.

"I'm glad you made good use of those documents you found." Lindel gives me a wink.

My brows raise in surprise. "That was you?"

"Yeah, I figured it out long ago. When your father died, I took it upon myself to clean up some of the messes he left behind. Paid off some women that were going to run to the tabloids. Saw to a bunch of accounts he had hidden, and that's when I found it. Ledgers in his damn filing cabinet. It didn't take me long to find out Tom was his son, and I took it upon myself to clean up the evidence."

"But why?"

"Your father left the board in such upheaval, we couldn't take that kind of scandal. I wanted you to get a fair shot on the board, so I held them back for as long as I could. I was in constant fear Tom was going to pull something, so I let some things slide that I shouldn't have. I just didn't want to rock the boat."

"Well, thank you." I can't say it enough. There simply aren't words to describe the torrent of emotions I feel seeing her go.

I turn to Ana. "You're finally right where I need you to be. I'd like you to take over for Tom as CFO."

Analise grins ear to ear. "Oh, baby! Put me in charge of that money, honey!"

Next, I look to Remi. "How does COO sound to you?"

Remi reaches for Analise's hand, beaming.

Oh great, they're friends. Just what I need is the two of them on the board ganging up on me.

Lindel's getting up from her chair, and I practically run to her, grabbing her up in my arms.

"I'm going to miss you more than Cregor," I say, and the room erupts into laughter.

"Looks like you'll be fine. You've promoted a couple ladies with questionable taste, but I think you'll pull through."

I'm crying now, tears streaming down my face.

"I've never imagined a board without you. I'm going to miss you so much."

"Well, you ain't kicking me out of the Tower, are ya?"

"Nope."

"Then step outta my way. I gotta cruise to book." Lindel glances over her shoulder at Cregor. "You with me, Creg? Bahamas?"

"You make the plans, just make sure to pack for me and tell me where to show up."

Cregor walks past me towards the door, turns back and says, "Gabriel, it was good working for you."

They leave, Ana following behind, and I'm left alone with Remi.

I can tell she's anxious, and before she can get a word out, I wrap her in my arms and cover her mouth with mine, while grabbing her ass.

After a full minute, I pull back and start to say, "I'm sorry, Remi. I was a fool, but I never intended to hurt you."

"I know," she says, a slight smile playing on her lips.

"Will you still have me?"

"Perhaps."

Perhaps?

"Can you ever forgive me?"

She looks at me square in the eyes and says, "Yes, but there will be conditions."

"Conditions? What conditions?"

"First, I get to tell Meghan everything, not that I haven't after that shitty board meeting."

"Condition met."

"And, you're not going to hide me. We either work together as professionals, or we work together as a couple. There's no secret fuck buddy situation anymore. I'm not made for that. I had to find that out the hard way."

"Well, then, instead of a press release being issued for my engagement to Sayo, I'll have one issued regarding my courtship to a Miss Remi Stone, single mother to Kibbles the Cat. It will go over great."

"I don't need a press release. I just need you."

She pulls me into a kiss, firmly, demanding, and as it turns out, I'm okay with her taking charge every once in a while.

Remi *Stone bags a billionaire…*

Holy shit! I think I've just been subject to a real-life PLOT TWIST!

Just four hours ago, I was feeling sorry for myself in Meghan's apartment, apologizing to some Chinese gangster lady, and now I'm wrapped in Gabriel Icor the 10's arms, being kissed in his fancy boardroom—as the newest member of his board!

And, on top of all that, I have my friend Analise back to serve with me on board.

And! We got rid of Crusty Cregor. Yep, that was all me.

Unfortunately, he didn't turn out to be so bad after all. Gosh, is this guilt I'm feeling. Damnit!

I have to admit, I didn't see it playing out this way. When Sayo asked me to attend the meeting, it was under the assumption that Gabriel needed my help. I was fully prepared to redeem my name and help him get some necessary items passed. I had no idea Sayo was trying to push Gabriel towards resignation, using me as bait.

Boy was she in for a surprise. I bet she regrets having me tag along now.

I wish I could say it was all for love, but the truth is, only a billionaire can afford Kibbles' kibble habits, so I must make some love life sacrifices to see to the care of those in my charge—yeah right!

This is 100% my dream come true.

Chapter THIRTY-FIVE

***Gabriel** has a brother from another mother…*

I walk into my brother's office. He's sitting in a chair, drink in hand.

"You never did drink much," I say.

"Well, if there was ever an occasion."

I slump into a chair without being invited to sit.

"I had no idea," I say, feeling rather guilty.

"Well, it took me a while to puzzle it together myself."

"Tell me about it."

"My mother was a maid. When he got her pregnant, he promised her the world. That is until your mother, Scarlet Primrose, showed up. Who can resist a movie star, right? Well, he sent my mom to France, where I was born. He'd come around, but I only knew him as dad, not the billionaire tech tycoon."

"So, he basically kept two families?"

"Yeah. My mother got pregnant again, but she miscarried. He was so angry with her for getting pregnant, that after that he didn't come around so much. I was devastated. He wouldn't allow my mother to date, threatened to take everything from her. My mother became a shell of herself. I wish she would have just moved on, taken another husband regardless of what he said—but no. She was insistent that one day he'd return."

"Did he?"

"After the miscarriage, I saw him once more on his terms, but he kept a distance. He was cold. When I finally figured out just who he was, I send him an email, demanding we meet. I was seventeen, sitting across from him, telling him what school I was going to attend, and what position I wanted upon graduation. He called me crazy and got up to leave. Then I threatened him. I threatened to tell my story. He said he had paid more than his share and owed me nothing. I told him I was going to go to the media. I've never seen the man so mad before. He threatened to cut me off. I told him to just imagine how that would look to everyone."

"Jeez, what a fucking asshole."

"Yeah, well, after that, he complied. I went to Yale, and he hired me on before graduation. The thing is—we got along great! We went golfing together, on trips together, picked up chicks together. Things he couldn't do with you because of your mom. Eventually, he even started treating me like a son."

"And he showed you the passages," I cut in.

"Ah, ya figured that out? Good for you. Yeah, we used them to spy. He was a real fucking pervert too. He used to look in on Analise, and boy, what a fucking body. Keisha too. Hot damn!"

"You're kidding me?"

"Nope. It's how I knew you were after Remi. I saw how you decorated her room, all the flower petals. There's only one reason why you'd do that. Bold move, being engaged and all. I ran up to your office afterward, to tell you I was taking our relationship on books, trying to get you to break it off."

That gives rise to my anger. "What you did with her is complete shit. Tangling her in all this!"

"I never intended for her to get involved in the first place. When she first presented at the Innovation Meeting, I wanted her to see how enthusiastic I was about her proposal—because it was good, and I wanted her on my future team, once I got rid of you. So I conferenced you in. I never expected you to promote her to director. I liked her."

"I guess she was just collateral damage to you."

"No, brother, didn't you listen to anything I said? I like Remi, more than any girl I've ever brought to any fancy dinner. I may make my way through women like our dad, but if there was ever a woman that would have made me stop—it's her. I was planning on marrying Sayo, but Remi had my heart in her hands."

It's ironic that we both had our eyes on Remi Stone,

seeing as how we could both have almost any woman in the world. And we were brothers.

"Anyway, back to good old dad. In the end, I think he counted me as his closest friend."

"I'm glad you had that time with him," I say.

"I wanted to take CEO when he died, and I almost made a bid for it—but he had mismanaged the fuck out of the company, and they were already gunning to out you."

"So you set out to deepen the hole. Force me into failure."

"God, it was so easy. Everyone wanted to hate you."

"Did you ever wonder what it would be like if instead of enemies, we were friends?"

He shakes his head. "Nope, not for a moment."

"Whose idea was it to bring Sayo and her family into this?"

"I approached Sayo's father two years ago with a plan. They've actually been struggling for quite some time. A significant portion of their money is made from shady business practices, and eventually, they know there will be a crackdown. I had him buy up significant shares in various companies we were dealing with, not enough to raise red flags, but enough for us to be listened to. Then we had them hire teams to spice up their platforms—quietly. We promised a grand unveiling and support from each of our companies when they brought their new systems online. There would be a slump, followed by a huge boost. You already know about the buyouts planned."

"Wow. That took balls."

"Then Sayo's father, Chenglei, approached me one

day, telling me he was worried about his daughter's sexual orientation. Why the fuck he gives a shit when he has five other kids, I don't know, but he basically wanted her out of the country so he wouldn't have to deal with it. He offered me her hand in marriage if I could get her on the board. That's when the plan began to formulate. I had him offer you his daughter's hand instead. This way, I could finish the fine details of my plan with your mind preoccupied. Then Remi came."

"Ironically, it's purely by chance I even met her. She came into the boardroom a day early, a complete mess thinking she'd overslept."

"God, it's part of her charm. I've had the companies I've been dealing with contact her to offer her a position. I wanted to see her land on her feet, and she would have been valuable to us during a merger."

"Well, now what are you going to do?"

"I have money saved. You haven't seen the last of me."

Tom gets up from his desk, throwing his glass against the wall. It shatters. Tom's last casualty at Icor Tech.

I watch him leave, wondering when I'm going to hear from him again.

Epilogue

*Gabriel's mother thinks **Remi** is a baby incubator...*

Boy, can Gabriel Icor cut a rug!

I mean, I could too, if I wasn't stumbling over my own two feet. Hopefully, no one saw that, but who am I kidding—everyone saw! Why? Because I'm at Gabriel's and my wedding.

That's right! We just got married.

Did we seek out the wildest and most exotic locations to get hitched?

Nope! We had a small ceremony, or rather a tiny one.

We got married in the boardroom at Icor Towers, where we first met. Cregor walking me down the aisle.

Then everyone met up at the Mother of Mercy Children's Hospital, where our reception is being held in the cafeteria. We turned it into a charity event, and the hospital is making oodles of money for the kiddos!

It's not what you'd expect a billionaire's wedding to be like, and there was more than one look of horror throughout the night, but it's perfect for us, and that's what matters.

Gabriel's mother looks beautiful as she glides across the dance floor with Mr. Sokolov, and I can't believe I'm going to be her daughter in law! I mean, I used to watch her on television growing up, and now, she's asking me to call her mom.

And…she's asking me how soon she'll have grandbabies. Like, every chance she gets. I go to dinner, and as I'm forking beans in my mouth, there it is again, "Do you track your ovulation," or my favorite, "I hear missionary position gives you the best chance of conception," oh, wait, there's this one, "If I were dating a billionaire, I'd want to get knocked up as quickly as possible!" said under her breath LIKE SHE'S PLANTING THE IDEA IN MY HEAD OR SOMETHING!

It's insane. But a crazy, insane loving mother-in-law is just what I need in my life right now.

Analise and Meghan act as my bride's maids, and Kibbles was escorted down the aisle by Gabriel's mortified mother to present the ring.

I get to meet Gabriel's friends, Cassius, Zev, Sven, and a bunch of others I can't quite keep straight, all accompanied by gorgeous and beautiful women.

I swear I saw Sven eyeing Meghan, though. It's something I'm going to keep my eye on.

Everything is going wonderfully, despite the fact that I'm scrambling to stay upright with the loud music, long dress, and my janky dance moves.

Oh, and Meg now lives at Icor Towers, filling some PR positions she's perfect for.

Lindel and Cregor are dancing together, and…it seems like they are really enjoying each other's company. Let's just say—it's enough to start some gossip.

Gabriel suddenly takes me in his arms, and I'm being whisked across the dance floor. He's staring intensely into my eyes. I'm totally lost in the moment.

"I can't wait to have you all to myself. For two weeks!"

"That's the longest you've been away from the company since you took charge, isn't it?"

"Yep."

"Aren't you nervous?"

"Not with Analise in charge. Enough talk of work, though."

He holds me close, and I'm in heaven. I never thought in a million years I could ever be this happy. That I could marry Gabriel the 10! But here I am, a blissful idiot—with an advanced degree and a high position in a billion-dollar company. Just to clarify that statement.

A video begins to play on a large screen at the head of the reception. It's various stills of Gabriel and me together, with a few short videos. My heart is near bursting when a video of me stumbling out of an elevator flashes on the screen.

He didn't!

The room is laughing, and I'm turning red. Gabriel grabs the microphone.

"That there, ladies and gentlemen, is a video I've watched no less than a thousand times since I met Ms. Remi Stone, or shall I call her Mrs. Remi Icor."

All eyes are on me, and I wave to the crowd.

He's so dead.

"This feed was taken right after we first met. Shortly after she stepped onto that elevator, I tracked down the feed so that I could see her one last time. I knew then that she was the one, even if I didn't know how to make it work."

Everyone's clapping now, and tears are streaming down my face. How can I be mad at that? Gabriel Icor the 10 is just so perfect!

I'm in his arms again, his hand around my waist, we're gliding across the dance floor.

So in love!

Remi and Gabriel get it on...

My heart is damn near bursting from my chest as I wait for Gabriel to emerge from the bathroom.

It's well past midnight, we've been married for under 24 hours, and I can't wait to finally be in his arms again —as his wife!

I wish I could say I look super sexy in some high-end lingerie, but that would be a lie. I have a form-fitting white tank top on and a pair of matching white boy shorts. I have plenty of sexy things to wear on the honeymoon, but for our wedding night, I want to keep it simple.

He saunters out, towel around his waist, and I see his sexy six-pack flexing. I can't wait to get my hands on it!

"God, what a day!" he says, stretching his arms in the air so I can get a good view of his flank.

"I'll say. I'm lucky I didn't roll an ankle out there on the dance floor."

He looks anxious. A grimace crosses his face.

"About that...it appears a video has already made it onto YouTube."

My hand shoots to my mouth. "No!"

He chuckles. "What's really funny is one of the replies, *Billionaire Marries Klutz to Get Out of Liability Claim!*"

"You're joking!"

"I'm not!"

"Well, it's been a busy day. I guess I'm off to bed," he says as he pulls back the blanket from the bed.

"Excuse me?" My hands are on my hips to show him I mean business.

"Getting married is busy work!" he says, feigning offense.

"Work? Is that what you call our union?"

"I mean, I can't think of a better word, but if you can, I'm all ears."

I climb up his body, throwing the covers aside and sit on his rock-hard abs.

His eyes brighten as he positions his hands behind his head. I lean down to kiss him before pulling off my shirt.

I never thought a man would enjoy staring at me so much, but Gabriel Icor goes into a trance every single time I'm naked. And I swear, once he even drooled.

"Hello, Sexy!"

I feel him beneath me, wanting me. I want him too, and soon, our bodies are pressed together, hungry and on fire.

"Remi Icor, I love you," he says between kisses.

I'm so lost, I haven't words to return to him.

He rolls me over, kisses down my body, pulls off my panties, and our night begins.

The End

Also By Lark Anderson

The Beguiling a Billionaire Series

The Billionaire's Board
The Billionaire's Fixer Upper
The Billionaire's Funding
The Bad Girl
The Dis-Graced
The Trainwreck

Reckless in Love
eBook Only

Love you…not!!!
Trust you…not!!!
Tempt you…not!!!

Savage in Love

Savage in the Sheets

The Glow Girlz Series

Stacey's Seduction
Tempting Teysa
Desiree's Delight

If you'd like to become an ARC reviewer for Lark, please email her at: mims@mimsthewords.com.

About the Author - Lark

Lark Anderson was raised near Syracuse, New York. She joined the USAF at 19 as a Flight Manager and eventually discharged in pursuit of a college degree. Her passion for writing manifested in elementary school, but she waited until she was in her 20's to pursue her dream. Now, she not only writes contemporary romance and fantasy, but she also writes for a sitcom!

Twitters: @mims_words / @lark_anderson
Goodreads: @Lark_Anderson
Instagram: @mimsthewords
Facebook: @LarkAndersonAuthor
Website: www.larkandersonbooks.net
BookBub: @mims8
Newsletter Signup: https://larkandersonbooks.net/subscribe/

A SNEAK PEEK AT.....

BEGUILING A BILLIONAIRE
BOOK 2

THE Billionaire's FIXER UPPER

Lark Anderson

Chapter One

*Let's start from the beginning... **Fiona** Fables... is homeless...*

What in the heck is this?

I rip the red sheet of paper off my door, waving it in the air, not that there's anyone around to see my act of rebellion.

"Evicted? I'm being evicted?" I yell as though I were not alone. "What coward left this on my door?"

I pace the hall, adrenaline coursing through my veins. Eviction is most certainly NOT how I had planned my evening to go.

"How is this even legal? Spoiler alert: It's not! How is it no one had the balls to come and tell me that I'm going to be homeless?"

I knock on my neighbor's door, then the door across the hall. I move from door to door, trying to get someone's attention.

Where the hell is everybody?

I continue down the hall until I reach the stairwell and turn back to see Mr. Everwell staring at me from his door which is opposite mine.

Mr. Everwell is an older gentleman, late 60's, a blues player. I've lost countless hours of sleep to him playing well into the night. Needless to say, there's a bit of a rivalry between us.

"Fi fi, why you actin' all crazy?"

Crazy? He has the audacity to call me crazy?

I take a deep breath, feeling much bolder than my usual rational, well-thought-out self. It's almost like I'm walking into battle, and I wonder if this is how it feels walking into a courtroom.

No, I don't think I'm being dramatic. If there's one thing I've learned in life, it's that we're basically always at war with something. For me, it's usually my lactose intolerance. Today—it's eviction.

Crossing my arms over my chest, I saunter up to Mr. Everwell, glaring daggers.

"Mr. Everwell," I hold up the eviction notice, "they're trying to oust me from my home when I haven't been late on even one payment."

"Yeah, but you got some janky shit over there on that side of the hall. Black mold. Rot. Faulty wiring."

My brow furrows. "Look, I'm well aware we live in a slum. I've had to put myself through college while living in one of the most expensive cities in the world. If you're trying to shame me for living in a shitty apartment right across from your own shitty apartment, then let me tell y—"

"Whoa, whoa, I don't think you heard me right."

"So, you didn't just bring up my mold, rot, and faulty wiring?"

"Your side was deemed unfit for habitation. They're redoing your row."

"Redoing my row?"

"Getting rid ah da mold. Fixing it up. Gettin' it up to code."

"Why wasn't I told about this? I know there's some city regulation that's gotta state how much time they're allotted before forcing me out."

"You were told. Everyone was told. They came around every day for two weeks."

Oh, no! Oh, no, no, no! Stay calm. Don't go nuclear.

"That's not fair! I've been studying for finals at the library. Why didn't they leave a note on my door?"

"They did, and if I remember correctly, you cursed them damn witnesses whenever you saw them."

Realization suddenly hits me like a slap in the face.

"Oh my God! That's what those were. Holy crickets! It looked like a damn coming to Jesus flier."

"Well, now you know."

Mr. Everwell turns to go back into his apartment.

"Wait! You can't go."

"Yes, I can. I got some shows about to come on."

He shuffles into his apartment, slamming the door

behind him, leaving me alone in the hall.

Where the hell am I supposed to go? They can't do this. Don't they need to tell their tenants in person if they're going to be kicking them out?

I try to remember the various rules and regulations regarding housing in New York City, but they elude me. For once, I wish I had paid more attention to things outside of entertainment law.

Think Fiona! You don't want to be going apartment shopping and job hunting at the same time.

My friends that I graduated with are off traveling the world, all on their parents' dollar. My one good friend left, Teagan from the coffee shop I work at, is a squatter, and chances are she doesn't have so much as a couch I can sleep on.

In other words, I'm completely screwed.

The stairwell door opens, and a man walks into the hallway. He's dressed in jeans and a red tee-shirt. A grey baseball cap is pulled low on his forehead.

What has my interest piqued is the toolbox he's carrying.

"Hey!" I say as he walks by.

He ignores me completely, continuing down the hall.

Who does he think he is ignoring me like that?

I follow him down the hall, eviction notice in hand.

"Hey—hello! Who do you work for? Hello? Listen, I just got this notice saying—"

He comes to a sudden stop before me, which I fail to do.

I walk straight into the man, but he doesn't budge even an inch, and suddenly, I'm on the hallway floor looking up at him through my frizzy red hair that's fallen over my face.

I'm startled. He's startled. Somehow, despite the fact that I was following him and yelling down the hall, he failed to hear me.

I gaze up at him, a mixture of embarrassment and anger.

Oh, wow—this man is smokin'!

He doesn't look at all like I expect a handyman in a slum to look like. Dark brown eyes, at least six-feet tall. Strong jaw and perfect white teeth. And those muscles—exactly what a woman needs wrapped around her.

His brow furrows in clear confusion, which doesn't seem possible with how loud I was shouting.

He takes something white from his ear, first one, repeating the process with the other ear.

Are those hearing aids? Is he deaf? Oh my God—he's deaf. Did he just not have them on? I'm such an asshole!

I try to remember the sign language I studied so long ago, but all I remember is certain letters.

C...A...N...

He's looking at me, confused. Like I'm crazy.

I hear a soft mumbling and look in his hands to see a small white earpiece.

"Are you okay?" he finally says.

"Are those...wireless earbuds?" I ask.

"Why, are you trying to rob me?"

My mouth gapes in offense. "Me? Trying to rob you?"

"Well, I'm not sure what the hell you're doing, lady. I just kno—"

I hold up the flier I've been gripping in my hand.

"I've just been evicted from my apartment! I need to talk to your boss—right now!"

His eyes shift downward as if he's ashamed—which he very well should be if he's had any part in this!

"Oh...weren't you notified four weeks ago?" he says. "About the renovations around The Shire?"

The Shire is what the group of buildings making up the apartment complex I live in is called, despite the fact that that it is FAR from fantasy living.

"No, I wasn't. And who the hell thinks four weeks is enough time to up and move in New York City! It could take ten months to find another affordable apartment."

"Well, you were given the option to relocate to another unit inside the complex."

"Good, I'll take you up on that."

"Unfortunately, they're all full now."

"No! No, they can't be! I need a place to live. I have nowhere else to go!"

There's no way I can afford another apartment in the city right now, especially before I'm actually accepted into an internship program. I got this one at a killer discount, and yeah, there's a bit of a smell, but it's within my means, and I've learned to accept its quirky charms.

"I demand to speak to the owner!" I say. "I just finished law school, and boy is he in trouble."

"Well, you probably wouldn't be in this situation if he were still alive."

I blink, confused. "He's dead? So who's evicting me?"

"The city. When his estate went to probate, there were a lot of inspections. Failed inspections."

That's actually kind of a bummer.

"Well, what exactly did you mean?" I say.

"I'm doing work on the entire complex, lining up contractors, getting it up to code. While I'm here, I've been given the maintenance apartment, but I don't need it except to house my tools. Since you are done with finals, you can stay there for free if you agree to help with some of the projects."

"Wait! So you expect me, with no credentials, to go around fixing the damn faulty wiring and shit?"

Now, he's laughing so hard her has to grab his gut, or rather, his rock-hard abs by the look of it. I want to be angry, but damn—all I can do is stare. Finally, he looks back over at me, regaining his composure.

"Let's start over," he says. "Hi, my name is Zev," he holds out his hand to shake. "Would you like a job?"

I take his hand, giving it a slight shake, furrowing my brow at him.

Say something, you idiot!

"Hi, my name is Fiona. I'm homeless and not qualified to do handiwork."

"Well, Fiona. You're in luck. I'm in need of a project manager that will line up contractors to get the work done, show them around The Shire, and assist in getting everything completed in a timely manner. In exchange, you can stay in the maintenance apartment for free during the duration of the renovations."

Coordinate contractors. It's not the worse thing I could be doing. And I won't be homeless.

But you need to be applying for internships. You can't be tied up all day in this slum. It could cost you opportunities.

"Oh, God! Oh, no! I don't know what to do? I just finished finals! I don't graduate for another month! I work as a barista for crying out loud. There is NO WAY I can afford to move."

"Do you have a friend you could stay with?"

"A friend? No, I have no one to stay with. Holy crickets, how could they do this to someone?"

I pull myself up into a sitting position, fanning my face with the notice. It's as if the air is scorching hot.

"I'm going to refuse to leave. They'll have to pry me from my apartment. I'll chain myself to the plumbing."

"I hope you know, I have bolt cutters."

Is he mocking me?

"Seriously? I find out I'm about to be homeless, and you're sitting here mocking me?"

"Well, you can't say you weren't warned."

"Wow! Just wow! It's not every day a guy takes a shot at a homeless woman."

The man sits down next to me, entirely too close for my comfort. Or rather, I'd like him to sit much closer if the situation were different. You don't see this kind of sexy every day. Dark eyes. Dark hair. Sly grin. And ALL those muscles.

"So, you need an apartment?" he says with a smirk.

The way he's staring at me has me anxious. As hot he is, there are rules when offering yourself up t woman. The biggest rule: Don't be a creep.

"If you're about to turn into some...pervert—I'r game. Holy sweet Jesus, when did my life turn i porno?"

He chuckles, turning red. "No, I didn't anything like that."

Not having an internet connection will cost me opportunities.

"I accept your offer, Zev. Now take me to my new home."

CPSIA information can be obtained
at www.ICGtesting.com
Printed in the USA
FSHW011104030221
78169FS

9 781087 884448